W9-BZX-304

CATCHING SANTA

FORGET EVERYTHING YOU KNOW ABOUT
SANTA BECAUSE IT IS JUST NOT TRUE!

THE KRINGLE CHRONICLES
BOOK ONE

CATCHING SANTA

MARC FRANCO

Pants On Fire Press
Winter Garden

Pants On Fire Press, Winter Garden 34787

Visit us at www.PantsOnFirePress.com

Illustrations and art copyright © 2011 by Pants On Fire Press

Cover art by Aurora Pagano
Interior illustrations by Drew Swift
Book design by Jill Ronsley

10 9 8 7 6 5 4 3 2 1

Printed in the United States of America

R. R. Donnelley and Sons, Crawfordsville, IN

Publisher's Cataloging-In-Publication Data

Franco, Marc, 1969-

Catching Santa / Marc Franco. – 1st ed.

p. : ill. ; cm. – (The Kringle chronicles ; bk. 1)

Summary: 11-year-old Jakob Jablonski has never met a snowman messenger or elf spies. All he knows is an ordinary life with his beloved adopted parents and their annoying daughters. But that life is about to change when a magical and frightening visitor demands the unimaginable, the impossible: that Jakob catch Santa ... or else.

ISBN: 978-0-9827271-5-7

1. Magic–Juvenile fiction. 2. Santa Claus–Juvenile fiction. 3. Friendship–Juvenile fiction. 4. Magic–Fiction. 5. Santa Claus–Fiction. 6. Friendship–Fiction. 7. Adventure and adventurers–Fiction. 8. Christmas stories. 9. Adventure fiction. I. Title.

PZ7:F71 Ca 2010

[Fic]   2010911471

For my three Js and the K who gave them to me.

Contents

I Get Drawn In

My index finger twitched uncontrollably. That's how it always starts and it was starting again. I looked up at the classroom clock. It was twenty minutes before dismissal. No, this isn't happening. Not after the day I've had. I tried to control my right hand, but it was no use. My pencil, captured by my hand like prey, was already rapidly sketching a comic of two commandos in armored battle suits. The scene took half the page. The commandos were crouched behind trees, dodging sharp icicles falling from the sky and return blasting a twirl of green-and-white energy from machines attached to their arms. It was the same battle scene I'd drawn last week. Now that the scene was sketched, my mind was being drawn in again—like the times before—into my comic, into the battle. Suddenly my head felt like it was being sucked through a vacuum. Then—just like that—the feeling was gone, but so was my classroom.

I was wearing commando gear, crouched between shrubs and looking through goggles at my familiar Florida neighborhood—but it was covered in snow. Suddenly there was a vicious shriek from above. Instinctively I glanced up, but a volley of deadly-sharp icicles forced me to run from cover. Snow, dirt and shrubs kicked up around me. There were more shrieks, this time much closer. I looked up again and was finally able to see what was threatening me from above. My first thought was snowmen gone mad. That was until I saw that they actually had icy, spiked skeleton heads; long, ice-skeleton bodies; and frozen-liquid wings. One thing was certain: they wanted to hurt me. Faces frozen in fury, hundreds of the figures swooped in from all directions. My only hope was to find cover. Suddenly a yellow light erupted from out of nowhere, and the sky was washed clean of the attacking ice skeletons. I sighed, but my relief was short-lived. Thick fog hung in the air, no doubt residual from whatever had evaporated the ice creatures. A terrible roar echoed from my right. I couldn't see anything but fog, when suddenly a flaming fireball whirled out of the darkness, straight at me. Just as I stood frozen in fear, a dark figure, wearing military armor with the nameplate DASHER, burst from the fog and threw me to the ground, rescuing me from the fireball's trajectory with barely a second to spare.

KA-BOOM!

"No!" I shouted and sat bolt upright in my desk, grabbing at the comics. I felt like I'd just awakened from a dream. Heart racing and head throbbing, I glanced around the classroom. Everyone was looking at me and, to make matters worse, my sixth-grade, gifted-class teacher, Mr. Swimdo, was walking toward me.

Suddenly a voice whispered in my ear from behind. "You were automatic drawing again." It was Logan, one of my *ex*-best friends.

"Don't talk to me. I'm mad at you," I hissed.

"Whatever. Just grab them, before he does," Logan said, reaching over my shoulder for the comics I'd just drawn. Too late. Rick Lang, jerk extraordinaire, grabbed them before Logan or I could.

"Look everyone. More crazy Santa comic drawings." Rick jeered as he studied the drawings.

"Shut up, Rick," I seethed, fist clenched. I wanted to feed it to him.

"That's enough," Mr. Swimdo said, taking my comics from Rick. He quickly paged through them, then dropped the papers on my desk. I studied the comics. Two pages of pencil-sketched images—everything I'd just experienced. But why was Rick calling it Santa stuff? My comics didn't have anything to do with Christmas. They actually looked more like something from Halo or Star Wars. Weird, but that's Rick for you.

"You're such a jerk. Wasn't what you did to him at recess enough?" I heard Logan say.

"Whatever. It's just a joke," Rick muttered dismissively.

"Jakob, gather your stuff." Mr. Swimdo ordered.

What? Dismissal wasn't for another ten minutes. Was I in trouble? Nervously and in record time, I packed up and stood as Mr. Swimdo motioned me to the door. That's when it hit me. He knew what happened to me at recess. He didn't say anything, and he didn't have to. Letting me go early and sending me off with a wink was telltale enough. It was a little unsettling that Mr. Swimdo knew, because that meant all the other teachers probably knew also. Wonderful.

Even so, I welcomed the head start he gave me. It settled my nerves a bit because I'd avoid all of the peering eyes, pointing fingers, and whispering voices as I walked across school to the bus.

I got to my bus without any problems and climbed aboard just as the dismissal bell rang. Grateful for the privacy, I walked down the aisle and sank into my usual seat, three rows from the back and on the right side. Christmas music was playing on the radio.

Boy was it was hot. I noticed the windows were open. Great, I thought, no A/C. Just because it was winter didn't mean it wasn't hot. It was Florida, for crying out loud. A song caught my attention. A man was singing "Let It Snow! Let It Snow! Let It Snow!" Yes, I thought, let it. All in rapid succession, I clasped my hands together, closed my eyes, and prayed. "Dear God, please let it snow!" Yeah I know, wishful thinking, but maybe God was listening and feeling really generous today.

Suddenly hooting and hollering kids poured from their classrooms to welcome the end of a very special Friday and the beginning of the weekend. But it wasn't just any weekend. It was Christmas break.

I wanted to partake in the celebration but was still mad—obsessing on my twentieth replay of what had happened to me at recess—when the bus moved ever so slightly. I looked up over the green vinyl seatback in front of me and saw a stream of kids boarding the bus. I stared out the window to ignore them all, then felt a tap on my shoulder. It was my eight-year-old sisters, Jordan and Jadyn. I didn't look anything like them because I was adopted. They, on the other hand, were identical twins down to the same number of freckles. But I could tell them apart—even with their perfectly braided brown hair and matching garb—by their voice. The difference was subtle, but enough for me to distinguish the two. That's why they didn't speak to me unless they really had to. It was some sick game they played.

"What?" I demanded, shrugging.

They didn't say anything, just pointed to the front of the bus. I looked. Ugh, it was my three best friends, although at the time I was so mad at them, I no longer considered them friends.

They walked, Shigeru Sugihara in the lead and heading right to me. He was really tall—definitely the tallest sixth grader at College Park Elementary. Shoot, he was already wearing size 10 adult sneakers. He went by "Shig" for short. Below his bowl-cut, straight black hair was a gentle face with a fair complexion, flat nose, and large lips that almost always smiled. He plopped down beside me but didn't say anything.

Logan Raffo was next, staring at me intensely with her dark, demanding, almond-shaped eyes as she forced an apologetic smile. She had black hair also, but hers hung long and silky over her tan complexion. She sat in the seat in front of me and slid over to the window.

Fleep Sanchez slid in next to her. His real name was Felipe, but he went by "Fleep"—something about his brother not being able to pronounce "Felipe" when he was little. His curly, long locks of blond hair swung from side to side as he walked. He had caterpillar-sized eyebrows, large brown eyes that seemed too big for their sockets, and thin, freckly cheeks. He was tall like me, but still not as tall as Shig. We were all eleven years old. I'd be the first to turn twelve though, just after the new year.

Shig tried to get me to talk, and Logan begged to read the comics I'd drawn in class, but I ignored them and just kept looking out the window. Then *he* got on the bus, the little pipsqueak Rick Lang, with one of his loser friends. His ferret eyes glanced around. I couldn't understand why kids would let him bully them. He was so short and skinny, and his shoulder-length hair made him look like goldilocks in skater clothes. Heck, I'd eaten cotton candy that was more intimidating.

Our eyes locked.

"I'll just sit up here in the front," Rick said, looking around and trying to act cool.

The ride home was pretty annoying because my friends kept trying to get me to talk. I guess that's what friends do, but I just ignored them and stared out the window. The bus finally stopped and we all got off at the same place, the entrance to our subdivision. Yep, we were neighbors and friends ... and most of the time it was cool, but not today. Today it was just plain irritating!

Rick and his bud were the first to exit and took off running like a pair of rats. I won't lie; I thought about chasing them, but Rick wasn't worth it. Besides, I still had my ex-friends to deal with. I stormed past Shig and made sure to distance myself from my bratty sisters and ex-friends, hoping they'd all get the message that I was really mad at them.

As I came up to my street, I spotted something odd over at Rick's house. Rick's older sister, Tiff, was out front. That in itself was odd because she was in middle school and wasn't supposed to be home for another forty-five minutes. Still watching Tiff, I walked across the street to my yard. She was looking through a pair of binoculars at Logan's roof, then Fleep's, then Shig's, and finally mine. That's when she saw me. I must have startled her because she immediately hid the binoculars by her side and waved distractedly. I waved back and walked to my front door, wondering what that was all about. I reached for the door handle but my curiosity won out. I had to know what was up with her strange behavior. Heart rate rising, I went into commando mode and stepped into the shrubs to watch whatever this was. Tiff was still at it with the binoculars, but now looking at an orange MINI Cooper parked in front of the house across the street from mine. The house was for sale and happened to be one of my mom's real estate listings. The tint on the MINI Cooper was dark, but not dark enough to conceal the silhouette of a man inside, peering back at her through his own binoculars. He was watching Tiff, and she was watching him. Weird.

Suddenly the MINI Cooper started and Tiff took off, running inside her house. When she came back, about a half-minute later, the MINI Cooper was gone. Whoever it was sure was in a hurry. It was all kind of strange but a bit boring. Just then I heard my little sisters walking up from the driveway. Awesome, I thought. Still hidden in the bushes, I waited eagerly then jumped out just as they passed by.

"BAAAH!" I shouted.

They screamed, and I laughed and chased them inside our house.

"MOMMY!" The twins wailed.

"In the kitchen," my mom announced. We raced to the kitchen. I won, of course.

"Jakob scared us," Jadyn whined.

"Yeah," Jordan gasped. "He was in the bushes." My mom kissed them.

"Okay, go do your homework. And Jakob, don't scare your sisters."

I nodded and gave my mom a hug, then sighed.

She held me back at arm's length and studied me. "Hey, what's wrong?"

"Don't let any of the three in," I said in a huff.

"The three?" she asked, releasing me.

"Logan, Fleep, or Shig."

She raised an eyebrow and stared at me as I grabbed my bulging backpack and ran upstairs to my room. I'd been messing around on my computer for about thirty minutes when the doorbell rang. Pretty confident it was one of the three, I didn't get up.

"It's Rick's sister, Tiff," my mom called up.

Hmm. What in the world does she want? She never comes over, I thought. I could hear my mom telling Tiff I was upstairs in my room. Tiff was thirteen and, even though she was in middle school, spent a lot of time with Logan because there weren't any kids her age in the neighborhood. I logged into Pandora Radio on the Internet and selected something Christmassy, then leaned back in my chair just as Tiff walked into my room.

"Hey," she said, waving her hand. Her red hair was pulled back into her usual ponytail, and stood out against her pale skin and green eyes.

"Hey," I said, waving back. "Done with your binoculars?"

"What?" Tiff answered like I'd accused her of a crime then quickly recovered her cool. "Oh, yeah, birds. I was watching a pair of cardinals. They just had a baby bird."

Birds, I thought, staring into her secretive eyes. You weren't watching birds. You lie like a fly, just like your brother. Tiff interrupted my thoughts.

"I heard what happened—Logan told me."

Logan and her big mouth.

"I just wanted to say I'm sorry. You know, about my brother and all. It was wrong, and I'll make sure my parents hear about it."

"Don't bother. It's not your fault he's a jerk." There was an awkward pause as she studied some of my drawn comics hanging on the wall. They were head shots of armored commandos in a wintery scene.

"Hey, at least you didn't curse yourself, right?" Tiff remarked in an exaggerated, yet relieved, way.

I cocked my head. "Curse?"

Logan Reads the Ten Christmas Rules

"What curse?" I asked suspiciously.

"You know, it's what happens when you publicly say that you don't believe in Santa."

"How do you know?"

"Oh, there's an entire chapter written about it in my dad's old German Christmas book. It's been in my—"

"I know about your book. Logan talks about it whenever I mention anything related to Christmas," I snapped, irritation in my voice.

"Yeah, well the thing's, like, *ancient.*"

I shot Tiff a doubtful look.

"Seriously, the book has been in my family for generations," she laughed. "Logan's been begging me since summer to let her read it, but my dad is a little peculiar about letting people see it. You know parents."

I nodded.

"Anyway, Jakob, the curse is real."

"Oka-a-ay," I said, drawn-out-like. So far she hadn't said anything convincing to make me believe the curse was real. Tiff stared at me hard.

"You really don't know about the curse, do you?" she said accusingly. I shrugged my shoulders. I wasn't going to tell her either way. "Well, whether you believe it or not, Logan, Shig, and Fleep cursed themselves the instant they told my brother that they didn't believe in Santa."

"Yeah, so now what happens?" I asked, not buying a word of it.

"No more presents from Santa forever; that is, unless of course they lift the curse. But they only have until six a.m. on Christmas Day," Tiff said somberly.

"That's the dumbest thing I've ever heard. Santa wouldn't do that!"

Just then the doorbell rang. She ran outside my room, I guess to see who it was, then ran back to my room as I got up from my chair.

"It's Fleep. Where's your bathroom?" Tiff said hurriedly.

"Outside my room, there on the right," I pointed, following Tiff out of my room.

My bathroom door shut as I got to the banister and looked down at the front door. Fleep was standing on the other side, looking up. My first thought was to hide, but he saw me and waved. I didn't wave back. A hard, cold stare was what he deserved and what he got. Why did you do it, Fleep? You're supposed to be my friend, and you sold me out in front of Rick and the other kids.

Fleep's cautious face quickly grew a smile the moment I finally, and reluctantly, waved him in. Before he could say anything, I turned on my heel and hurried back to my room, plopped in front of my computer and stared at the screen. Fleep ambled into my room a few seconds later.

"Jakob, you still mad?" he asked.

You can't tell? So much for my upset look.

"Look, I'm sorry. I didn't mean it. It's not what I really believe. I was embarrassed—we were all embarrassed—and you, well, you were the first to answer Rick's question. And you answered so fast that by the time everyone stopped laughing at you, well, we all knew we had to answer no. But I believe in Santa. Really, we all still believe in him!" Just then the doorbell rang, again.

Fleep and I raced to the banister and looked over: it was the rest of the gang—Logan and Shig. I sighed, then waved them up and walked back to my room. I could hear them racing up the stairs. They sounded like a herd of horses. I imagined Logan in the lead. She had to win and would, one way or another.

"Is he still mad at us?" Logan asked, slightly winded as she entered my room. I glanced over at her. Her long, black hair was pulled into a ponytail, her face shiny with sweat. She leaned against my navy blue wall and glanced around at my Star Wars-themed room. I had a giant mural of an Imperial Star Destroyer crashing through the wall over my bed, several starfighter models hanging from the ceiling and a Star Wars Imperial Commando poster that read, 'I Want YOU For The Empire!'

"I don't know," Fleep began. "I told him that we believe, then you guys rang the doorbell, but he still hasn't said anything."

"Come on, Jakob, you would have done the same thing if it was one of us they were laughing at," Shig said, hopping backward up on my bed.

I stood up and faced Shig.

"No way," I said, pointing my finger in his face. "I'd stick up for you guys no matter what. That's what real friends do and I'd say it again—a million times if I had to. I believe in Santa! He's as real as God."

"What? You can't see God," Shig said.

"So what? It doesn't mean I don't believe in him," I said defensively.

"Yeah, but that's a bad example to use," Logan protested.

"Why? Because it's not written in Tiff's mysterious Christmas book—a stupid book you've been talking about since summer, a book that you haven't even read. Have you?" I pressed.

"No, I haven't read it," Logan admitted.

"Speaking of Tiff, she's in my bathroom."

Logan looked surprised.

"No way, Tiff's in your bathroom?" Shig said. "What in the world is she doing here?"

"I have no idea. I mean, she came over and apologized for her brother but then started talking nonsense about you guys being cursed," I told Shig.

"We're cursed?" Fleep asked nervously.

"No, you're not *cursed*," I said, annoyed.

"Yes, we're cursed, but I know how we can fix things," Logan said.

"Are you insane? People don't get cursed. Tiff's up to something. I even caught her in a lie." I looked firmly at Logan. "Just remember, she's Rick's sister—you can't trust her!"

"Yes I can. She's my friend," Logan said, taken aback. "Besides, hating her brother doesn't give you the right to be a jerk to her. She's trying to help us."

I got in Logan's face.

"Help us? Was her brother trying to help me when he asked me if I believed in Santa? Oh, no wait, he was mocking me out in front the entire fifth and sixth grade." I stood back and stewed for a moment then looked at Logan. "Get it through your thick head, she's making the curse stuff up. Even the book is bogus," I said, my voice raising.

"Okay, *smarty*, what's she up to?" Logan asked.

"What's she doing in my bathroom?" I replied.

"You can't answer me with a question. I asked you first," Logan said.

"I just did," I snapped back. "What's she doing in there?"

Logan sighed. "Gee, what most people do in a bathroom, genius!"

"Not for that long and, besides, she ran in there as soon as she saw Fleep at my front door. I'm telling you, you can't trust her."

"Yes, you can," Logan insisted.

"No, you can't."

Logan was about to say yes again, when I shouted, "Shut it!"

Then there was silence, and everyone waited for the inevitable intervention from downstairs.

"Hey, what's going on up there?" my mom called. And there it was, right on cue. I scrambled, knocking Shig's knees as I ran past him and into the hall. My mom stood in the kitchen looking up the stairs.

"Just a small misunderstanding," I said, real innocent-like.

My mom cocked her head. "You and Logan?" She asked. I nodded. "You two have *got* to stop this arguing."

"I know, we will." I ran back to my room, plopped into my chair and studied my friends' faces.

Logan sighed then began, "Look, we know you're upset. We're sorry about today."

"Yeah, we should have had your back," Shig added.

"Yeah," Fleep made the apology unanimous.

I smiled. My best friends were back. "Apologies accepted," I said.

"Good, because we have our own problems to worry about," Logan said.

"Like what?" Fleep asked, surprised.

"The *curse*," Logan declared.

"Oh yeah," Fleep said dejectedly.

"Saying you don't believe in Santa because of a little embarrassment means no more Christmas presents from him forever," Logan said.

"What do you mean, 'no more Christmas presents'?" Fleep asked with alarm.

"I'm talking about the Ten Christmas Rules," Logan said.

First curses, now rules? What in the world was Logan babbling about? I looked at Shig and Fleep. They looked as confused as I probably did. I'd never heard of the Ten Christmas Rules—the Ten Commandments, yes, but Ten Christmas Rules? It sounded like more nonsense from Tiff.

"I've never heard of Christmas rules. You can't get cursed. Just ignore her," I said. Thinking of Tiff reminded me she was *still* in my bathroom.

Logan continued. "Just after I got home, Tiff came over. I told her what happened today between her brother and you."

"Yeah, thanks for blabbing," I said.

"Well I'm glad I did, because we would have never known about the curse. I didn't even believe her until she showed me the rules on Wikipedia. Tiff said there's also an entire chapter in her father's book about them." Logan paused for a moment, studied our faces, then continued. "Guys, Tiff's very knowledgeable about Christmas and Santa."

"Here we go again," I said sneeringly.

"The curse is real," Logan snapped.

"Yeah, right," I scoffed. "So because Tiff says there is a curse, we should go ahead and believe her. I can't believe I'm listening to this."

Logan ignored me then dug into her right pants pocket and pulled out a folded, printed copy of the Wikipedia article. "Okay, the Ten Christmas Rules are:

1. Believe.
2. Be faithful.
3. Be kind.
4. Be joyful.
5. Love.
6. Be peaceful.
7. Be patient.
8. Be good.
9. Have self-control.
10. Be gentle.

You need to worry about the first rule," Logan said to Fleep and Shig. "The only rule that carries a blessing or a curse is 'Believe'. According to this rule, you have to publicly believe in Santa. If you believe, you'll get presents on Christmas. That's the blessing. But if you publicly deny believing in Santa ..." she touched her index finger to her thumb and made a zero, "you get nothing, zero! No presents on Christmas. And that's just what you two are looking at getting." Fleep and Shig looked stunned.

"Wait a minute, you said you didn't believe either," Shig cried. Just then I heard the bathroom door open and watched as Tiff emerged and settled in unnoticed against the doorframe of my room.

"Yeah, but like I said before, I know how to make things right," Logan shot back.

"Christmas Rule Eleven—The Lost Rule," Tiff said coolly.

Logan whirled around to see Tiff then clapped so fast you'd think she was welcoming a movie star. "Oh my gosh. I'm so glad you're really here. Jakob doesn't believe me."

Tiff's green eyes stared through me.

"I thought there were ten rules," Fleep interrupted.

"Nope," Tiff replied. "My father's Christmas book also mentions an eleventh rule."

"Yeah, the rule has to do with lifting the curse," Logan said, then dug into her pants pocket again and pulled out another folded sheet of paper. I could see the Wikipedia banner and the title "Christmas Rule Eleven—The Lost Rule."

How many articles did she have tucked away? "Now you're carrying Wikipedia articles around in your pockets?" I asked sarcastically.

"I just printed them," she said, snide-like, then began reading. "Rule Eleven states that 'in order to lift the curse and restore present-receiving privileges from Santa, you must do two things. First, confirm to the person who asked if you believe in Santa that you do indeed believe, and second, make that person become a believer, if they are not so already.' " Logan looked up at us and smiled.

"I don't understand," Fleep said.

Logan sighed. "It's simple. We tell Rick we believe in Santa and then get Rick to believe in Santa too. We can do this."

"Guys, I don't know, Rick's pretty thick headed. You'll need help," Tiff said. "Jakob, will you help them lift the curse?"

What? Who, me? That was a surprise question considering this curse business had nothing to do with me and, besides, I was still processing Logan's dumb comment about getting Rick to believe in Santa. This conversation was bordering on insanity.

I looked over at Fleep and Shig. Tiff had them hooked like a fish. Well, it was time to cut the line.

I shook my head and crossed my arms. "No way am I helping," I said. "This is all nonsense and you guys—"

But before I could finish, Tiff was in my face. "You listen to me. The curse is real. This isn't some dumb game. If they don't tell my brother they believe in Santa and get him to believe before six a.m. on Christmas Day, they will never get presents from Santa again."

No matter how many ways I heard it, even said angrily, it still sounded like the dumbest thing on earth. Santa doesn't curse people and stop delivering presents. "You have to follow Christmas Rule Eleven and lift the curse. I mean it!" Tiff sounded desperate.

I tried not to laugh at her, but couldn't hold it back. "HA-HA-HA," escaped and that was it, I'd lost it. After my laughing fit I came face to face with an angry-looking Tiff. She stared at me for another second then pushed past me and stormed out of my room with Logan and Fleep at her heels. Logan even called for her to stop, but it was no use. A few seconds later, the front door slammed shut. There was silence.

"That was different," I said, sitting at my desk. Shig nodded.

"You totally upset her, Jakob," Logan said, walking in my room with Fleep. "I've never seen her so mad. She's only trying to help us."

"Why? Why is she so interested in helping us?" I asked.

"Because," Logan said.

"Alright, well, how are we supposed to make Rick believe?" Shig, always the level-headed one, interrupted, probably sensing another argument brewing.

"I don't know," Logan said then looked at the Christmas Rule Eleven article again. "Wait, there's an e-mail address, cursed@thekringlechronicles.com. It says to contact them if you suspect you have cursed yourself."

"I can't believe we're cursed," Fleep said gloomily.

"Hey!" I snapped. "Stop saying that. A Wikipedia article doesn't prove you're cursed. Shig, back me up."

"I don't know, Jakob," Shig faltered. I couldn't believe what I was hearing. Disappointed, I faced my computer screen. Shig, by far the smartest of the group, was buying into the curse. I shook my head. This curse business was just the next chapter in Rick trying to get me. And now Tiff was helping him.

"Holy smoke," Logan yelped, interrupting my thoughts of a Tiff-and-Rick conspiracy. She was captivated by the stack of sketched comics on my desk. "How often are you doing the auto-drawing thing?" Logan asked.

"Once, sometimes twice a month," I said, studying her. "You didn't tell anyone, did you?"

"No," Logan said, shocked.

"What about you guys?" Two head shakes.

"They're pretty freaky though. When can I read them?" Shig said, thumbing through some of the comics.

"You can't. No text," I said, grabbing a page.

"Almost like it doesn't want you to read it," Shig said. "Awesome armor!"

"Yeah," I pointed to the comic. "See, I'm wearing a futuristic-looking armored suite and holding a small pointed rod."

"Cool, you have a heads-up display," Fleep said.

"Yep, the scene is always the same though—our neighborhood, transformed into an icy battlefield with fierce commandos. What does it all mean?"

"Maybe it has something to do with you being adopted," Fleep said.

"Yeah, right!" I said, sounding unsure and feeling a bit uncomfortable. Truth was, the adoption thing had me thinking. I didn't know who my parents were or where I'd come from. I just knew the story of how my adopted dad, a fireman, had rescued me as an infant from an abandoned burning building. And now that I think about it, the circumstances surrounding where he found me were just as unusual as the comic writings. He found me covered in soot and black dust in a room where the temperatures and smoke should have killed me. But I survived. I guess that's why my parents always said I was special.

"Guys, figure it out later," Logan interrupted. "Jakob, e-mail that cursed address."

I stared at her for a moment then shook my head. "No way. Bad idea, Logan. I'm not e-mailing anyone from some paper you printed off the Internet."

Fleep charged at me and tried to grab my keyboard, but I managed to swivel the chair and block him. "I want a new skateboard this Christmas. If we don't e-mail that person, I won't get it," he cried.

"Hey, chill out," I said, swiveling back around in my chair. "You'll get your skateboard without the e-mail."

"Jakob, actually we have nothing to lose by sending the e-mail," Shig said carefully.

"Ugh. Not you too, Shig," I mumbled.

"Let's e-mail them," Shig said.

I stared at them for a moment. "You seriously think you guys are cursed?" I asked Shig.

"Actually, I don't know," he said, a little unsure. "But I don't want to risk it."

"Yeah, me either," Logan said.

"Me either!" Fleep joined the chorus.

I stared some more. They believed Tiff and the nonsense from the Internet.

Logan clasped her hands together and pleaded, "Come on Jakob, you're on the computer. Just e-mail them. I'd do it for you."

I stared at the screen. I liked Logan a lot and would do anything for her despite our occasional fight, but sending an e-mail to a stranger was a bad idea. But I believed what she said, that she'd do it for me if I asked. "Please!" Logan pleaded again. I looked up at her over my shoulder, and sighed. She smirked. She had me, and she knew it. I faced the flat-screen monitor. The rest of them scurried around me, with Logan hovering over my left shoulder.

"What's the e-mail address?"

"Cursed@thekringlechronicles.com," Logan read from the paper.

"Okay, so what do I say?"

"Start off by telling them that you have been cursed and that you need help. Keep it simple."

I read aloud as I typed.

Dear Cursed,

I just found out that I am cursed. Can you help me?
I really want Santa to bring me presents.

"Sounds good, now type your name," Logan ordered.

I signed the e-mail, "Stormtrooper TK421."

"Stormtrooper TK421? You can't sign it that way," Logan cried.

"Why not?" I asked, still looking at the screen.

"They'll think it's a prank or that we're a bunch of kids," Logan said.

"Hello? We *are* a bunch of kids!" I said, facing my friends. "Besides, I am not signing my name, no way!"

"Okay, whatever," Logan conceded. "Just send the e-mail." I swiveled around and reread the e-mail and then clicked Send. There, it was off and on its way to whoever cursed@thekringlechronicles.com was. Before my friends left, I told them not to get their hopes up for a response.

Boy was I wrong. The e-mail response arrived five hours later.

Dear Stormtrooper TK421,

I, the esteemed S.R., will help you. Please respond with details of the event in which you denied your belief in HIM. Time is against you, Stormtrooper TK421. There are only six days before HE takes to the sky to bamboozle the children of the earth. Of course, you wish to participate in that evening's euphoric event; therefore, you must do exactly as I say, or there will be no presents for you … *FOREVER!*

First, you must recant your disbelief to the person who asked you if you believe. That is a simple task; the next is not. You must then get that person to believe in HIM. I know of only one way to do this and, unfortunately, it has never been done before. You will be the first to lift the curse if you are successful.

What must you do, you ask? Well, my young boy, you must catch and present HIM to the unbeliever! I can help you catch the portly man. I offer my services. If you so choose and accept them, I will need the full names of your parents (including your mother's maiden name). We must hurry if we are to formulate a plan and catch HIM.

S.R.

I stared at my screen with a triumphant smile. There was no doubt in my mind the e-mail was a hoax, and Rick and his sister were behind it. First, it made absolutely no sense; neither did Rick. Second, Tiff often used big words, sounding like an adult. Third, the sender called me a young boy, which was impossible for him to know. So having figured it all out, I grabbed my mouse and was about to click Delete when I suddenly changed my mind. It was Logan. She needed real convincing, not Fleep and Shig. Telling her that I'd received an e-mail from Rick masquerading as someone named S.R. wouldn't persuade her to my side. No, Logan had to read it. After all, she was just as smart as me and hopefully would then come to the same conclusion … that Rick sent the e-mail.

Now determined to dig into this e-mail full force, I grabbed a notepad and pen from my desk and wrote myself a note to look up the meanings of some of the big words I didn't know, such as *euphoric and portly,* at Webster.com.

I looked at the time on my computer. It was almost eight-thirty. Bible time, I thought. My dad would be in my room any minute to read two chapters from the Bible like he did every night before bed. Just as I was moving the cursor to close out the e-mail program, a new message arrived. It was from S.R. I hesitated for a moment, deciding whether to shutdown the computer or read the e-mail. I quickly opened it.

Stormtrooper TK421,
   Six days remain. Time is running out, and I impatiently await your response. Please reply immediately.
                        S.R.

Reply? You want a reply? I'll give you a reply, Rick Lang. Without a thought, I clicked Reply to fire off a heated response and end this charade, then suddenly heard my dad's voice in the hall. Oh no! I was out of time. What was I thinking? I should have been in bed and not replying to an e-mail, much less one that appeared to be from a stranger. My dad would go ballistic. I quickly closed the e-mail window expecting the program to instantly close, but it didn't.

To my horror, a Checking Mail window popped up on the screen. The computer was auto-checking for new e-mail. Argh! Not now! I banged on the keyboard. My dad was just outside my room, yelling back to the twins. Frantic and heart slamming hard against my chest, I repeatedly clicked Cancel. The unimaginable happened next: the computer froze with Rick's, a.k.a. S.R.'s, second e-mail splashed open on the screen. This isn't happening, I said under my breath.

My dad walked into my room just as I reached back from pressing the main switch on the power strip. The screen blinked off as the computer came to a hard stop. I sighed and knew I was in trouble. My dad had lectured me one too many times for doing what he'd just seen me do, and I was about to get the speech again. I stared at him from the chair, guilt written all over my face … guilty, guilty, guilty.

"Jakob! How many times have I told you?" my dad said in utter disbelief.

He didn't want an answer, but I gave him one anyway.

"A lot," I replied, sounding more like I was asking a question.

"Break the computer and you're paying for it." My dad went on and on, talking about the repercussions of killing the power and corrupting the hard drive, but I wasn't listening. All I could think about was the computer as I climbed into bed. Would it restart? Losing Rick's, a.k.a. S.R.'s, e-mail to a system crash before Logan could read it would be my luck. Tuning back into my dad's voice, I endured my fiftieth or so lecture on how lucky I had been so far since hard drives couldn't take that kind of abuse. Was this it, though? Was the fiftieth time going to be the switch of death for my computer? I could only hope not. I really wanted Logan to read the e-mail.

Logan Spams Santa

It was night, and I was outside in the cold being chased by a tall man wearing a hooded, dusty cloak and carrying a sack over his shoulder. Suddenly I heard panting to my left and realized someone was running beside me, but I couldn't see who because the moon had gone behind a cloud. Then I heard the cloaked man shout, "It's too late! I have you, my wooden boy."

Just then I stumbled and collided into the figure running beside me, and both of us tumbled to the ground. As I lay momentarily dazed, the moon reappeared and I could clearly see who, or what, I'd crashed into. What I saw horrified me. It wasn't a person at all, but a humanoid, wooden creature. I could see the wooden, grainy texture of its arms and neck, but where there should have been a head … there was nothing. The thing was quickly disintegrating before my very eyes, dissolving into a dusty trail that led to a black rock-looking thing. With a start, I realized the creature was being transformed into a lump of coal! I watched, frozen in fear, as the transformation became complete. The cloaked man swooped in, scooped up the rock and stared at me ominously. His confident, glowing eyes locked with mine as he held up the coal and said, "You are next, Jakob!"

I sat bolt upright in bed. It was December 20, five days before Christmas, and I'd just had a nightmare. I wiped the sweat-soaked hair from my forehead, then peeled off the covers and climbed out of bed. I tried to brush the nightmare aside, but couldn't rid my mind of the image of the disintegrating wooden creature.

When I came downstairs, my mom was in the kitchen with her back to me, standing by the sink holding a package. She was in mid-sentence talking to my dad, who was seated across the counter at the bar.

"… just strange, that's all I'm saying. Normal people don't do this kind of stuff."

"What stuff?" I asked. My mom turned around.

"This stuff." My mom held up a package about the size of a hardcover book. "Mr. Raffo just dropped it off." Logan's Dad, I thought. It was a standard, white envelope padded with bubble wrap, the same kind Mr. Raffo always dropped off. I shrugged my shoulders.

"We have a business arrangement. You know that," I said.

"Why doesn't he just place it in our mailbox instead of giving it to you? I don't like you handling a package and not knowing what's inside," my mom said.

"He wants Jakob to work for his money," my dad said.

Every so often, Mr. Raffo would give me a package to mail with my home listed as the return address, and I always had to put it in my mailbox. It was the easiest five bucks I'd ever made. My dad was cool with it and thought it was pretty entrepreneurial of me to do. My mom and Logan, on the other hand, were extremely suspicious, especially since they had no idea what was in the packages. Logan was certain that her dad was some sort of spy. My guess was that because Logan's paranoia had gotten so far out of hand, Mr. Raffo needed me to mail his goods to prevent her from opening the packages. She wouldn't dare reach into my mailbox.

I reached for the package. Hesitantly, my mom gave it to me. "Logan's right; only spies and criminals do this kind of stuff," my mom said.

"He's not a criminal," my dad said with a chuckle.

"Okay, explain why I saw people wearing hazardous suits at the Raffos' house," my mom said.

Hazmat suits, that's what my mom was talking about. Yeah, I'd seen them, too, but not just at Logan's house. I'd also seen them at her dad's shop, The Teashroom, when it was being built. Holy smoke, I'd never really given it much thought before, but it was very odd. Construction people *do not* wear hazmat suites, especially in Florida. Maybe there is more to Mr. Raffo than meets the eye. Maybe Logan is right and her dad is some sort of spy. I laughed at the thought.

"Not that again," my dad said, sounding irritated. "He's already told us what they're doing."

"And you believe him?" my mom said.

"Yeah, I do!"

"Well, I don't. Workers finishing an attic do not wear hazardous suits, period," my mom countered.

"Haz*mat*. They can if they're dealing with fiberglass. You don't want to be breathing that stuff. Heck, I'd wear a suit."

"Yes, but the fiberglass was removed two weeks ago. He's moved on to polished steel and a lot of it. Trust me, there's something else going on over there." I watched my mom as she talked about Mr. Raffo. Man, she was seriously suspicious of him and getting feisty too, probably because she still had a lot to do before Christmas.

I left the kitchen, walked outside and placed the package in my mailbox for Logan's dad. Even though it was Africa-hot outside, it still felt pretty Christmassy, thanks in part to the neighbors who had decorated their homes. It was obvious that retro lights were all the rage this year, and there seemed to be a competition for the yard with the largest animated Christmas-whatever. I kid you not, the house beside Logan's had a twenty-foot-tall, animated snowman, and the house across the street from Shig's had a giant mechanical elf that jumped out of a present. All I needed now to have that true Christmas feel was a bone-chilling wind like when we visited my mom's home state of New Jersey. Fat chance on that happening here in Central Florida, though.

I gave my house a disappointed look. It was a big, brown two-story with no Christmas lights. Not a one and it was all because of my dad. My mom had one word for him. Cheap! He had promised last year that, after Christmas, he'd buy lights on clearance to put up this year. He hadn't and, yet again, we were the dullest house in the neighborhood.

I looked at the house to my right and felt a little better. It was Shig's house, an olive green two-story, also bare of Christmas lights. But at least he had an excuse. They were going "green" this year. Shig's dad, Mr. Sugihara, was out front washing his white, unmarked police car with Shig's younger brother, Koji. Koji was seven. Mr. Sugihara was actually Lieutenant Sugihara of our local police department. I looked down past the Sugihara's to the next house, a tan single-story where Logan lived, and saw her walking my way.

Then my eyes wandered across the street to the house where Rick lived, and my face suddenly flushed with anger. Fleep and Shig were shooting hoops with Rick. I crossed my arms in a huff and glared at them, hoping they'd see me.

Fleep saw me first, then Shig. They waved, but I didn't wave back. I was really irritated with them. I mean, come on, they were hanging with the enemy. Rick just stood there for a second, real cocky-like, with his hand on his hip, staring at me, then he finally shot the basketball.

"Miss!" I said, hopeful. He did. I smirked, and was just starting to put up the flag on our mailbox when Logan finally reached my driveway.

"What's in there, one of my dad's packages?" she said accusingly.

"Yeah."

"Let me see it!" Logan demanded, as if asking sternly would make me give it to her.

"No."

"Well, did you at least shake it?"

"I don't do that anymore. You're the one who thinks he's a spy."

"He is and I'm going to prove it. I'm going to open it," Logan said, walking to my mailbox.

"Open it and you'll go to jail. Ask Shig if you don't believe me."

"Spies go to jail too, and so do their accomplices," Logan retorted with a flip of her hair and started to walk back home.

"Wait, stop." She didn't. "I got a reply to my e-mail." Logan quickly turned around. I thought her eyes were going to pop out of their sockets.

"No way," she exclaimed, running back to me. "What did it say?"

"Well—"

"Stop! Don't tell me. I want to read it. Besides, you'll get it all wrong."

I groaned. "You are so rude sometimes, you know that?"

"I don't mean it like that. It's just that, well, you're a boy and you'll forget something. I'll just read it. Come on, let's go," she encouraged me, really amped up and ready to go. We were already halfway up my driveway when we heard a loud HONK. Logan's Dad pulled up in his SUV and impatiently waved for her. Mr. Raffo was a muscular man with a light-skinned face that looked like it had been cut from stone, and long black hair pulled back into a ponytail. He was really nice, but not the kind of guy you kept waiting. In that instance I realized something that sent chills up my spine: Mr. Raffo looked cool … spy cool.

Logan cupped her hands around her mouth and shouted. "I'm not coming!" Her dad shook his head disapprovingly. "Ah man, he's making me go. It's not fair. I want to read that e-mail," she said, frustrated, "This is all because I have to meet some dumb new guy my dad hired."

Her dad owned The Teashroom, a tea and herbal shop that was built in the shape of a giant mushroom and designed to appeal to both kids and adults. It was really cool looking. The outside looked like a giant mushroom from a Japanese video game. Definitely one of the coolest places to hang out. The inside was awesome too. There were four soundproof gaming rooms, each with its very own gaming console and flat screen. Being friends with Logan was like having your own personal arcade.

"Just let me tell you what the e-mail says."

"No thanks. I'll read it later. In the meantime, I'll do some more undercover surveillance on Dad. I'm going

to prove The Teashroom's some sort of secret spy place."
Logan winked, walking off.

Rolling my eyes jokingly at Logan, I glanced down
the street and saw that Fleep and Shig were walking
my way. Perfect timing I thought, then went inside and
waited for them in the kitchen. A minute later Shig arrived, followed by a sweaty Fleep. I stared them down.
Yeah, I was upset that they'd been playing with Rick,
but I would never admit it. Not that I had to anyway; it
showed on my face.

"What? I was bored, and he asked me to play," Fleep
protested with open arms.

"I don't care who you guys hang with, but you'll
never find *me* hanging with Rick."

"Water, I need water," Shig panted. While they raided
my refrigerator and got what they wanted, I told them
about the reply e-mail.

"From the curse people?" Fleep said.

"Yeah, the curse people, now—" The sound of three
knocks at my front door broke in.

I had a pretty good view of the front door from the
barstool, and sighed at what I saw.

"What is Rick doing here?" I said, a little disgusted.

My dad shot us a glance as he reached for the door.
"His dad and I both agree that you two need to fix your
little problem. So get outside and figure it out."

"Yeah, but I was—"

"No *buts*, Jakob. Go!"

"Fine," I said, defeated.

"Never find you playing with Rick, huh?" Shig beamed.

"Whatever," I said, frustrated.

"Come on. Rick and his friends are waiting outside for you guys!" my dad called, half outside.

"Let's just get this over with. I'll show you the e-mail later," I said then ambled to the front door with Fleep and Shig on my heels.

"And hey, we're talking about showing a movie at poolside tonight with the neighbors—so no fighting!" my dad said as we walked past him. We have this really cool, lagoon-style pool with a huge deck and an outdoor fireplace, and my Dad had rigged a ten-foot-tall screen so we could watch movies outdoors. I popped into the garage to grab my bike and helmet, when Rick walked up to me.

"Man, you need to chill and learn how to take a joke."

I got in his face. "What you did was no joke. You mocked me in front of the entire school." Okay, so I was exaggerating.

"I'm sorry, alright? You want to believe in Santa—that's your thing, even if you're the only sixth grader who does."

"Actually, since we're on the topic ..." Shig began. "Fleep, I think that now's a good time for us to, well, set the record straight and—"

I interrupted Shig. "What are you doing?"

Shig shrugged. "Doing what the Eleventh Rule said—in case the curse is real. Right, Fleep?"

"Uh, yeah, okay—well ... I believe in Santa," Fleep said, looking at Rick.

"Yeah, and so do I, and so does Logan. But she has to tell you herself, right?" Shig said to Rick.

"I don't know," Rick said, shrugging.

"Come on, Rick. Does Logan have to tell you in person?" I asked suspiciously. Not that I really cared. I had one thing on my mind—prove that Rick was behind the e-mail and this curse business.

"You're strange, and I don't care what you guys believe. What happened at recess was just a joke. We had fun."

"*You* had fun," I said, correcting Rick. I leaned in closer to him and whispered. "I'm onto you, man. I know you're up to something and I'm going to prove it."

Rick backed away, holding his hands up. "Look—I apologized. Now what's your problem?"

"You. You're a jerk to me, to us! That's *our* problem. Right, guys?"

"Right," Shig said. Fleep didn't answer. He was enviously watching Rick's skater friends out in the street doing tricks on their boards.

"Hopeless," was all Rick said as he left to meet up with his friends. A minute later, Logan's dad pulled up in my driveway and Logan got out. The Teashroom was only a two-minute drive down the road, so it was no surprise she was back already.

"Did you meet the new guy?" I asked.

"Yeah, he's a little strange," Logan said, seemingly lost in thought for the moment. "So hey," she shot back, "let's read the e-mail now."

"We can't," I said. "My dad kicked us out."

"What? No! Come on!"

"Chill out. You'll read it later. I promise." I watched Fleep. He was still mesmerized by the skaters. I have to say, they were doing some pretty cool tricks. Wistfully, Fleep mumbled something about never getting the skateboard he asked Santa for. We heard this every Christmas.

Logan tapped Fleep on the shoulder. "Fleep, I'm going to tell you my secret to getting what I want from Santa. It's simple, really. Just send him, like, twenty e-mails a day until Christmas Eve."

"You *spam* Santa? That's not right," I said, shaking my head.

"Yeah, that's not going to get him a skateboard!" Shig said dismissively, then turned to Fleep. "It's your parents; they're probably not signing your Santa wish list. They have to sign it," Shig insisted.

"How do you know?" I asked.

"I just know. Parents are the ones who send the final letter to Santa," Shig said.

"I can't believe my parents tell Santa what to do."

"Fleep, you are living proof that I'm right. You've asked for a skateboard three years in a row," Shig said.

"And remember last year? You even mailed Santa a magazine clipping of the exact skateboard just to be sure he didn't get confused. Face it, nothing you've done has worked, and spamming Santa is not going to help."

Just then Rick and his skater pack rode over to us on their boards. And, to rub salt in an already infected wound, Rick showed up riding the very skateboard Fleep wanted.

"Face it, your parents don't want you to have one right now," I said.

"Have what?" Rick asked, removing his helmet.

"A skateboard like yours," Fleep said.

"Who wants to give you one?"

"Don't answer that," I said, warily studying Rick and his friends. I faced Fleep, stood inches from his nose and whispered, "I have a really bad feeling about this."

"No, it's okay. Rick said he was sorry, remember?" Fleep said, real upbeat, then brushed me aside. I crossed my arms, shaking my head. Fleep was always so trusting, and it invariably got him in trouble.

"Shig's trying to tell me that my parents have to sign my letter," he explained. Rick and his gang looked confused.

"What are you talking about? What letter?" Rick said.

"The letter to Santa! I keep asking for—"

"Wait, you guys write letters to Santa?" Rick interrupted Fleep. He didn't wait for our answer. Rick knew the answer. And with that, Rick and the rest of his gang fell to the ground, laughing hysterically. They were laughing so hard they couldn't talk. My face flushed with frustration. Recess was happening all over, only this time it was a smaller crowd, and it involved all four of us.

"All of you write letters to *Santa?* Goo-goo ga-ga, anyone?" Rick said, pretending to suck his thumb. "I told you there is no such thing as Santa."

I couldn't believe Rick was doing it again, making a fool out of us. Just a couple of minutes ago, he had said he didn't care what we believed. Well, I wasn't going to back down.

"Santa's real. He's as real as you or any of us," I said.

"Oh yeah, and so is the Tooth Fairy and the Easter Bunny and, gee, let me think, who else? Oh, I got it— Yoda, he gives us free light sabers every May for Jedi Spirit Month." Rick and his friends laughed stupidly. I *really* didn't like them. "Look," Rick said, as he stood up and brushed himself off. "Santa is a fake. Your parents buy the presents, wrap them the night before, and eat the cookies and drink the milk. Wow, you guys are dumb— still believing in Santa!"

I stepped in closer to Rick. "Well, we believe in him, so whatever. You don't want to believe in him, then don't. But don't try to tell us he's not real."

"Prove it!" Rick said mockingly.

"Yeah, right," I said.

"I mean it. Prove it, and I'll give you this skateboard and whatever else I get for Christmas. In fact, we'll give you all of our boards—right, guys?" Rick looked over at his friends. From their looks, none of them seemed eager to offer up their boards. "Come on, give me a break. There is no Santa Claus."

"How am I supposed to prove it?" I asked.

"I don't know." He walked away, then stopped and stared at me for a moment "*Catch him*. That'll prove that Santa is real and it's not your parents who give you the presents!"

From out of nowhere, Tiff walked up to Rick, grabbed him by the neck and shoved him to the ground.

"Take it back—*all of it*," Tiff demanded, standing over her brother. Rick looked up at his sister with devilish eyes, then at his friends, then back to his sister. He was embarrassed and, honestly, I felt good.

Rick picked himself up and ran off, then stopped just before his house and shouted over to us, "Santa's a fake! I hate him!"

I shouted back, "IS NOT!"

Tiff ignored her brother, said something to his friends to make them disperse, and then did something really odd. She walked over to Fleep and said gently, "Santa is not a fake. He is a real person, a special person. You believe that, right? Don't listen to my brother. He doesn't believe in Santa, because he never gets what he wants."

Well, I got what I wanted—proof that Rick was S.R. and that he wrote the e-mail. He had messed up big time by asking me to catch Santa, just like he'd done in the e-mail. That was proof enough for me. But one thing still bothered me. Was Tiff also part of Rick's scam? It was hard to tell now. Judging by the way they got along, maybe she wasn't helping her brother; I just wasn't sure. But as I walked away, Tiff grabbed me.

"Hey, Logan said you e-mailed someone about the curse?"

Logan the blabbermouth, I thought.

"I just want you to know that I'm glad you're helping them, and I'm sorry about freaking out yesterday."

"It's okay, we all freak out sometimes."

Tiff cracked an easy smile. "Cool, well let me know when you get a reply from the e-mail, okay?"

Well, at least Miss Blabbermouth didn't tell her yet that I'd gotten a reply. "Sure, no problem," I said, lying through my teeth. Don't get me wrong, I hated having to lie, but I had made up my mind. I wouldn't tell her anything until I knew for sure whose side she was on.

SNOWMEN RING DOORBELLS

I'd been home for about thirty minutes when my doorbell rang. It was Shig, Fleep, and Logan. I'd been expecting they'd want to read the e-mail before we started movie night, and was surprised they hadn't burst in earlier.

"Wow, the temperature is dropping," I shivered as I let the gang in.

"Well it's not cold enough for *snowmen*," Logan said, unhinged.

I shot her a puzzled look.

"We would have been here sooner, but something happened. Follow me," she said, then stormed past me with Shig and Fleep not far behind. They headed out back toward the pool, carrying what looked like twigs, black rocks, and some other stuff. Odd.

"Sit down," I said, motioning to some pillows.

"I'm too freaked to sit," Logan's voice quaked.

"Okay, what happened?" I said inquisitively and, honestly, a little worried.

"Snowmen, oh-my-gosh, snowmen!" Logan said, hugging herself and rocking. "A snowman just came to my door."

I didn't say anything. What do you say when your best friend tells you a snowman came to her door? Remember, we live in Central Florida.

"The curse is real. This proves it," Logan said, handing me two twigs, black coal, and a carrot. "See this?" She held up a wet, blue paper. "Do you know what this is?" Logan's voice quaked as she shook the paper. I'd never seen her like this. She was beyond freaked out.

"It's a wet letter, a wet letter that's melting. And do you want to know why it's melting?" Logan was hyperactive.

"Because it's trick paper from a magic shop or something—I don't know."

Logan caught her breath. "No, it's not magic trick paper. It's a curse letter ... delivered by a *snowman*. Did you hear me, a snowman? We have five days ..." Logan was hysterical. She started crying.

"Will someone tell me what happened?" I said.

"Logan, calm down. I'll tell him," Shig said, patting her on the shoulder.

Shig did a parent scan. The coast was clear. My mom and dad were in the kitchen doing something. "She's telling you the truth. Fleep and I also were just visited by a snowman."

I didn't say anything at first. I just stared at Shig then said, "Do you know how crazy that sounds?"

Shig leaned into me and said, "Yeah, I do, but it happened. I was in my house, walking past my front door when I saw him. He was on the other side of the glass, three snowballs high and about six feet tall … a snowman." Shig pointed to the twigs and the coal. "He had twigs for arms, and coal for his smiling mouth and eyes, and the carrot was his nose. The snowman looked like he was staring at me. At first I thought it was some kind of a joke. It's not unlike someone from the police department to play a joke on my dad by making a snowman and leaving it at out front door; the fire department has a snowmaker too. I opened the door. That's when I noticed the thing was moving. Scared to death, I quickly stepped back inside and slammed the door. I watched it for a few seconds. The snowman wasn't just moving—he was alive. His arm, the right twig, was trying to open the door while the other twig held up the blue letter thing. I could tell he wanted to give it to me. Slowly, I cracked open the door just enough to snatch the letter. In that instant, the snowman melted, leaving this stuff behind. I bent over to pick up some of the coal when I heard a bloodcurdling scream come from Logan's house. I sprinted to her front door just in time to see her snowman melt. Left behind were two twigs, a carrot and coal in a pool of water and …"

"I was like … oh my gosh, did you see that? Did you see the snowman?" Logan interrupted Shig. "That's when we remembered Fleep and took off to his house. Sure enough, he was outside holding a carrot and staring at twigs and coal in a pool of water."

"Fleep's story was the same as mine and Logan's," Shig said.

"Except I didn't scream," Fleep said as he reached down, grabbed the carrot and bit into it.

"Gross, that was his nose," Logan said, now a little calmer.

Fleep quickly spit out chunks of carrot while Logan and Shig stared at me. I didn't say anything. I was thinking. I knew they weren't kidding around. I've seen Logan cry and she wasn't faking it. She was really worked up over this snowman business.

"Let me see one of the letters," I said.

Logan handed me her letter. I examined the blue paper. It was wet and felt sponge-like. The text was written in a fancy white cursive. The bottom part of the letter, the part that was supposedly melting, really was disintegrating. I could see tiny specs of the paper slowly dissolving and forming into drops of liquid. The letter read:

> *With great sadness I deliver, to you, your curse letter. The letter will melt in just five days. Lift the curse by then or it permanently stays. Only the Pole can help you.*

"Creepy, but explainable. Here, look." I showed them the letter. "The bottom part, here," I pointed to the drop that was forming. "This paper has to be made of some type of dissolving material. Add a little water to it and bam, you've got a melting letter." Shig and Fleep were examining their letters.

"Let me see that," Logan demanded.

I handed Logan her letter. "I bet if you tear off the dissolving part, it will stop melting."

"Interesting," Shig said, already tearing his letter. We watched and waited.

"It worked. It's stopped melting," Shig said after another minute.

"Trick paper from a magic shop," I said matter-of-factly. Fleep quickly tore off the lower section of his letter. Logan didn't. She held on tightly to her letter, then went into a tirade.

"Are you guys insane? You just shortened your curse time. The paper was going to melt in five days. Who knows how much time you have left now that you've torn it. I'm not tearing this thing, no way," Logan said.

"Come on, Logan. I think I did a pretty good job of explaining the paper," I said.

"You can't explain the snowman. It moved. It was alive," Logan said.

"Whatever, Rick probably built the snowmen, wrote the letter and rigged a timer to melt them," I said.

"Rick built the snowmen? With what snow?" she demanded.

"A snow-making machine," I said. "The fire department has a snow-making machine. Remember, my dad's a fireman. Come on, Shig; help me out here."

"Okay, but it doesn't explain the thing melting before my very eyes," Shig said.

"Look, sometimes, when you are excited about something, you end up seeing things. Your brain does it. Trust me, I've seen it on TV."

"I don't know ... maybe," Shig said, unsure. "Well, what about the Pole?"

"The what?" I asked.

"The letter says that only the Pole can help. Who is the Pole?" Logan asked.

"I don't know and don't care. Come on. Let's go. Do you want to read the e-mail or not?" I said. Tired of snowman talk, I took the gang up to my room.

Logan Translates S.R.'s E-mail

"**B**efore you read this e-mail, you have to promise not to tell Tiff about it," I announced as we settled in around the computer.

"Why?" Logan asked."

"Because I'm trying to prove her brother sent the e-mail and you'll mess things up by telling her. Okay?"

"Not that it matters, he didn't. But whatever, I promise," Logan said, followed by two more promises, one from Shig and one from Fleep.

I opened the e-mail then stood back and studied their faces as they read. *Enthralled* was the simplest way to put it. That didn't matter though. All I needed was one of them—just one of them to say that they thought the e-mail was from Rick. Then we'd counter his hoax somehow.

They took their time reading, I think because they were trying to figure out the words they didn't know. Finally Logan spun around in the chair and stared at me, wide-eyed.

"Okay, I am officially freaked! Print it," she said, pressing buttons on my printer.

"Stop that," I said.

"I know how to turn on a stupid printer. Just print it."

"You know how to turn on a printer, but can't press print yourself?" I mocked.

"I'm not touching your computer. Last time I did, you had a hissy fit."

"Stop saying I have hissy fits. Girls have hissy fits, not boys!"

"Just print it," Logan demanded.

"No, I'm not wasting ink."

"Jakob, please," she begged.

"Fine!" I said, rolling my eyes.

I didn't want to argue with Logan anymore. She was my friend and the bickering *was* getting old, but it was hard dealing with someone as thick headed as her. In her mind, she was right and I was wrong, even if I was only trying to protect her from Rick. Maybe with a little nudging on my part, my friends would come to the same conclusion I had: that Rick was orchestrating all of this. I reached past Fleep and printed the e-mail, then handed it to Logan. She began reading.

"The e-mail's author, S.R., tells us to catch 'the portly man,'" she said as she walked over to the end table beside the printer. There was just enough room to sit down. "And notice how S.R. doesn't mention Santa by name, not once," she said, referring to the e-mail. "That's odd and—"

I interrupted Logan. It was time to throw her some bait. "Yeah, you are right, it is odd. And what about S.R. instructing me to catch Santa and then Rick telling me to do the same thing? It's almost like it's too much of a, a ..." Come on, one of you, say *coincidence,* I thought.

"... a sign that we should do it," Fleep said.

Ugh! I glanced over at Shig. He was smiling but in an anxious way, like he had something to say and couldn't wait to say it. Spit it out, I thought.

"I know who ..." Shig began, but Logan held up her index finger to shush him then looked over at me.

"Have you looked up the words?"

I shot her a blank stare.

"The *words.* The big ones, the ones we don't know the meanings of," Logan said, shaking the printed e-mail in exasperation. She stepped over to the computer chair, brushed Fleep aside, then sat and logged onto the Internet. "We need to substitute the words we don't know with ones we do and then reread it. Trust me, it will make more sense."

This was a complete waste of time. It's a hoax, a trick, a scam. Look *those* words up, Logan. I ambled over and glanced at the computer screen. Logan was logging onto Webster.com, and had a pencil and the printed e-mail in front of her.

"I've circled all the words we don't know or are not sure of: *esteemed, bamboozle, euphoric, tedious, recant,* and *portly.*"

"Wait a minute," I barked at the back of her head. "How do you know what words we don't know?"

She sighed, then grabbed the paper and held it over her head, still looking at the screen.

"If I don't know them, then *you* definitely don't," she said, as condescendingly as she could. Ugh, she didn't even have the decency to offend me to my face. Why did I put up with her? She was so arrogant, but also so right. Maybe that's why.

"Oh wait, *portly* is … *fat!*" Shig blurted.

"Are you sure?" Logan asked.

"Pretty sure."

"That's not good enough—we have to be sure," Logan snapped. She was quick, and within seconds had her first word looked up and substituted on paper.

"Here," Logan said a couple of minutes later, shoving the e-mail into my chest as she got up from my chair. "Read it with the new words, please. Oh, and substitute the name *Santa* whenever it references 'he' and 'him'."

I liked the *please*. It definitely helped to ease the pain of her pushiness. I cleared my throat and began.

Dear Stormtrooper TK421,

I, the [respected] S.R. will help you. Please respond with details of the event in which you denied your belief in [Santa.] Time is against you, Stormtrooper TK421.

*There are only five days before [Santa] takes to the sky
to [trick] the children of the earth. Of course, you wish
to participate in that evening's [joyous] event; therefore,
you must do exactly as I say or there will be no presents
for you ... FOREVER!*

*First, you must [take back] your disbelief to the per-
son who asked you if you believe. That is a simple task;
the next is not. You must then get that person to believe
in [Santa]. I know of only one way to do this and, unfortunately, it has never been done before. You will be the
first to lift the curse if you are successful.*

*What must you do, you ask? Well, my young boy,
you must catch and present [Santa] to the unbeliever! I
can help you catch the [fat] man. I offer my services. If
you so choose and accept them, I will need the full names
of your parents (including your mother's maiden name).
We must hurry if we are to formulate a plan and catch
[Santa].*

S.R.

"I know who S.R. is!" Shig said, almost shouting.
Logan placed her hands on her hips.

"Really? Who?" Fleep said.

"Yeah, who?" I asked, extremely interested in the answer. Come on, buddy, don't let me down.

"Rick. Rick is S.R.," Shig said. *Finally,* I thought,
someone's using his brain. I smiled and so wanted to do
a victory dance.

Logan turned to me and said, "You told him to say that, didn't you?"

Ugh, she was killing me.

"No, he didn't tell me to say it," Shig fired back.

Logan was ready with more ammo, but I cut her off.

"Search your feelings, Logan," I said, making a Darth Vader breathing sound. "You know Shig is right. It's just too much of a coincidence." I stopped the Vader act. "Catch Santa? Come on. It's Rick," I said.

"So, just like that, we go from being freaked to 'Oh! Rick did it!'"

"Uh-uh, don't include me in the freaked-out moment. You're the only one freaking out."

Fleep interrupted us, raising his hand like he was in class or something. "The snowman freaked me out," he admitted.

"Rick is S.R.," I said.

Logan threw her hands in the air then smacked her thighs. "No way, I don't believe it. Rick is not S.R., guys," she said to Fleep and Shig. "Remember the snowmen and the melting curse letter." She turned to me and said, "We're cursed, running out of time, and you're not helping with all of this negativity!"

"Me, negative? What do you call believing in a curse?" I asked. "Guys, I'm right. All I need is a little more proof, and you'll be thanking me for not having to worry about a fake curse."

"Then prove it or shut up about Rick!" Logan said.

"Fine. I'll prove it! Check this out. S.R., a.k.a. Rick, is sending me an e-mail every hour on the hour, twenty-four e-mails a day."

I showed them my deleted items folder. It had a lot of e-mails from S.R., each entitled "Time Is Running Out."

I started a new e-mail.

"I'm going to reply to S.R.'s last e-mail and tell him I know he's Rick. Once he realizes that I'm onto him, I bet the hourly e-mails will stop.

I read as I typed.

You are so busted, dear respected S.R.! How about I call you by your real name, Rick Lang? Logan, Shig, Fleep, and I know. The e-mails, the Wikipedia articles, and even the curse are all bogus. Nice try, man. We know it's you, Rick, so stop sending me the stupid e-mails. You are really in for it. Wait until I get my hands on you ...

"No threats. You shouldn't make documented threats," Shig said.

"Okay, Officer Sugihara," I said, then pressed the Delete key and watched my threat disappear. There, now it was short and to the point. The last thing I wanted to do was waste any more of my Christmas vacation on it or Rick.

I clicked Send.

"There, done!" I said, hopping out of the chair. "Just remember this night. This is the night that I proved that Rick is S.R."

Logan shook her head. "You're brainless."

I gave her a dismissive look as we left my room to go outside and watch the movie. We all sat around the outdoor fireplace since the weather was still getting strangely colder, and tried to forget about curses and quarrels. If our parents noticed that we were a little distracted, they didn't say anything, probably just chalking it up to Christmas excitement.

An hour later, everyone had gone home, my parents had tucked me in, and I was in bed staring at my dark ceiling. Surprisingly, I was a little anxious thinking about the e-mail. I wanted to find out if the hourly e-mails had stopped; that would prove Rick is S.R. I glanced over at my clock. It was almost eleven p.m. It didn't matter; I had to check. I got out of bed—probably not as quietly as I should have—and started my computer. Drumming my index fingers on the keyboard, I waited anxiously for the computer to boot. A minute later, I stared at the mail icon. This was it: the moment of truth. I clicked open my e-mail program, then just as I was about to click Check Mail, my dad walked in. And would you believe that I did it *again?* What was wrong with me? Like a spastic game show contestant, I reached over and pressed *the* button— the button that killed the power to my computer.

"I thought I tucked you in?"

"You did, but I wanted … I mean, I'm just going to bed now—"

"You can quit your bumbling. I saw what you did. Actually, I heard it. You see that switch over there, the one you can't stop pressing? Well, it makes a *clicking* sound. You know, *click, click!* The sound should be very familiar to you, considering the number of times you've pressed it."

Ugh! Man, I wish I could take it back, but it was an instant reaction based on pure instinct. The excuse I offered up didn't matter, so I'm sure you can guess what happened. Yep. I lost the computer. But it wasn't too harsh a punishment this time; probably because of my dad's forgiving Christmas spirit. I lost it for a day. Not harsh, but still a bummer, because I wouldn't know for another twenty-four hours if the e-mails had stopped. I sighed, said my nightly prayers, and fell asleep.

An Old Friend Calls Rick

I saw something in the darkness, growing bigger as it came toward me. Suddenly the moonlight revealed a tall man wearing a dusty hooded cloak. My heart raced. It was the man from my dreams. The same man who had threatened to turn me into coal. I tried to run, but my legs refused to move. My arms wouldn't budge. Only my eyes were free to look. A prisoner in my own body, I gazed upon the frightening man. His black hood concealed most of his face, but I could see his cold smile, the whiskers on his cheeks, and a long, braided goatee that reminded me of the Egyptian King Tut.

"For me? You shouldn't have," the cloaked man said gleefully, motioning downward.

My eyes cut to the ground, to snow, and to the unconscious body of a very large, muscular man lying on his back. His face was shadowed by a black military helmet. He was some kind of soldier. But before I could look at the rest of him, some hazy movement next to the soldier caught my eye. It was a serpentine trail of black dust particles. The trail led to a lone pair of pants and combat boots that stood about five feet from the soldier. The pants were definitely military issue because of the many bulging pockets and the way they tapered around the combat boots. But, even in my fear, something struck me as odd about the pants. They were way too small to belong to an adult.

That's when I realized what was happening. A kid, dressed in soldier gear for some reason, was being transformed into a lump of coal. The small pants and boots were all that remained of him. Horrified, I tried to speak but couldn't. So I watched helplessly. A moment later, the last of the boots disintegrated and floated away.

"The Wayward are mine. They always have been ... and always will be!" The cloaked man announced then rushed over to the unconscious soldier, bent down, and without hesitation reached for something. I couldn't see what he touched on the soldier because it all happened so fast. But whatever he was trying to do didn't work. He was instantly shocked by a flash of blue light that threw both him and me back several feet.

I sat bolt upright in bed. It was the next morning, December 21, four days before Christmas and I'd just had my second nightmare in two days. This was Rick's fault. He and the stupid fake curse were interfering with my sleep. Regardless, the nightmare really scared me. I tried to put it out of my mind by thinking about the e-mails. I stared at my computer. I was one keystroke away from finding out the answer to the mystery question. Did Rick, a.k.a. S.R. reply to my e-mail? I walked over to turn it on, then remembered last night—that stupid kill switch. I peeked out into the hallway. No Dad. Cool, the coast was clear. I ran back to my desk and reached for the computer's power button.

"Jakob!" I jerked my hand back like I'd just been burned.

"Breakfast! Get up!" It was my mom calling from downstairs. Only her voice sounded like it was just outside my room.

It took a couple of dry swallows, but I finally cleared my heart from my throat and managed to answer. "I'm awake. Be right down."

I gave the power switch one last longing look then left my room. Yeah, maybe I could have stalled coming to breakfast and turned on the computer without my dad ever knowing, but was it really worth it? No, it wasn't. Instead I'd try a classic kid approach: begging. So that's just what I did at the breakfast table, and it worked. Dad said I could have the computer back after lunch. I did the elbow thingy you do when you've just scored, then looked up at my mom.

"Can I have lunch at eleven?"

She smiled.

"It doesn't work that way, and you know it," my dad said between laughs. "You'll get it back *after* lunch. Got it?"

"Yeah," I said, shoving a fork full of pancake into my mouth. Just then the doorbell rang. My twin sisters took off from the table and beelined it to the front door. I stood up halfway, peering my head high enough to see the front door. It was Logan.

"Wow, it's only nine o'clock. You two have something special planned?" my mom asked, walking back to the cook top.

"Yeah, the two of you've been hanging out a lot. Nice." My dad winked at me.

"We've all been hanging out. Shig and Fleep, too. We're on vacation, remember?" I said, getting up from the table.

"It's Logan!" Jadyn shouted in a sing-songy voice.

"We know!" I sang back, then returned my dad's wink. He smiled as I walked away. Parents are so odd, I thought.

"Hey," I said, opening the door.

"Hey."

"I'll be out in a minute—just finishing breakfast."

"Did the e-mails stop?"

I sighed. "I don't know. I can't use the computer until after lunch."

"What?"

"Chill—I'll be out in a minute."

"Unbelievable." And with that, Logan walked off.

Logan wasn't hanging around waiting when I came out after breakfast. As I walked down my driveway, I was blasted with a gust of cold air. Man, it was chilly out—too cold to be wearing a t-shirt and shorts, which of course was what I had on. I spotted Logan on her driveway talking—no, yelling—at Shig and Fleep, and holding up what looked like the melting blue letter the snowman had delivered. Wow, was she animated. Shig and Fleep had their letters too; that seemed to be the topic of argument. I took my eyes off the drama for a minute and looked across the street at Fleep's house. His mom, Mrs. Sanchez, a big woman—larger than most men, stood in the driveway talking to Tiff. She appeared to be consoling Tiff, then gave her a hug that swallowed her whole. I wondered what that was about. Sappy girl stuff, probably.

Glancing back to my friends, I let out a whistle and waved. Logan was now talking to her dad, but she managed to acknowledge me. Fleep wasted no time and jogged over right away. He was smiling from ear to ear.

"Why are you smiling? You look dorky."

"Guess whose parents left last night for a couple of days?" Fleep asked, wiping sweat and his long, blond hair from his forehead.

How in the world was he sweating in this cold?

"Uh—I give up," I said, spotting Shig a few feet away.

"Tiff and Rick," Fleep said excitedly. "We're watching them."

"Is he joking?" I asked Shig as he ambled up to us. Shig shrugged.

"Well, you're not watching anyone, your parents are," I said loftily. "So is Rick sleeping in your room?"

Fleep looked at me, smile gone, face serious.

"Yeah, but, it's not like we're friends or anything."

"Whatever," I said, standing. The wind kicked up. I crossed my arms and shivered with cold. "You two can shoot hoops and be skater friends for life," I said condescendingly.

Fleep looked hurt then got up to leave.

"Hey," I said, quickly grabbing his arm. "I'm sorry. I was being a jerk. It's just that I'm still mad at Rick. Come on, so tell me what happened with Rick's parents." I sat down, hoping he would do the same. He did.

"Family emergency. Someone's really sick; I think it's a grandparent, but I'm not sure."

"My parents would never leave me or Koji alone, even if it was a family emergency," Shig said.

I didn't say it, but I was thinking the exact same thing. My parents would have taken us, especially during the holidays; but, hey, different parenting styles, I guess.

"Well, I hope whoever it is gets better," I said. Shig and Fleep agreed. That's when I looked for Logan. She was just passing Shig's house, almost to us. "So ... four more days until Christmas, including today," I said excitedly.

"Yeah, and I'll finally ..." Fleep stopped in midsentence and suddenly looked deflated.

My smiled faded. "And what? You'll finally what?" I asked.

Fleep frowned. "I was going to say get a skateboard, but we're cursed, remember?

"Don't be stupid, Fleep! I told you, Rick is tricking you."

"You guys fighting already?" Logan asked, walking up and waving her magic melting letter.

"Yeah, round two of curse vs. no curse," Shig said.

Logan held up her melting magic paper. "Well this might help decide the winner. Look at my curse letter. Over a quarter of it has melted."

"Yeah, because you didn't tear it. It's trick paper," I said, a little frustrated we were going through this again.

"I knew you were going to say that," Logan said. "Guys, show him."

Fleep and Shig dug into to their pockets and pulled out their letters.

"It started melting again. Even the part I tore came back. Really weird," Fleep said.

"Yeah, mine too. I even put mine in the freezer, hoping it would stop melting," Shig said, shaking his head. "It still melted."

"Of course it did! And you want to know something else, Jakob?" Logan's tone was mysterious. "Tiff said *you're* the Pole mentioned in the snowman letter. You are the only one who can lift the curse."

"What! Tiff's crazy."

"I'm serious," Logan insisted.

"Me too," I said, shivering. "So did you hear why Rick's parents took off?" I asked Logan, hoping to change the subject. She placed her hands on her hips and stared at me for a moment, as if to say I know what you're doing, then finally spoke.

"Yeah, it's terrible."

"Yep, bummer. And we're still cursed," Fleep said.

"What does that have to—?" I began.

"Guys, don't make the Pole mad," Logan warned Fleep. "We need his help."

"Don't call me a Pole!" I was so annoyed. My friends had lost their minds. Just then Rick rode up on his bike. Feeling both surprised and excited, I moved past Fleep and approached Rick real casual-like. Rick had no idea he was about to confess everything.

"What's up … *S.R.?*"

"What did you call me?" Rick asked.

"S.R., that's your alias, isn't it?" Shig asked.

I motioned to the gang. "Surround him." I sat on his front tire and squeezed his brakes while Logan stood to his left, Shig to his right and Fleep took the rear. Confronting Rick for the answer was quicker than having to wait to get my computer back.

"Admit it—you're busted," I demanded.

"So busted," Shig said, leaning into Rick's ear. Annoyed, Rick jerked his head to the left.

"I don't know what you guys are talking about. Move out of the way."

"Grab him!" I shouted.

Logan grabbed Rick's left arm while Shig grabbed his right arm. Rick struggled for a second then broke free from Shig. I reached up and snatched his arm back.

He wasn't going anywhere.

"Let go of me, you weirdoes!" Rick said.

"You are S.R. You're the one who wrote that stupid Wikipedia article about Christmas Rule Eleven and the curse. Admit it. You know what I'm talking about. You got the e-mail that I sent you last night!"

"Wiki-e-mail, what? I didn't write anything, and I'm not S.R." Rick's face was turning red. He was filled with anger—mad enough that he jerked his bike violently to break everyone's hold. We backed away for a second then grabbed the bike again. I'd never seen Rick so angry.

"Look, we just want answers, so relax," Shig said. He paused, saw that Rick had settled, and began again. "So you're saying that you're not S.R.?"

Rick nodded. "I am not S.R., or whoever."

"Did you make the snowmen and the magic melting paper?" Fleep asked innocently.

"*What!*" Rick said in utter disbelief. "Snowmen—*are you insane?* Wait, is this more Santa stuff?"

We didn't answer.

"Look, if you guys want to believe in a man in a red suit and snowmen, then be my guest. But leave me out of your wackiness."

"I don't believe you. I need proof," I said, now inches from Rick's face. "Isn't that what you want: proof that the fat, I mean *portly* man, exists?"

"Hey, Rick! Rick!" It was Tiff. She stopped at Shig's driveway, ignoring the fact that we were holding her brother hostage and, in some sick sister way, probably feeling happy about it. Even so, I motioned for the others to release Rick, and we backed away.

"What?" he asked Tiff as he jerked away his bike and pedaled toward her.

"The phone. A friend, says it's important. Someone named S.R.!"

Rick Starts Smoking

Tiff shouted *S.R.* pretty loudly and with unmistakable emphasis. Yeah, right … this had *setup* written all over it. And this answered my question about Tiff: she was definitely helping her brother. Why wasn't it obvious to Logan and Fleep? How much more proof did they need?

"Did you hear that?" I asked. "A friend named S.R.?"

"Yeah, I heard," Shig said, nodding.

"We are about to get scammed if we fall for this S.R.-and-curse garbage," I said, a little worked up.

Shig nodded again. "I think you're right, Jakob. The way she said S.R. was kind of obvious."

"You're right, Shig. And what's she doing inside her house? Isn't she supposed to hang out at Fleep's until her parents get back? This has something to do with the fake curse," I said suspiciously.

"Shut up about the curse being fake," Logan said.

"Just don't believe, then. I already told you guys: Tiff wouldn't help her brother. They hate each other."

"Whatever, let's catch up with Tiff and settle this once and for all. She'll fess up," I said, sprinting ahead. I could hear Logan behind me, protesting that I'd only upset Tiff again and should let her handle it. We caught up to Tiff a few seconds later at Fleep's driveway. "Hey, Tiff, who is S.R.?" I asked in a calm voice. I didn't want to come across as confrontational, not yet.

She stopped and turned around. "I don't know. Rick has never mentioned him."

Not entirely satisfied with her answer, I pressed further. "But you said he was a friend."

"Yeah, because that's what the guy said," she said, a little annoyed.

"It's a guy, like a man and not some kid?" Logan asked, nudging me as she passed.

"Come to think of it—yeah, he sounded older." Tiff was eyeing us suspiciously. "What's all this about?"

"Oh, you already know," Logan said dismissively with a chuckle, trying to lighten the growing tension.

"Whatever," Tiff said testily and turned to walk away.

"Tiff, wait," I said. She didn't stop. I turned to Logan. "Ask her," I demanded. Logan shot me a piercing look to shut up. It had no effect. "Fine! I will."

I shouted at Tiff's retreating back, "Are you helping your brother?"

Tiff stopped, slowly turned around, then pursed her lips and folded her arms. "What are you talking about?"

"You don't know that your brother has an e-mail address listed in that Wikipedia article about the Eleventh Rule? And that he calls himself S.R.?"

Tiff looked confused. "The e-mail in that article was cursed@thekringlechronicles.com, not S.R., or whoever."

"Look, just sneak into your house and see if he's even on the phone. If he is, listen in and find out what he and the S.R. person are talking about. It'll prove you're not helping him," I said.

"I'm *not* helping him," Tiff said disgustedly.

"Then go and see what he's up to so we can forget about this curse and catching-Santa nonsense."

Tiff visibly jerked. "Wait, what did you just say?" she asked, grabbing me by the shoulders like a parent does when you're in trouble and have to listen to what they say.

"We can forget about the curse ..."

"Not that. The catching-Santa nonsense," Tiff interrupted.

I sighed. "I got an e-mail reply from someone named S.R., who is actually your brother." Tiff suddenly released me and turned to Logan. Strong grip, I thought.

"You got a reply and didn't tell me?" Tiff said forcefully. Logan stepped back and folded her arms, obviously uncomfortable with Tiff's behavior.

"... and the e-mail said that we have to catch Santa," I said, trying to steer Tiff back to her original question.

"Catch Santa—" Tiff said to herself then turned, panic stricken, and grabbed me again. "He used his initials and disguised his voice." Tiff's eyes were insanely wide. It was scary. "If anything happens, it's your fault. You hear me? Your fault! You should have told me!" Tiff snapped over her shoulder as she ran to her house.

"What in the world just happened with Tiff?" Shig asked. Good acting, that's what happened, I thought as I rubbed my arms. Tiff was really strong.

"Just a guess, but I think she knows who's on the phone with her brother. And based on her reaction, it's not good," Logan said.

"Exactly," Shig said.

"Yep," Fleep added.

Pathetic, I thought.

So there we were—Fleep, Shig, Logan and I—tensely pacing along the sidewalk near Fleep's driveway. Five minutes later, we watched a terrified Tiff sprint from her house like she was being chased. She was as white as a ghost and covered in sweat.

"Something's wrong!" Logan shouted.

We sprinted to Tiff, preparing to meet her halfway, but she didn't stop. "Run! Run!" Tiff shouted over her shoulder as she passed us. "He's after me!"

"Who?! I don't see anyone!" Logan shouted as she chased Tiff. I quickly glanced around. Logan was right, we were the only ones outside. Tiff finally stopped just past Fleep's house, crying, in a panic, talking so fast it was hard to understand her. All we could understand was something like, "He's gone."

"Who's gone? What happened?" Logan asked, leaning into her.

"We have to go, get away from here—no, we have to get the book. Yes, the book, we have to close it," Tiff said hysterically.

"What? You're not making any sense," Logan said.

Tiff's mad eyes cut to me. "This is all your fault, Jakob. You won't believe in the curse and now he's gone."

"What?" I asked puzzled.

"Tiff, who's gone?" Shig repeated, begging her to answer.

"Rick!" Tiff snapped. "I was hiding just outside the kitchen, behind a wall. I could hear Rick talking on the phone, answering questions about Jakob, and then his voice suddenly changed. At first I thought he was choking, so I peeked from around the wall. Rick looked right at me, so I knew he saw me. Then he dropped the phone and that's when I saw it—the smoke, coal black and billowing out from the cordless phone at Rick's feet. My instinct was to shout *fire,* thinking the phone was on fire. I sprinted toward Rick, and as I opened my mouth to warn him, it attacked me."

"What? What attacked you?" Fleep asked nervously.

"The smoke, it formed into a hand and covered my mouth. I tried to scream but couldn't. I could barely breathe, and Rick was inches from me, gagging and coughing. I watched helplessly as another strand of smoke billowed out from the phone and surrounded Rick in a black, cloudy pillar."

Oh, my gosh, this is getting ridiculous, I thought. Logan was in my periphery, rubbing her arms. She had chill bumps again, which meant she believed every word of Tiff's story.

"Then I watched the impossible happen, something that will give me nightmares for the rest of my life," Tiff continued softly.

"What?" Logan asked, her voice full of dread.

"The pillar of smoke spun around Rick like a mini-tornado, and I watched as my brother's legs, then waist, and then the rest of him turned to smoke and got sucked into the phone. He looked like a genie being sucked back into its bottle. Then, before I knew it, Rick was gone and the smoke that was wrapped around me disappeared. I could suddenly move my legs and ran as fast as I could."

I stared at Tiff for a moment to digest everything she had said, then waited for the punch line ... waited for the "Ha-ha, I got you" ... waited for Rick to come running out his front door spouting something obnoxious. I waited, but nothing happened.

"Rick's gone? This isn't some sick joke of his?" I asked, breaking the silence.

"No!" Tiff said, crying, "He's gone. Gone and it's your fault!"

I can't explain it, but there was something in Tiff's expression that made me ignore the accusation for the time being. She was either the world's greatest liar or was telling the truth. I had no way of telling. Tiff plopped down heavily on the sidewalk and crossed her legs. Logan, Shig, and Fleep joined her.

"Seriously … the phone sucked him in?" I asked, folding my arms.

Tiff looked up at me. She looked so sad, so fragile; her green eyes were pooled with tears. She blinked and the tears ran. Logan put her arm around Tiff.

I sighed and sat down. "We need to go back in there," I said. "This has to be one of your brother's pranks."

"It's no prank. Rick is gone. S.R., as he's now calling himself, took him and now he's coming for you three," Tiff said, referring to Logan, Shig, and Fleep.

"Why's he coming for us?" Fleep asked nervously.

Suddenly Fleep's garage door opened, startling us. The door rose like curtains to reveal Fleep's dad staring at us from behind his sunglasses. Keying in on Tiff's tears, he began to walk down the driveway toward us.

We stood as Mr. Sanchez approached.

"Did Grandma die?" He sure was a just-the-facts kind of guy. No soft emotional lead in, no couth; just cut to it and ask the question. That's definitely how my dad would have done it too. I guess that's why they got along so well. Tiff shook her head.

Fleep chimed in. "Dad, Rick and her had a little …"

"Fight?" Mr. Sanchez asked.

"Something like that," Logan said. Tiff wiped her tears.

"Oh, well, it happens. You'll be fine," Mr. Sanchez said reassuringly, rushing away to the garage. The situation was obviously a bit too emotional for his comfort. "And listen, remind that brother of yours to check in with me whenever he's done sulking!"

Tiff nodded, and we all breathed a collective sigh of relief that it was just us again.

Secretly, I still was convinced it was a prank. But by now I also was convinced Tiff was Rick's latest victim. He had terrified his own sister, his own blood, to tears. Clearly he had no limits or loyalties. I was determined to prove Rick was hiding somewhere in his house. So, while everyone else watched Mr. Sanchez walk away, I kept a close eye on the front windows of Tiff's house, expecting to catch Rick peeking out at us. But it never happened.

We Learn Why
Smoke Is Bad For You

We relocated to my house and sat out back around the unlit fireplace. Tiff said it was time to tell us who S.R. was. I secretly didn't care what she said; I knew who he was. I had my own agenda, and it meant getting everyone out of sight to give Rick some breathing room. He was in his house, I was sure of it. Something magical would have to happen for me to believe otherwise.

"You need to tell my dad what happened to Rick. Kidnapping is a crime," Shig counseled a somber-looking Tiff. Just then the "Feliz Navidad" song began blaring from the poolside speakers. The happy tune created a bizarre backdrop to our serious tone.

Wrong approach, Shig, I thought. We need the truth. I walked over to Tiff, placed my hands on my hips, and said, "I can't believe Rick was taken by some magical smoke. Maybe the smoke was actually coming from a prop like a hose or something."

"I don't care what you believe. I know what I saw. I don't need this." Upset, Tiff stormed off to the sliding glass door and opened it. My mom met her on the other side holding our phone. Tiff backed away from it like it was toxic.

"Oh, sweetheart, it's only a phone. Hand it to Jakob for me," my mom said, puzzled, as she handed it to Tiff. Tiff held it like it had cooties, which drew another odd stare from my mom.

"It's for you, honey," my mom said to me. "I'm running up to the store with the girls." She smiled then closed the slider.

"Here!" Tiff said, quickly shoving the phone into my chest.

I looked straight into Tiff's anxious eyes and said, "Hey, I'm sorry. Please stay." I put the phone up to my ear. "Hello."

"Jakob Jablonski?" I didn't recognize the voice, but it was strangely loud, like the phone was on speaker even though it wasn't. Tiff was staring at the phone intensely. I hesitated then pressed speaker and held the phone out so the others could hear better.

"Yeah," I said, eyeing the gang.

"You do not answer your e-mails," the voice said.

"Oh no!" Tiff cried, stepping back.

The voice was male, slow and deliberate, and rolled its Rs as if Scottish. The accent reminded me of Fleep's mom, who was born in Scotland and did the same thing when she got excited or angry. Suddenly there was a sniffing sound coming from the phone.

"Oh, what is that smell?" the voice asked. "Tiff? How conveniently perfect." Tiff's eyes widened. The voice continued, "Jakob." I was too stunned to answer him and too busy reminding myself that you can't smell through the phone. "Jakob!" the voice shouted, demanding my attention.

"Yes," I said, startled.

"I have someone you want to speak to."

"Who—"

"Don't do it! Don't believe him! Whatever he says is a lie! Listen to Tiff. She knows everything. I can break out of here! Tiff, light the wall in the—" It was Rick's voice. Then we heard a struggle and rustling.

"Rick! Rick!" Tiff shouted. Tiff held her hands over her mouth and started crying. This was no joke!

"That will do," the Scottish voice said calmly. I could still hear Rick shouting in the background, then there was a thunderous crackle, like a lightning strike, and Rick's voice was no more.

Tiff charged the phone. "What was that noise? What did you do to him? Let me talk to him!" Tiff demanded.

"He is … napping," the voice said coolly.

Tiff was seething and paced around like a caged lion. "You let him go or I'll—"

"You'll what?" the voice cut in angrily then sighed. "I'll tell you what you'll do. You will have Jakob make things right. That's what *you'll* do. This is all his fault."

"*What?*" I blurted out. "How is any of this my fault?"

"You don't believe in the curse, and I'll wager that, up until now, you didn't believe Tiff's story about Rick disappearing. You have to see it to believe it. Isn't that right, Jakob?"

"No, I don't," I said, taken aback. It wasn't like that. I didn't trust Rick; everyone knew that. It had nothing to do with seeing.

"Well, how about I give you something to *see*. Watch as I take your friends and teach you a lesson you'll never forget. Then maybe you will do as you're supposed to."

I looked around but didn't see anything out of the ordinary. Then the pain hit me just as Logan screamed. "Jakob, your hand is smoking!"

I looked down and saw it was actually the phone that was smoking. It had suddenly become burning hot. My hand felt like I had just touched a hot stove. Yeah, I've touched a hot stove and don't recommend it. I dropped the phone and shouted some indiscernible words on my way to the pool's edge. I punched my hand into the water and held it there for a minute. Surprisingly the pain was already subsiding, leaving no throbbing, nothing. Odd, I thought. Slowly I removed my hand from the water, expecting to see red, blistery flesh. But I was fine. How could that be? Not that I wanted my hand to look like zombie flesh, but the pain I'd felt was so real, so intense, and yet there was no sign of injury or lingering pain.

"Nashash smoke!" Tiff stammered then pointed to the phone. It was billowing thick, gray smoke that seemed to be transforming into a large hand—a King Kong-sized hand.

"Nash-what smoke? What's happening?" I begged.

"It's him!" she said, backing away from the smoke. "It's S.R.!"

Ever curious, Shig stepped closer to the phone just as Tiff shouted, "Watch out!" I spun around as the giant, smoky hand grabbed Shig.

"Say good-bye to your friend," the amplified voice said from the phone.

We charged for Shig but didn't get far. Another gray, smoky hand instantly surrounded us, then transformed into a spinning, tornado-like cloud. Seconds later I was lifted off my feet, forced to the center of the mini-tornado, and pressed against Fleep, Tiff, and Logan. We screamed as the force held us captive.

The spinning continued, going faster and faster, pressing us closer to each other and forcing unbearable pressure against my body. It felt like I was on a carnival ride gone bad. Just before the last of my consciousness drained from me, the pressure dwindled, but there was still no break in the spin. Now wind began pressing down on us from above. I could barely move; breathing became difficult. The air was being sucked out of whatever it was we were in. Struggling and gasping, I felt sheer terror. Was this my last breath of air?

Tiff Almost Loses Her Head to a Sharp Tongue

My knees took the brunt of the impact as the powerful force slammed me down on the pavers. Another blast of unseen and unrelenting pressure was pressing against my back. I tried to fight the force by holding myself in a push-up position, but the heaviness was too great. My arms buckled, collapsing me slightly forward through the smoky tunnel. As soon as my body touched the smoky wall, I heard a loud, crackling shriek. The mini-tornado instantly stopped—the spinning and crushing force were gone, and the smoky tunnel was disintegrating. I quickly stood and came eye to eye with a groggy Tiff, Logan, and Fleep. As I walked through the remaining smoke, there was another loud shriek and the smoke slithered and retracted back into the phone. Was the smoke injured?

84

"Did you just do that? Did you just stop the tunnel?" Tiff yelled.

"No—I don't know. It just stopped," I yelled back.

"*It* doesn't just stop!"

Suddenly I heard more wind to my right. Shig! He was still struggling in the smoky, hand-shaped cloud. It looked like he was suffocating. I ignored Tiff and ran over to Shig, expecting the gray smoke around him to fade away too, but it didn't. In fact, things got a lot worse.

Another smoky wind tunnel grew out from the phone, only this one was as black as coal, and quickly surrounded Tiff again. Panic-stricken and struggling, she managed to reach out through the smoke. It was a short-lived plea for help. Her arms were thrust to her side, her long hair flew out of control, and her clothes rippled against the strong wind. Tiff tried again to raise her hands but couldn't. Then I saw her finger struggling to touch the smoke. It was almost like she was sending me a message—to touch the smoke. That's when I remembered what she said … it doesn't stop on its own. I must have stopped the gray smoke before by touching it.

I shifted my weight from foot to foot. I had a decision to make and soon. I wanted to help Tiff, trust me I did, but Shig was in worse shape. Still in the smoky cloud, Shig was on his knees, holding his arms up. His hands were now beginning to disintegrate into smoke too and were being sucked into the phone. What had happened to Rick was happening to Shig!

"Leave him alone!" I cried, diving into the smoke and tackling Shig. There was an immediate and terrible shriek like before, then the smoke cleared. I quickly stood, helped Shig to his feet, and looked at what was left of his arms—very little.

"Close your eyes!" I barked. Shig didn't listen. He was terrified and probably in shock. We stared at what used to be his hands, but were now two strands of smoke leading into the phone. "Don't worry, buddy, I'll get you back together," I said, hoping my words would come true. I instinctively grabbed the left strand of gray smoke then the right one. Another loud shriek echoed from the phone as soon as I touched the strands. I don't why, but I felt like I knew what I was supposed to do, even though I'd never had to rescue a disintegrating friend before. This is going to sound weird, but the smoke actually felt like tire rubber, which allowed me to get a pretty good hold of it and even pull some of Shig out of the phone.

"Pull back with your arms. Like tug-o-war," I ordered Shig.

"It's working," he said excitedly. "They're changing back." It took a few seconds of tugging on the smoke before the rest of Shig's arms and hands returned to flesh. I spotted Logan over by the screened door, hopelessly spraying more smoke with a garden hose. Fleep cowered several paces behind her. I grabbed Shig by his restored hands and gave them a firm squeeze.

"Get over there! Stay together" I shouted, shoving Shig toward Logan and Fleep. That's when I caught a

glimpse of Tiff. Tiff! She really needed help, but so did my friends. And S.R. had made it very clear—he was going to take my friends, not Tiff.

When I looked back at the gang, I saw that strands of wiry black and gray smoke had encircled my friends and wrapped them up like mummies. My eyes followed the smoky trail to an area by the outdoor fireplace. A pair of branch-like hands was holding what looked like a hose made of smoke. The arms were attached to a five-foot-tall, evil-looking, three-legged, log-like monster. It stared at me with fierce, glowing eyes. Its cavernous mouth, rimmed with teeth like daggers, was open wide and also spewing clouds of gray and black smoke. The creature reminded me of a fireman by the way it held the smoke as if it was a powerful hose. Where had the thing come from? I glanced over at the outdoor fireplace. The log was gone. Could it be the log? How? How was any of this possible?

The thing stared at me, as if daring me to come closer. I was scared but also smart. All I had to do was touch the smoke, right? I grabbed the strands in one swooping move like I was putting them in a headlock and immediately let go, screaming in agony as the burning pain traveled over my hands and underarm. Unlike the gray smoke, the black smoke hurt me. But I'd still made the lasso disappear, and that's what I wanted. The weird log creature was still there, staring at me with arms out as if to say, "You want some of this?" I shot it a fierce look then inspected my hands. The skin was singed and my shirtsleeves were burnt and smoking. Suddenly I was hit with a sharp stream of water. It was Logan, spraying me with the hose.

"Okay, Logan, stop!" I yelled.

"Ah, now it hurts *you* to touch the smoke. How wonderful," the delighted voice said from the phone, sounding as loud as the school intercom system. I ignored the voice and ran over to my friends.

"You need to get outside!" I said.

"No, you need to help Tiff," Logan countered.

I could barely see Tiff through the black smoke. My hands were pounding like a heartbeat, reminding me of what waited for me if I charged into the black cloud— the same smoke that had just burned me. I knew I should dive into the tunnel and tackle Tiff, but I couldn't get past the thought of burning pain all over my body.

"Jakob, hurry!" Logan screamed.

With that plea, my body thought for me. I sprinted and jumped through the tunnel, tackling Tiff. We instantly fell to the pavers, and the smoke was gone ... but there was a terrible burnt smell—my clothes, my hair? I didn't know, but there was no time to look. Just know that I took what felt like a zap of electricity for that girl, Tiff. Unless you've been shocked before, you have no idea what it feels like, and I'm not talking about the shock you get from sticking your tongue on a nine-volt battery.

My friends were yelling as I stood. The log monster was holding smoky whips and advancing on them again, taking advantage of my distraction. They needed help yet again. I quickly reached down for Tiff. She was semiconscious, frazzled, and moaning.

"Here, grab my hands," I said as I pulled her up.

She saw the log creature and yelled, "Logart! Evil wood spirit!" How she knew the name of this freaky creature was beyond me, but I didn't have time to think about it.

"Guys, get outside the screen!" I shouted.

Logan ran just as the log monster came within striking distance. Wide-eyed, she jostled back and forth to avoid the smoke trails and reached for the screen door with Fleep and Shig on her heels. But they weren't quick enough. One of the smoky whips found its mark and wound around my friends, jerking them together and pulling them back toward the log monster.

Without a second to lose, and unprepared for the pain that awaited me, I rushed toward my friends. Then, just as I was within inches of them, the black smoke disappeared. I heard a *poof* and looked over at the Logart. I caught a glimpse of a mini-mushroom cloud as a pile of logs fell, lifeless, to the pavers.

"I think that's enough. No sense in hurting the Pole," the devious voice echoed from the phone. "However delightful it may be to see you in pain, I still need you, Jakob!" The voice suddenly turned jubilant. "Although

I can't believe it's true. Finally after all these years of searching."

As the voice spoke, silvery smoke slowly slithered out of the phone and began to transform into the silhouette of a huge, hairless face. With no eyebrows, lashes, or hair, it looked like a giant mannequin head.

"Well, well—what have we here?" the face said excitedly in its Scottish voice. "You know *most* children would have run off by now. Oh, but not you, Jakob. Not a Pole. I still can't believe it," he was smiling.

"Let Rick go!" I demanded.

"Ha!" The face snickered then stared at me for an uncomfortable minute or so, smiling.

"Who are you? What do you want?" I asked, breaking the silence.

"I am the esteemed S.R. The better question is: do you know what you are?"

"He doesn't know," Tiff said flatly.

"*Hey* … yes I do," I said, frustrated that Tiff was speaking for me. "I'm a person, a—a boy—"

"Ha!" S.R cut me off and turned to Tiff elatedly. "Dedicated yet untrained? Faith strong enough to defeat smoke? Finally!" He studied me with his devilish eyes and said, "You're not just a boy," then turned back to Tiff and eyed her suspiciously. "Did your brother chose him?"

"Yes," Tiff said nervously.

"Are you sure? Maybe someone else chose him, hmm?" S.R. asked slyly.

"No!" Tiff said.

S.R. looked up and let out an evil hollow laugh, then poked his head at Tiff like he was going to headbutt her, but he didn't. "Liar!" he said. "The tongue deviseth mischiefs; like a sharp razor, working deceitfully." He let his words soak in then continued, "Isn't that right, Tiff?"

Tiff motioned me away.

"What is he talking about, *Tiff*," I said, walking backwards into Logan. Just then S.R. opened his mouth and stuck his snake-like black tongue out at Tiff.

"No, I'm telling the truth," Tiff said, her voice quivering. I sensed something bad was about to happen and it did.

A puff of black smoke filled S.R.'s mouth. Then there was a clanking sound—like metal against metal—and the smoke quickly faded. The tongue was gone and in its place were two razor-sharp, shiny black spears. I don't know how, but S.R. managed to speak with the spears coming out of his mouth.

"Come now, Tiff. You're a terrible liar," S.R. said, turning his nose up at her. The spears moved off of Tiff for a second.

Tiff didn't say anything.

"Your breath ... it wreaks when you tell a lie." Tiff cupped her hands and breathed into them and smelled. I couldn't tell the verdict, if her breath stunk or not, but that was the least of her worries. The spears were now inches from her face.

"We have to do something," I said to Logan under my breath.

"Are you crazy?" Logan said.

"Yes, are you crazy—Jakob?" Ugh, S.R. had heard us. "Touch the spear and die. Don't believe me? Try." He looked pleased with himself. "Hmm ... I made a rhyme." Accidentally touching smoke and learning that you can fight it is one thing, but being warned of imminent death is entirely different. I heeded S.R.'s warning and watched Tiff helplessly.

"I'm going to ask you one more time—who chose the Pole?"

"The fire test confirmed him a Pole three times," Tiff said crying. S.R. sniffed the air, sounding like a dog. He seemed satisfied and the spears retracted instantly, like a switchblade, into his mouth and disappeared. I guess Tiff wasn't lying, but what was she talking about?

"Hmm, maybe I acted a little premature in dealing with your parents," S.R. said, thinking out loud. "No, they left me no choice."

"My parents? You took my parents?" Tiff asked, horrified.

Annoyed, S.R.'s eyes cut to Tiff.

"Oh come now, girl; don't act so surprised. You and your family should have found one of his kind hundreds of years ago," he said, facing the rest of us.

I looked at Tiff, dumbfounded by the prospect that I was staring at a girl who was *hundreds* of years old? It couldn't be. She was thirteen—looked thirteen. My mind raced with questions, but S.R. interrupted before I could ask the first one.

"Listen to me, you lazy brats!" S.R. said, speaking to my friends. "You three are cursed. And in three days, a blood-red X will appear on each of your roofs confirming the curse. When that repulsive, overweight, lard of a man sees the X on your roof, he will know to pass over your house, and guess what that means?" he asked mockingly.

My friends looked confused and terrified.

"No presents! Not a stinking one!"

I shot Tiff a puzzled look. I remembered spotting her looking at our roofs a couple of days ago through the binoculars. Looking for Xs? I wondered.

Tiff remained stone-faced.

"We don't care about the presents. We want her family back!" Logan said, pointing to Tiff.

S.R.'s face tensed for a moment then relaxed.

"Jakob," S.R. startled me by saying my name. "You have to make things right. You have to catch the fat man—"

"What—why me?" I asked.

"Because, you stupid pig-eared monkey," S.R. was enraged. "You are a Pole. Haven't you been listening?" Evidently when he got angry, his language deteriorated from the level of an aristocrat to an 11-year-old kid.

Oh, this freak was making me mad. I had just about enough of the name calling.

"I'm not catching anyone! And you can't make me!" I said.

"I'll take your friends," S.R. said matter-of-factly.

"What? Wait a minute. You just said—"

"I'll take your friends. *That* is what I just said! Don't think I can't."

I stared at the face then cracked a smile. Why? Because, I'd been right all along in saying there was no curse to lift, and S.R. just proved it by threatening to take my friends. It also proved something else I'd been saying since Friday—Santa doesn't curse people.

"What about the curse and Christmas Rule Eleven— The Lost Rule?" Logan asked, sounding devastated.

I rolled my eyes at Logan. "Isn't it obvious? It's just like I told you guys. It's all made up, the curse, the eleventh rule. Lies!" I said coldly.

"So what. So you figured it out. *Big whoop!*" S.R. said mockingly.

"Once you realized I wouldn't help my friends because I didn't believe in the curse, you came up with another plan ... to take them. You just want Santa. That's all you want. And you want me to catch him!"

"Argh!" the face shouted. "Do not say that despicable name in my presence." S.R. shook his head so violently that the smoky face blurred then disappeared.

Five seconds passed before I finally said, "Hello?" The face reappeared, inhaling deeply.

"How in the world am I supposed to catch—"

"Use your Pole brain, punk and figure it out," S.R. broke in. "I can't help you directly. There are rules!" It was hard to believe this person, this thing, followed rules. "But I can point you in the right direction. First, agree to catch the blubbery ape. Do it and I'll leave your pathetic friends alone. Don't do it … and your three bratty friends will be coal by tomorrow."

Coal! A wave of fear washed over me as I remembered my nightmares of a cloaked figure who turned people into coal. Was this thing before me the cloaked man from my dreams? Had I dreamt of my friends' demise? I glanced over at Shig. He was sweating bullets. Logan was fidgeting with her nails, and Fleep, well, he was crying.

"I don't have all day!" S.R. barked.

"I guess I have no choice," I said, defeated.

He smiled smugly. "*No,* you don't."

"Fine, I'll do it," I said, still looking at my friends.

"Splendid. Very well then. Catch me the fat man and bring him to the vacant house across the street—the one that is for sale. We'll do the exchange there—Rick and family for the blob," S.R. said, then quickly turned to Tiff. "Don't worry, naturally I left the book—otherwise how would I return? And, as for that point in the right direction, Jakob," S.R. continued, "go to thekringlechronicles. com. It's the slob's Web site."

"How do I know it's not your Web site?" I asked.

"You don't," S.R. said matter-of-factly, "but it isn't. I wouldn't have all of the stupid faith and heartsy-fartsy trash if it were my web site. Listen to me: thekring-lechronicles.com is just a cover. The real information is on his secret Web site."

"How do I get—?"

"Backdoor hack. Once on the Web site, find and solve this riddle:

'Stories of man, hang from the vine. Picked by the woman, forbidden by the divine.' Solve it and you'll access the secret section. I'd love to tell you more, but I'm not allowed. Rules."

The riddle made absolutely no sense. Logan and Shig were reciting it quietly, no doubt memorizing it. "And, if any of you amoebas tell your parents, I'll take them— all of them. It isn't hard to do, you know. They're all just a phone call away." And with that warning, the face disappeared.

Uncertain and cautious, I approached the phone. It was still on. As I was contemplating picking it up, S.R.'s face suddenly reappeared again, almost giving me a heart attack.

"I'll be in touch, Jakob Jablonski."

My friends screamed. I yelled and without thinking, kicked the phone into the pool. We ran to the poolside and watched as it sunk to the bottom.

Positive the phone was no longer a threat, we avoided the pile of logs and walked past the empty fireplace and flopped down on chairs. Tiff joined me on the smaller sofa.

"Jakob, that was amazing—fighting the smoke and—" Logan voiced quivered then cutoff. Her eyes were glossy. She was doing her best to hold back the tears.

"Incredible," Fleep said with a sigh.

"Yeah, thanks Jakob, seriously ... thanks for saving me," Shig said somberly. "I wish I had a smoke-fighting super power."

"Oh come on, it's not a super power," I said. I was a bit worried, sure, but surprisingly not as somber as my friends. I guess there was a part of me that felt that we could handle this.

I sat there motionless, staring into the fireplace, my mind trying to absorb and make sense of all that had just happened. Tiff had to have the answers. I sat up. Logan's eyes were open and tearing. Shig's and Fleep's eyes were now closed. My heart went out to my friends. They were trying their best to be brave and not cry.

Tiff looked to be taking it the hardest and rightly so. She had watched her brother transform into smoke and get sucked into a phone. And who knows how S.R. took her parents. Probably by phone as well. I sighed and said, "Unbelievable," under my breath.

It was a story that only thirty minutes ago was un-imaginable. But now it was real ... and I was bursting with questions. Like who is this powerful, evil S.R. guy? What about Tiff? What was she? Surely people can't live hundreds of years. And was she working for S.R.? How was I able to do things that no one else could?

Yep. It was time for some answers.

Tiff Spills
Some of the Beans

Tiff was wiping her tears when our eyes met.

I cleared my throat, thinking it would make me sound firm. "I have so many questions and my mind feels like it's in its own tornado. First of all, what was S.R. talking about when he mentioned you and your family? Do you work for him?"

Tiff sniffled. "Oh, not now, Jakob." She ran her hands through her hair. "I'll tell you later."

"I don't think so!" Logan demanded, using her right shoulder to dry her cheek.

"It's complicated," Tiff said.

"Complicated or not, you *owe* us answers. It's a simple question. Do you work for S.R., yes or no?" Logan pressed. The tension was growing.

"Kind of" Tiff said tensely. "We're spies working for S.R. We have one job … find a Pole."

"Okay, wait," I said. "What's a Pole?"

Tiff shot me a blank stare.

"They're special people. I've heard them called the chosen ones. They're the only ones who can see Santa. And if you can see him, you can catch him."

I stared cockeyed at Tiff.

"It's true and that's all I know. S.R.'s not the kind of person you ask questions. So, we just did our job and searched many years for a Pole. But last Christmas, after we still hadn't found one, S.R. really freaked out and threatened us, saying this would be our last free Christmas if we failed again. Well, we were pretty sure we'd fail again this year, so my parents contacted Santa's elf spies and secretly made a deal. Basically, my family and I are now double agents—S.R. thinks we work for him, but we are really helping Santa's forces instead."

Forces? Elf spies? I mulled that over in my head … definitely not the Santa I'd imagined all these years.

"What was the deal?" Logan asked, moving to the edge of her seat.

"We'd help them catch S.R."

"Holy smoke! Santa wants S.R.?" Shig asked.

"Yeah, he's been trying to catch S.R. for centuries, but S.R. stays well hidden. He fears Santa's power. The elf spies told us that the only way they could ferret out S.R. was if we actually caught Santa. That required finding a real-life Pole, which Santa's spies did. They directed us to you almost immediately. It was incredible, really, considering we'd been looking for someone like you for centuries. They obviously keep track of you Poles. So anyway, they told my parents exactly what to do. We moved to this neighborhood, got to know everyone, and targeted you specifically. Then, a couple of days ago, we tried to trick you into thinking your friends were cursed and the only way to save them was to catch Santa. And, well, you know how that turned out."

I shuffled around in my seat, feeling uncomfortable with what I was hearing. I'd been selected by Santa's spies. I still wasn't clear on the whole Pole thing. Were Poles people of the North Pole? How could I have special powers? So many questions and no answers.

Tiff thought for a second then continued.

"My parents freaked because they had to tell S.R. that you didn't believe in the curse and refused to catch Santa. But then they wondered if maybe Santa's spies were wrong about you. Maybe you weren't a Pole. We still had time to check. There's this test that we do to see if someone is a Pole. It's usually done as a last resort, because it alerts Santa's forces to our location, but that didn't matter since this time we were secretly working for them anyways." Tiff studied us for a second and keyed in on our inquisitive stares. "Ugh," she said. "You want to know about the test?"

"Yeah," Fleep said eagerly.

"*Fine.* We have portrait-sized pictures of all of the kids in this neighborhood. My mom has this pale green crystal with a burning flame inside it, called a Lahavyor, that she holds up to each picture. If the kid is a Pole, a flame shoots out like a flamethrower and torches the picture. We torched three of your pictures. It was true, Santa's spies had found us a Pole. My parents were ecstatic but still worried. You were the right person, but refused to believe in the curse and help your friends catch Santa. They didn't know what to do.

I did, well kind of. I had an idea to shake you up and make you believe: magical snowmen delivering curse letters. But that didn't work either. Then I remembered that, when I was hiding in your bathroom, I overhead you talking about your loyalty to your friends. And, well ... that was good news, because it meant that you would probably do anything to protect them. I went home and told my parents. That evening they told S.R.; I wasn't privy to their conversation, but they seemed upbeat after telling him and said he'd come up with his own plan."

"Yeah ... to kidnap my friends. But I stopped him."

"Don't get so cocky. He could have taken them if he wanted to," Tiff said.

"Well what about the red Xs he said would appear on our roofs? Are they real?" Shig asked.

"Yeah, they're real, but S.R. is a major liar. You actually *want* a red X on your roof. If you don't have one, that means you're on the Wayward List, you know, the Naughty List," Tiff said.

Fleep gulped. "Are any of us on the Wayward List?"

I was about to say of course not, you dummy, when Tiff shook her head and said, "Not yet."

"What does that mean?" I asked, surprised.

Tiff hesitated. "I shouldn't have said that. Just forget about it."

"Tiff," Shig said somberly, "just tell us. We can take it." I could sense that she was about to say something I wouldn't like. She kept looking sideways and biting her bottom lip.

"One of them," Tiff finally said, pointing to my friends, "will be wayward by Christmas Eve at sundown," she said regretfully.

"How do you know this?" I snapped.

"I dreamt it."

"Impossible. Dreams don't come true." I briefly thought of my own scary dreams I'd had lately and sure hoped I was right.

"Look, I'm sorry. I shouldn't have—"

"Guys, not helping!" Shig interrupted. "Her dream scares me, but the idea of that S.R. thing taking my parents scares me even more. We need help and we need it now, or bad things are going to happen to our families. We need to help Jakob catch Santa. That means we need to be ready by Christmas Eve," Shig said, getting right to it.

Fleep was counting on his fingers. "That's in four days," he added.

"Yeah, so we need to hurry up and learn what we can about Santa," Shig said. Secretly, I was glad that my friends were shrugging off the dream talk. Maybe they didn't believe it would happen. Personally, I was scared. And after all we'd been through in the past hours, it wasn't farfetched that Tiff could foretell the future.

"I think we should try to solve the riddle on the Web site," Logan said, interrupting my thoughts. "So let's break up into two groups and whoever solves it first calls the others."

"Good idea. Shig's with me," I announced, walking over to Shig. I needed a dose of his cool-minded objectivity right now.

"Okay, Fleep's with me. And Tiff can research her dad's Christmas book," Logan said.

Tiff was already shaking her head. "I'm not stepping anywhere *near* my house!" She said, crossing her arms.

"I'm sure it's safe," I said. "Think about it. He would have taken—"

"Don't you get it? This was all about catching S.R., remember? But now that S.R. has my parents, and my brother, I don't know what to do. And the stuff you guys want to do isn't going to help me get them back. You don't even know how to catch Santa. We need the elf spies. Our only hope is that they make contact with us, but I don't think they will. Too many things have gone wrong.

They'll probably just abort the mission." Tiff looked miserable, and I could tell she'd given up all hope.

I countered back with strength and determination I didn't know I had. "No way! I don't care what the elves do. We are doing this and we'll figure it out. Santa's the only one who can fix all of this. We have to catch him … with or without the elves help," I said.

"Fine," Tiff said without enthusiasm. "I'll research my dad's book." She still looked sad, but at least was agreeing to help. Fleep jumped up and put an arm around Tiff to console her. He may be a worrier, but he was also the most sensitive of us all, and I was glad to see him try to snap Tiff out of her funk.

Logan jumped up. "Alright then. We'll be over at Fleep's."

Just before she headed out, I pulled Logan aside and spoke softly so that only she could hear. "Hey, I know it will be hard, but try and convince Tiff to grab her dad's book."

Logan glanced over her shoulder at Tiff, who was still being consoled by Fleep.

Logan nodded. "Yeah … we need to see that book now more than ever. I just hope she cheers up." She exited out the sliding glass door. Fleep and Tiff got up to follow, with Tiff slightly hunched like the weight of the world was on her shoulders.

After they left, Shig and I jumped into gear. First priority: straighten the pool area so my mom wouldn't suspect anything unusual … not that she'd ever in a million years guess what *really* caused this mess. I reached over and picked up a pillow and threw it on the sofa, while Shig arranged the chaise, then walked over to the pool's edge and looked down into the water.

"The phone," he said with a grimace.

"Leave it." Mom's fury or not … I wasn't going to risk picking up *that* thing again.

He shrugged and finished picking up around the pool as I waited by the sliding glass door.

"You know," he said, walking toward me, "she didn't tell us everything."

"Who?"

"Tiff. She didn't tell us everything."

I opened the sliding glass door and walked inside. Shig followed.

"Continue," I said slowly.

"She knows why S.R. wants to catch Santa, she's just not telling us."

Shig and I went straight to my room and got on my computer. Figuring that Shig needed to use his newly-reclaimed hands as much as possible, I asked him to drive (use the mouse and type on the keyboard). He'd been staring at and wiggling his fingers the whole way up to my room. I couldn't blame him after what he'd been through, but it was driving me crazy and he needed to put them to work.

We got on thekringlechronicles.com Web site, the one S.R. said was Santa's. We browsed around, clicking on some of the links and searching for the hidden riddle. Before I knew it, an hour went by. We had browsed every page, read every word, and scrutinized every picture on the site ... and still we had nothing.

I sighed in frustration. "We're not doing something right. Maybe we're being too literal."

"What do you mean?"

"We've been looking for the riddle, but I don't think it's written anywhere."

"Yeah, but we've looked at all of the pictures too," Shig said.

That's when I noticed my Bible and suddenly it hit me. I slowly recited the riddle, "Stories of man, hang from the vine. Picked by the woman, forbidden by the divine." I smiled. The riddle was so obvious to me now. "A woman, not allowed by the divine, by God, to pick—" I waited for Shig to catch on.

"Forbidden fruit ... the apple," Shig blurted out. "But apples don't grow on vines."

"Doesn't matter," I said. "Remember the painting of the woman standing behind the plant?"

"Yeah, I remember," Shig said, clicking the mouse to find it again.

A minute later we found the painting of Eve. She was standing in a vibrant garden, beside a tree whose trunk was wrapped in vines, and she was reaching for a dangling silver book. Shig clicked on Eve, but nothing happened. He clicked on the tree, still nothing. Then he clicked on the book. A password prompt popped up.

Bingo! For thirty minutes, we guessed various passwords with no success. We tried the obvious like Adam, Eve, Eden, Bible … all with no luck.

"We're never going to figure it out," Shig said, crushed.

"Don't give up. We need to think," I said. "Have we really solved the riddle?"

We both thought for another five minutes or so, until Shig asked, "What was the name of the tree Eve couldn't eat the fruit from?"

"The Tree of Life," I exclaimed.

Shig tried again. "Nope. Didn't work. Wait, not life … knowledge." He faced the computer. "Tree … of … knowledge," Shig said as he typed.

"Man!" I said. "That's not it."

"No—tree of knowledge has to be it. Maybe it's a language thing."

"The entire web site is in English," I said frustrated. "We're over thinking this." That's when it hit me. We hadn't tried the most obvious—the fruit. "I think I've got. Apple." Shig looked over his shoulder and gave me an embarrassed nod then quickly typed apple in the password window and hit the enter key. Voila, the dangling silver book opened. We high-fived each other. We did it, we were on Santa's private Web site!

We found ourselves overwhelmed by the information on the site. Most of it seemed pretty outlandish at first, until I reminded myself about S.R. and the attacking smoke. *Nothing* was too bizarre in that world. The site was filled with a bunch of strange-but-cool (and not-entirely-believable) things—like Santa having Special Forces units and regional command centers throughout the world, and also a long list of his powers. I won't bore you by listing each and every power here. Now that you know the password, you can go out to his Web site at thekringlechronicles.com, access the private section, and read them yourself. That is unless Santa's webmaster elf changes the password.

As we read through his powers, my computer rang. It was Logan video-calling me on Skype. Shig clicked on the Answer button and Logan appeared on my screen sitting at her desk.

"What's up, Logan?" Shig asked.

"Where's Jakob?"

"I'm right here," I said, crouching beside Shig until I could see both of us in the little window on my screen. "Logan, you're not going to believe it. We solved the riddle. We're on Santa's secret Web site."

"Awesome. How?" Logan asked. After I told her how to get to the site, she started telling me about Tiff.

"Tiff was just at her house reading her book. She said that things had changed. I don't know what she meant by that. And, yes, I asked her. She said she couldn't just tell me—that she had to show me."

"Well, at least you're finally going to see the book," I said excitedly.

"Yeah. Tiff also said that her book mentions something about Santa and caffeine and that he's aller—"

"That doesn't make sense. We want to slow Santa down, not jack him up," I interrupted.

"Right, it doesn't make sense unless you're seriously *allergic* to caffeine," Logan said.

"For real?" I asked.

"Yeah, caffeine is supposed to really freak you out if you're allergic to it."

"I assume that, by freak out, you mean Santa will slow down in some way?"

"That's what Tiff said. And that we'll need to create a special drink; because of his allergy, he won't touch coffee or sodas. Hey, I have to go. I'll see you guys later," Logan said hurriedly.

"Bye," Shig said.

"Later," I said, but her video had already disappeared.

"Interesting," Shig said. "So, where do we buy the world's strongest caffeine drink?"

"Mr. Raffo's place, The Teashroom. That's why Logan dropped off the call so fast. She's probably already on her way there."

"Or she's going to see Tiff," Shig suggested. I shrugged. It was certainly possible.

We went back to reading The Kringle Chronicles Web site for another ten minutes, then Shig was called home for lunch.

After he left, I finished reading about reindeer landing tactics and the fact that, contrary to popular belief, most of the landings did not occur on the roofs but actually happened on the lawns between the houses. This was done for tactical and defensive reasons. There was even a picture of the reindeer and sleigh parked between two houses. I studied the picture. I had a feeling I was missing something. Then I noticed it and couldn't believe my eyes. Both houses had a red X on their roof. Thinking that I'd be able to confirm what Tiff said the red X meant, I clicked on them, and what I read blew me away.

First off, I learned that S.R. was indeed a *major* liar. S.R. had said that the red X was a sign telling Santa to pass over a home—because someone living there was cursed. Not true. Not a word of it. In fact, it was just like Tiff had said—the red X was actually meant for the servant, instructing *him* to pass over the house, that the child inside belonged to Santa. Secondly, I learned that the initials S.R. stood for Servant Rupert. So I knew his name ... but not his story. I mean, why did he hate Santa so much? I poked around some more, hoping to find the answer to my question, but didn't find anything else.

Shifting gears, I decided to research the authenticity of the Kringle Chronicles Web site. I turned to Google. It wasn't easy to find information, but I kept at it and, after about thirty-six mouse clicks, I learned that it was owned by The Kringle Corporation. And would you believe the address was listed as North Polanshalem, Earth? Yeah, it actually said Earth, the planet. What happened to the North Pole? More weirdness. Thankfully, almost all of the Google searches led me to U.S. and foreign military Web sites, so that put to rest any doubt I had that The Kringle Chronicles site was concocted by S.R. It really was Santa's Web site.

Logan and I Are
Attacked by Vampire Owls

After dinner I called the gang over to my house. We met in the Red Room, appropriately named because of its red walls and red sofa. It was the coolest room in my house, and the perfect location to plan a mission. It had the latest techno gadgets, video game system, and even a high-definition projector that displayed onto a nine-foot screen. Everyone got comfortable and we ended up lounging in the middle of the room. I went first and told the gang what I'd learned on The Kringle Chronicles website—the meaning of red Xs, how Tiff had been right and even S.R.'s real name. Tiff reacted with a repulsive look and loud gag when I mentioned Servant Rupert. I was about to remind the gang that there were only four days before Christmas and that we needed a plan, when Logan interrupted me.

"I have good news." She paused for a moment. "Benji is going to tell us how to catch Santa," Logan started. I didn't like what I was hearing.

"Who in the world is—?"

"He's my dad's new assistant. I was at The Teashroom this afternoon and, well, while my dad was in that secret room of his doing spy stuff, I searched for the energy drink with the most caffeine. That's when Benji came over and said real mysterious-like that I wouldn't find what I needed to catch Santa."

"Did you freak out?" Shig asked.

"Yeah! But I played it cool. I wanted to know who Benji really was, but he never said—just that he was here to help us."

"I'll bet Benji's an elf spy," Tiff said excitedly. "Probably the one my parents were working with."

"Or, Benji might be a spy for S.R.," I said, shaking my head. "It's too weird."

"A little late to be thinking things are weird, don't ya think?" Fleep said.

"Benji said you'll need his special tea mix to catch Santa," Logan said, looking at me.

"Me?" I asked, totally creeped out that I was again singled out by someone I didn't even know. Logan nodded.

Shig leaned in and asked, "Did he actually say *Santa*? Remember, S.R. doesn't say Santa."

"Good thinking," I said, patting Shig on the back.

Logan looked around, not sure of herself.

"I—I don't know. I can't remember." She made a weird face as she was thinking.

"Describe Benji," I said.

"Okay, he's tall with curly red hair, a reddish tan face, and a Scottish-English-type accent," she said slowly.

Shig and I gasped. "A Scottish-type accent and doesn't say Santa? Holy smoke, Benji's S.R. Your dad has S.R. working for him at The Teashroom!" I said disgusted.

Logan's eyebrows knitted together. "You can't say that. I can't remember if he said Santa or not," she said defensively.

Then Tiff hit me with a painful reminder. "Jakob," she said, sounding more like a mom than a teenager, "you also thought *Rick* was S.R., remember?"

Ouch. I stewed for a minute then finally gave in. "Fine. When are we supposed to meet Benji?" I asked, defeated.

"Tomorrow," Logan answered.

Now, I know what you're thinking. Why in the world would I agree to meet a perfect stranger and take his advice on how to catch Santa? Well, I think Tiff pretty much answered that question when she kindly reminded me of how wrong I'd been assuming Rick was S.R. She was right; look how that turned out. So I decided I'd forget my suspicions for the time being. If Benji was S.R., we'd know soon enough.

Tiff glanced at her watch then stood suddenly. "It's seven o'clock. I better get back to Fleep's house. Mr.

Sanchez will want to know why Rick hasn't checked in," Tiff said, walking to the door. She gave us a flip-of-the-wrist wave and left. I motioned to the gang to wait as I listened for the front door to shut behind her then spoke.

"It's four days before Christmas, we don't have a plan and she takes off in a hurry."

"She just said she has to talk to my dad," Fleep said softly.

"Yeah, and don't worry about the plan. Benji's going to tell us what to do," Logan said reassuringly.

I nodded. "Maybe you're right."

"I usually am," Logan forced a smile.

Shig brushed past me on his way out the door. "She sure is. I'll see you guys tomorrow," he said.

"Me, too," Fleep seconded, walking a foot behind Shig.

"See, everything is going to be fine. So just chill. I've got to go, too," Logan said, standing.

Great. So much for a plan; everyone seemed content to wait for Benji to help. I stood just as Logan popped her head back in the red room and whispered, "Oh, Tiff still hasn't shown me the changes at her house. We should go check it out ourselves and see the book."

"Let's go now," I said eagerly.

I swear Logan's tan face turned five shades lighter.

"In the dark? No way. Tomorrow, before we meet Benji. Call me as soon as you get up."

That's right. I'd forgotten how skittish Logan was at night despite her toughness. "Hey," I said. She turned around at the doorway.

"I'll walk you home."

I'm pretty sure I saw a hint of a smile on her face.

Minutes later, just as I followed Logan up her driveway, I asked a question that had been bothering me since we'd left my house.

"Logan," I touched her shoulder. She stopped and turned around. "Why didn't this Benji person just give you the special tea?"

"Because, he said he knows you're a Pole, and he has to meet you." Before I could respond, Logan grabbed me by shoulder and said, "Get down."

We hid behind the front of her parents' SUV. "I don't think she saw us, but let's wait a few seconds just to be sure."

Who saw us, I wondered. Did she mean Tiff? I couldn't wait to see. Slowly I stood and peeked over the SUV hood.

"Whoa, what in the world?"

Tiff was across the street on Fleep's driveway, wearing a pair of sunglasses. I turned to Logan and made an odd face. The way Tiff was holding the glasses was strange. It was like she was *using* them, not just wearing them … if that makes any sense. "Wait a minute, is she looking at the roofs?" I asked.

"Yeah, maybe, now that you mention it. I thought

she was looking up at the sky or over the houses, but yeah, you might be right … weird."

"She did the exact same thing Friday with binoculars."

Logan shook her head. "It doesn't make sense."

Tiff stared at her house for a few more minutes then ran around back.

"Come on," I said as I motioned for Logan. "Let's see what she's up to."

We followed Tiff behind her house and caught up to her just as she entered her parents' poolside bedroom door. Quietly, we slipped in behind her. As we cut through her parents' room, Tiff took off hurriedly to the front of the house, muttering strangely to herself there were only twenty-five minutes left. It felt creepy, passing through the quiet rooms. I didn't like being in the house at all. I never thought I'd say this, but it needed parents. To make matters worse, we were following Tiff toward the kitchen—the same place where Rick had been attacked by the smoke and sucked through the phone. Logan and I stopped in the nearby family room and hid behind a sofa. All I could think about was the possibility that S.R. was on the phone waiting to attack Tiff. He'd already taken her entire family. What kept him from taking her?

The sound of Tiff grunting interrupted my thoughts. It sounded like she was trying to lift something but wasn't having much luck. I wanted to get a better look inside the kitchen, but it was impossible to do without being seen. Tiff struggled for a few more minutes—doing whatever it was she was doing—then suddenly gave up with a sigh. There was a moment of silence, then the weeping began. Logan gave me a look that said we had to go to Tiff. I shook my head and mouthed, "No." Then, from the kitchen, we heard a terrible screech mixed with a girl's scream. Tiff! We charged into the kitchen just in time to see the backside of Tiff as she raced out through the other side yelling "Blood-sucking Strix! Blood-sucking Strix!" Logan called to Tiff but another shriek drowned out her voice. Tiff still hadn't realized we were in the house.

As Logan ran after Tiff, I turned to the source of the shriek—the island counter in the center of the kitchen. It had transformed to crystal, and on it was a giant open book. The book was the size of a kid's mattress. The hardcover and binding also looked like glass or crystal, definitely a clear solid, and supported a three-foot-high heap of gilded pages. The two crimson ribbon markers were partially burned and lay across the pages. What I saw next blew me away. There was an opening inside the giant book—hardwood steps on the lower half of the right page that led down into the book. Talk about 3-D; this was crazy.

Just then I heard the shriek again and four beautiful, powder-white owls flew out of the book. Snow owls! I'd only seen them in pictures. They were even more majestic-looking in person. I couldn't take my eyes off them. But something was off. I realized that they didn't have beaks; instead they had fangs, like vampires, and razor-sharp talons. Whoa! I wanted to run, but I couldn't. I tried to look away but couldn't take my eyes off of the owls. I was under some kind of trance and about to be clawed to death. That's when I heard Logan's voice.

"Close your eyes and run toward my voice." I closed my eyes and was suddenly able to move. It worked. I blindly sprinted from the kitchen, collided into Logan's arms and opened my eyes. We quickly shook out of the hug like we'd just given each other a year's supply of cooties.

The vampire owls shrieked again. The four owls were circling the kitchen, taking turns diving. One of them stopped in midflight, shrieked, then bared its white fangs at us.

"The front door!" I barked then sprinted with Logan on my heels.

Seconds later we were at the front door. Logan quickly grabbed the handle and shook it violently, but it was no use. It was locked from the inside; we needed the key. Another screech from the kitchen sent Logan into a panic attack. I grabbed her by the shoulders and told her to chill, but she was too hysterical. I slowly turned around, expecting to be face-to-face with the owls but, oddly enough, they hadn't left the kitchen. I turned around so I was nose to nose with Logan.

"Logan, think. You've been in this house a million times. Where is the key to unlock the door?"

Sobbing, Logan thought then finally said, "Inside the big vase, the brown one by the dining room." I pivoted on my heel, spotted the vase and ran over to it. But when I reached inside, my arm was too short. I couldn't reach the key, and the vase was too heavy to pick up.

Another terrible screech came from the kitchen. I looked up and counted only three owls circling above. The fourth owl was diving on a course for me—just about to fly out of the kitchen. But before I could even think about being scared, the owl exploded into a cloud of flour-like dust as soon as it crossed the threshold. My first thought was that I'd been hit with a pound of flour. I was instantly covered in the stuff and even had some feathers on my head. It seemed the creatures couldn't leave the kitchen. With a relieved sigh, I began to wipe the powder from my eyes.

Boy was I wrong. Charging out from the cloud of powdery smoke came the skeleton of the owl. Just the bones ... and just as furious. I guess it lost some of its being when it flew too far away from the book, but it still clearly had one thing on its mind—me. Logan shouted a warning and I, still not seeing well, backed away just as its sharp, bony claw shattered through the vase.

"The key!" Logan yelled. I quickly spotted it in the shattered debris, snatched it up and sprinted to Logan. Thankfully, the owl's claw was stuck in the vase, which gave me just enough time to insert the key into the lock before the creature broke free. I don't think I've ever moved so fast in my life. We opened the door then slammed it right on that vicious thing as we ran out. I heard terrible clawing on the door as we ran away.

After dropping Logan off at her house, I beelined it home. What was happening to my quiet neighborhood? Even walking a friend home had become dangerous. Sheesh!

By the time I got to my bedroom, I was exhausted and mad—mad at myself for not trying to close the book. Who knew what evil was still lurking deep inside it, waiting to come out.

I Watch a Boy Turn to Wood

I got up early the next morning, around seven. It was three days before Christmas. Tiff's once mysterious and now scary giant book popped into my head just as I hopped out of bed. I got dressed, charged downstairs to the kitchen, and called Logan. I had an idea but would need Logan's help.

"Hello," Logan answered. She sounded froggy, like she just woke up.

"Did I wake you?"

"Yeah, what's up?"

"I've been thinking about the book! We need to close it."

"No way."

"But we—"

"Hold on." I heard what sounded like the bedcovers being thrown off and Logan getting out of bed. Then a door shut. Logan whispered. "Jakob, I'm not going near Tiff's house. Not with those freaky, white Dracula owls flying around."

"My gut tells me that they're gone. Owls are nocturnal creatures, right?" I asked.

"Yeah, but I don't want to chance it."

I sighed. Getting Logan to come with me wasn't going to be as easy as I'd hoped. But I couldn't blame her for not being her usual gung-ho self … the owls were scary. But, oddly enough, the thought of going back to Tiff's excited me. The thought of closing the book had me all jacked up; something told me I could do it. But I wanted Logan's help. I remembered something from last night.

"Logan, just before the owls attacked, I read some of the book." There was a long pause. She was thinking.

"Impossible, I saw the pages. They were blank."

"Nope."

"Seriously?"

"Yep."

She sighed. "Okay, let me get something to eat then I'll meet you out front. My house—five minutes."

"Okay, later." I hung up feeling satisfied. I knew Logan couldn't pass up the chance to read the book, or at least having me read it to her.

I quickly made myself a bowl of cereal and devoured it in record time, then got the okay from my mom to go over Logan's. When I sprinted out the front door, the temperature outside stopped me in my tracks. It had seriously dropped. It was, like, New Jersey-cold. I looked at my T-shirt, thinking a sweatshirt would have been better. I contemplated going back inside for heavier clothes, but figured sprinting down to Logan's would warm me up. I ran quickly and within seconds met up with her.

"Follow me," I said over my shoulder, not stopping. We jogged up to Tiff's house and stopped at the front door. I spun around, face to face with Logan.

"I'll peek inside and make sure there are no flying bird bones. Okay?"

Logan nodded.

I reached up, grabbed the handle, and opened the door slowly. I looked around. The coast was clear, but that didn't mean the vampire owls weren't still in the kitchen, or even in the book. Hopefully they followed vampire tradition and slept during the day like all good vampires should. I walked toward the kitchen, careful to stay in the sunlight shining through the dining room windows. The kitchen was clear.

Logan was peeking in through the cracked open door. I motioned her in with one hand while pressing my index finger up to my lips with her other. We still needed to be quiet until we knew for sure the house was clear of creatures. Logan entered without giving it a second thought. That was a good sign; fearless Logan was coming back.

Suddenly there was a muffled roar, not a shriek, from Tiff's parents' master bedroom. I brushed past Logan and motioned for her to follow. Before I knew it, we were tiptoeing lightly through their master bedroom. The roaring sound led us into the master bedroom closet. From what I could tell, it looked like your average parents' closet, really huge with clothes, shoes, and stuff. Then I noticed a large heavy-duty flashlight strangely propped up on a shoebox. Here we go again. Tiff's house was full of weird surprises. The flashlight was on and must have been for some time because its light was dim. But it was still strong enough to light a section of exposed closet wall. I followed the beam of light—then saw something moving on the wall! At first I thought they were bugs until I got closer and saw they were actually thumbprint-sized individual pictures. They were everywhere, hundreds of them. As I stared at the pictures, I realized that they weren't pictures at all, but prison cells with people inside, and the people were moving—they were alive. I got closer, but the images were still too small to tell who they were.

"It's hard to see—" I whispered.

Logan tapped my shoulder with an object. It was a magnifying glass.

"It was beside the flashlight," Logan said. I took it, ran it across some of the thumbprints, and for the first time truly realized what I was looking at: kids, in each and every cell. I felt like I was in a video monitoring room, watching them.

I got even closer to the wall, adjusting the magnifying glass to get a better look and scrutinize the faces. Who were they? Where were they? These and many more questions popped into my head, and then I saw something that made my heart skip a beat. One of the thumbnails had Rick in it! What were the chances that, of all the hundreds of images on the wall, I would find Rick? He was dirty and looked exhausted. I couldn't chance losing sight of him in the sea of kids. Then I heard a faint scream come from further down the wall. It came from the area to my far left … too far for me to go and still keep an eye on Rick.

"Logan," I forced a whisper. "I found Rick … here—my right hand."

"No way!" she whispered then followed my hand to Rick.

"Remember this spot. I heard a scream," I said, moving to my left.

"I didn't hear anything."

Then it happened again, and by the look on Logan's face, she'd heard it, too. Only this time, it was louder and like a yelp, almost like a creature's cry. I scanned the area to my left, row by row, cell by cell. Then I heard it again, and zeroed in on the right square. What I saw stopped the world for me. At first I wasn't sure what I was looking at. Then I caught glimpses of a human-looking face. It was a boy. He was transforming into something. I couldn't stand the continued yelping and covered my ears as the transformation continued. When it was over, the boy's clothes lay torn atop a muscular wooden body ... the only remnants of his humanity. His skin was ridged and the color of chocolate. The creature panted and seemed exhausted from the ordeal. I was horrified and frustrated that I couldn't help. Just as I leaned in closer to get a better look at him, Logan accidentally moved the flashlight.

"Hey!" I complained, forgetting to keep quiet.

A chorus of shouting began at the sound of my voice.

"Hey!"

"Help us!"

"In here!"

It came from all directions. Hundreds, maybe thousands of voices cried out for help. Even the wooden creature gave a nasty roar. I covered my ears and backed up in a hurry, falling over the boxes. Logan bumped past me, turned off the flashlight, and quickly turned on the closet light. I got back up and charged for the wall. Nothing—it was now blank. The pictures, or whatever they were, had disappeared. I grabbed for the flashlight, but Logan was too quick.

"Hey, come on, they heard me—bring them back!"

Logan shook her head. "No, I wanna go!"

I regarded her. "Logan, they need help. We should talk to them, figure out where they are," I insisted.

"No way. I knew something bad would happen if we came back here."

I sighed. Brave Logan was gone again.

"That roar was a *boy*. He transformed into some weird wooden creature. We need to find out who he is. What he is."

"Then let's go ask Tiff."

"No, I want to know now," I said stubbornly. "Give me the flashlight."

"No, I don't like it here. We need to go."

"But I found Rick."

"Then let's get outta of here and tell Tiff."

Before I could tell Logan how heartless she was sounding, another loud roar echoed. But this one came from somewhere else in the house, like the kitchen.

"The book!" I said, hurrying out of the closet.

"The book *roared*?" Logan asked disbelievingly.

"Come on," I said, ignoring her question.

Stealthily, I led Logan through the master bedroom then walked across the hall and into the dining room. We stopped, looked for owls, then continued toward the kitchen. That's when I saw the vase debris in the dining room from last night. I grabbed one of the dining table chairs and placed it beside the wall adjacent to the kitchen, then climbed up on it and motioned for Logan to do the same. I knew the kitchen was the last place we should have been—especially with that roar—but I just had to try closing the book.

Logan glanced back over her shoulder at the front door, visually marking the distance in case we needed to escape ... or maybe she was just staring at the vicious-looking claw marks made by the skeleton owl. Finally, she grabbed a chair, set it beside mine and stood on it. I stared at the book's text.

Logan nudged me. "Are you reading the book?"

"Yeah."

"You better not be messing with me. I see blank pages."

I ignored her and kept reading. Logan nudged me again.

"Well, what does it say?"

"Hold on," I said, a little annoyed.

I read from the left page and continued onto the following page, where the text seemed to just float over the open stairwell.

"It's talking about the Wayward List. It lists ways to punish or dispose of those named on the Wayward List."

"That doesn't sound good."

"No, it doesn't."

My curiosity suddenly shifted to the steps that led down into the book itself. What was down in that dark abyss? I shifted and struggled to get a better look down into the book, but I couldn't. All I was doing was bumping into Logan. I hopped off the chair and stared into the kitchen.

Every part of my curious, eleven-year-old being wanted to get closer to the book, to use the flashlight to look down the stairs, and maybe even to take a few steps down. But that sudden spike of confidence was washed away by one tidal wave of fear when we heard the monstrous sound of a second—and much louder and closer—roar: a roar that emanated from *within* the book.

I've been to the zoo and heard a lion roar. This was no lion's roar; it was a hundred times louder and fiercer. That was it for me. Logan and I beelined out the front door and sprinted to her driveway.

Once there, we watched Fleep and Tiff come outside with Mr. Sanchez. Mr. Sanchez pointed a baseball bat at Tiff's house as he spoke to them. From the sound of that roar, I expected to see something—a huge beast, a monster maybe—behind us, but there was nothing in Tiff's yard. I noticed that a lot of neighbors had come out of their homes, which I thought was pretty crazy. If you heard something that sounded like a monster's roar, the last thing you should do is go outside.

Then Mr. Sanchez's voice came into earshot, "... the panther, the one that lives along the pond behind Jakob's house."

Logan and I dashed over to Mr. Sanchez.

"Yeah, it had to be the panther," Tiff said, overly anxious.

"It sure sounded close, like it was right next door," Mr. Sanchez said.

"Probably," Logan said. "Tiff has a lot of rabbits in her yard. What are we going to do?"

I know what I wanted to do: involve a parent and tell him all that was happening, but I knew that was impossible. S.R. was a real threat and I knew that the moment he learned we told a parent, things would get much worse.

"Nothing. Whatever it is, it's gone. I'm going back inside," Mr. Sanchez said. "I'm just glad I didn't have to use this," he said, laughing as he walked off with his bat. Tiff had started walking over to Logan and me when Mr. Sanchez added, "Come on, Tiff. I want to finish our talk about your brother."

Her brother! I wanted to give her the news about Rick, that Logan and I had seen him on the wall under the magnifying glass in her parents' closet. Boy, that sounded weird even in my head. I also wanted to ask my questions: who were the kids on the wall, where were they, and what was that wooden creature thing?

Tiff gave me a somber stare. She looked like she wanted to tell me something, too, but couldn't—not with Mr. Sanchez there. She just gave us a slow and deliberate shake of the head, then offered a weak wave and followed Mr. Sanchez inside the garage.

Logan and I walked across the street and parked ourselves on her driveway.

"Did you hear Fleep's dad?" I asked.

"Yeah, I heard him."

"That wasn't a panther. You know that, right?" I asked.

"Yeah, I know. I'm not *stupid*. I was there. There's something inside the book."

"And in the pictures—don't forget the pictures. Those kids need help. I bet Santa can rescue them. We need to call the cops or at least tell Shig's dad. Technically it has nothing to do with me catching Santa," I said.

"Call the police?" Logan held her hand up to her ear and mimicked talking into a phone. "Police? Uh, yeah, there's a giant book inside our neighbor's kitchen, and the book has a stairwell that leads down inside its pages. And there's some scary roaring creature down there, too, so be careful. Oh, and in the closet is a view into a prison-like place with hundreds, maybe even a thousand kids in it, but don't forget you have to stand in the dark in the closet and use a flashlight to see them." Logan looked at me and shot a cutesy smile. "Oh, and then after you do that, our parents turn to smoke and disappear."

I rolled my eyes. She was right. "Okay, then what do we do?" I asked, staring at Tiff's front door. Logan started rambling on about being safe, but I zoned out and didn't hear a word. I was thinking about the giant book … I *knew* I had to close it. When I tuned back in, Logan was snapping her fingers inches from my face. "Hey, did you hear me? We stay away from Tiff's house!"

"No, I need to close the book, or at least try."

"What? No *way*! Whatever's in that book—"

"Isn't a problem," I finished her sentence, but Logan shook her head worriedly. I placed my hands on her shoulders and looked into her deep brown eyes. "Come on, Logan. Think about it logically. If the creature was going to come out, it would have by now. I think we're safe."

"Fine! Maybe for now … but I'm sure S.R. has something else up his sleeve." She turned, stepped away, then held her finger up like she was the lead detective in an investigation and was about to make a proclamation. "Those creatures are in the book for a reason." Logan sighed then continued. "They have a purpose; they are part of something bigger. Jakob, we can't do this alone. I hope Tiff's right about Benji being an elf spy."

"We'll find out soon. Is your mom still taking us to The Teashroom?"

Just as Logan nodded, her garage door opened behind us and startled her.

"Relax," I said. "It's just your mom."

She exhaled and tried a fake laugh, but I knew she was anxious. I wanted to make her feel better but couldn't find the words.

"Hey, you two, I'm going to get my nails done. I'll be back after lunch. Be ready," Mrs. Raffo said hurriedly.

"We will," Logan said.

"We need to tell Tiff about seeing Rick in one of those cells," I said, watching Logan's mom pull away.

"I really don't think that's a good idea."

"I'd want to know if it was my family."

"She's not going like that we were in her house," Logan said.

"I know, but it doesn't matter. We have to tell her."

Logan sighed, then we walked over to Fleep's house. We got Tiff and Fleep to come out and told them everything. As Logan expected, Tiff was pretty upset that we went into her house, but she quickly got over it when we hit her with the Rick bomb. Knowing Rick was okay brought Tiff to tears of joy.

"I'm glad he's okay, but there's nothing we can do to help him. I can see and hear the prisoners on the wall and they can hear me also, but that's it. I can't just reach into their cells and pluck them out," Tiff said.

"What is that place anyway?" I asked.

"It's Diyu, S.R.'s prison for the wayward," Tiff said regretfully.

"Wayward, like from the Wayward List ... the list that's mentioned in your book. Bad things happen to kids on that list," I said. "So all of the kids I saw on the wall—they're wayward and waiting for their punishment?"

Tiff nodded.

"Yeah, but that's S.R.'s form of punishment. The only punishment Santa ever intended was for naughty kids to get a lump of coal instead of presents."

"What in the world happened?" Logan asked.

"S.R. happened. He wants Santa's power. He always has. Never mind all that. Just know that bad things happen at Diyu ... very bad things. Now, you said you saw a boy get transformed into a wooden creature?"

I nodded.

"He's rebuilding ..." Tiff mumbled. "There'll be more transformations before this is all over."

"Rick too?" Logan asked worriedly.

"I don't know. I don't want to think about it."

"Ah man," I said grabbing my hair. "This is not good. Where is this prison? Where's it located?"

"I don't know. But even if I did, it would do you no good. You can't see it. It's hidden, just outside of time," Tiff said.

"That's impossible," Logan said.

Tiff looked at her and said, "You *did not* just say that."

"Yeah, you're right—never mind. So what about calling Santa to come? I mean there's got to be a way to call him. Maybe it's on his Web site somewhere."

"He's not Batman, Logan," Tiff said then turned to me. "It's all up to you, Jakob. You have to catch Santa. It's the only way."

I Meet an Elf Spy

Logan's mom dropped us off in the parking lot at Mr. Raffo's teashop, The Teashroom. It looked like a giant brown-stemmed, green-capped mushroom—like something from a fairytale.

Logan and I first became friends when it was being built, and we'd explore the construction site together. I have to admit, there were some really strange things happening even back then. We'd watch the odd workers wearing mirrored sunglasses and yellow hazmat suits, kind of like what firemen wear. I remember repeatedly asking Mr. Raffo why we didn't have to wear the suits too when we walked around the site. He'd just shrug and quickly walk away before I asked any more questions. And some days we weren't allowed to come on site at all—it was completely closed to anyone except the strange workers. It was odd now that I thought about it.

On our way to the door I noticed something new hanging outside The Teashroom. It was a red-and-white flag blowing in the wind. As I got closer I could see an image of a standing polar bear in the center of the flag. I shrugged and followed Logan toward the front door— an exaggeratedly large, round, glass door I had entered a hundred times before. As I reached for it, Logan punched me in the arm.

"What was that for?" I asked.

"Don't say anything dumb to Benji. He's *not* a spy for S.R.," Logan said.

I didn't say anything and walked in. The chime sounded, announcing our presence. A tall, freckle-faced, skinny man in his thirties, with a red 'fro that covered half his ears, walked out from the back room. We met by the counter.

"Hi. Welcome to The Tea—oh, it's you ... and your friends," the man said, suddenly excited. His accent caught my attention—the way he rolled his r's.

Jingle Bells was playing over the speakers.

"Hi, I'm Benji," he smiled and looked pointedly at Fleep, "And who might you be?

"I'm Fleep." Fleep turned his head curiously, studying Benji. "Are you a Scot?" he asked excitedly.

"Aye," Benji said.

"My mum is a Scot," Fleep said, almost sounding Scottish himself.

"Well, it is a pleasure to meet you." Benji shook Fleep's hand firmly.

"Likewise," Fleep said.

"Yeah, and I'm—"

"Jakob, the Pole," Benji said, stepping forward and beaming widely. Odd greeting. We shook hands.

"Guys, let's play some video games," Fleep said, looking past the counter to the back of the shop where the games were.

That's all Fleep ever wanted to do—walk in and head straight to the gaming area. Logan reached out and grabbed his arm. "I don't think so," she said matter-of-factly then jerked him back. "We didn't come to play video games."

"That's right. I'm going to tell you how to catch Santa," Benji said. My eyes bulged. He said *Santa!* That knocked out my suspicion he was S.R. Was Tiff right? Was Benji really an elf spy? I moved closer to Logan.

Benji smiled and continued, "You need elf tea. High in caffeine and irresistible to its drinker. One sip and Santa will drink the cup dry." He leaned against the counter and peered at us over his sliding black-rimmed glasses. I stared at his ears and tried to see the slightest hint of a point. I had to ask him if he was an elf.

Just then a woman, probably my mom's age, came in.

"Meet me over by the caterpillar aisle. I'll be but a moment," Benji said.

Benji was referring to one of the four merchandise aisles where all the health-related items like teas, vitamins, and herbs were stocked. The first aisle looked like a giant, lifelike, yellow caterpillar. The second aisle looked like a red snake, the third aisle like a blue earthworm, and the fourth was like a giant, black, African millipede. I'd never seen an African millipede before, but Miss Know-It-All always corrected me if I didn't call it by its proper name. Speaking of whom, Logan was reading a bottle she'd picked up from the snake aisle, no doubt looking for elf tea. She was so literal.

While I waited for Benji, I looked around the shop at the four faceless glass figureheads hanging high up on the wall. The red and yellow figureheads were female. The red one held some type of a rod, and the yellow one had massive, textured glass wings and held a crossbow-like weapon. The other two figureheads were male. The blue one held a sword in one hand and a knife in the other while the black one held open a gleaming white book that contrasted against his onyx black hands. They were beautiful. It was probably the shop's light, but they had this magical glow about them. I just wish they had faces.

I glanced back at the snake aisle, looking for Logan, when I thought I saw the snakehead move. I did a double take, looked again, and saw it frown at me.

"Did you see that?" I shouted at the top of my lungs.

"What?" Logan shouted back, equally loud.

"The snake—"

Logan screamed the loudest girl scream I'd ever heard her do. It was painful on the ears.

"Where is it? Kill it!" Logan said, sprinting toward the counter.

"I'm talking about the aisle, the snake, you … just forget it." I was seeing things; maybe this business of catching Santa was catching up with me.

I forgot about what I thought I saw and found Fleep leaning against the counter on his tiptoes, still looking toward the game rooms. Benji was on the other side of the counter, pouring something into a cup.

I walked over to Logan and said, "You're not going to find elf tea just sitting around. He has—"

A lady's scream broke. "Oh my, are you okay? Do you need me to call someone?" The woman cried out. I sprinted to the counter, while Logan ran around it.

"What happened?" Logan asked, placing her hands on her hips.

"He poured scalding water over his hand!" the lady said.

"It was an accident. I'll be fine," Benji said.

"Aren't you in pain? Run it under water! Hey, are you in shock?" The lady was snapping her fingers in his face. Benji stepped back.

"Lady," Benji's said, clearing his throat, "I'm fine. I work in a teashop. I burn myself all the time. It's called tolerance. I'll be okay."

He resumed what he was doing before and finished making her drink, all the time watching me. What was his deal? Maybe he healed from burns like I did with S.R.'s smoke. I pulled Logan by the shirt and forced her to follow me away from the counter, away from the woman. As we walked away, I whispered to Fleep, "Wait here. We'll be right back." Fleep nodded.

I glanced over at the counter. Benji was still watching me while the woman chattered on. "I think Tiff's right. He's an elf ... or something. Boiling water burns, and he's acting like nothing happened. We just don't know whose side he's on," I said.

"Come on, let's ask him," Logan said, walking toward the counter as the lady was leaving. Benji was already strutting over to us carrying a green denim backpack.

"I've been watching you, Jakob. You need to relax a wee bit. I'm on your side."

"How do you—"

"I can read lips," he said with a smirk. "A rude but useful talent that is quite handy in my line of work." He stopped and looked around to be sure no one was listening, even though we were alone in the shop. "Yes, I'm an elf spy. I work for Santa."

There was something in the way he had said the name Santa, a certain pride in his voice that made me trust him. Something innate, deep inside me, knew that he was a friend.

I cracked a smile and could see that Logan was relieved too. Suddenly I didn't feel so alone. I had magical help, Santa help. He looked us over then said, "You're a smart bunch. By now you've probably learned that Santa has caffeine anaphylaxis." Fleep offered a blank stare then walked to the internet lounge area and sat at a computer.

He was so easily distracted. There we were, meeting one of Santa's elf spies, and he just walks off. I gave Logan a look. She shrugged her shoulders and went after him.

Benji seemed to shift gears and reached into the green denim backpack. "Jakob, take these. They are special glasses that make it possible to see the Xs on the roofs."

"I know what the red X means," I said.

He nodded. "Good. Keep them handy. You'll want to know which home is missing an X on Christmas Eve." Benji discretely glanced over his shoulder at Fleep and Logan.

"Do you know something about my friends?"

He shook his head, like he was keeping a dark secret. "Not yet. Just wait for further instructions." There was no doubt what Benji had done. He'd looked at my friends funny. Did it have something to do with Tiff's dream? Was one of my friends really going to be wayward by Christmas Eve? Benji smiled warmly as Logan and Fleep rejoined us, then continued back on the conversation about Santa.

"Listen, Santa's allergic to caffeine. Once he sips the elf tea, he'll begin to lose focus. He'll forget what he supposed to be doing and may exhibit bizarre behavior, even run into walls. Jakob, you and only you will be able to see him. So make sure you get to him quickly and sit him down so he doesn't get hurt. He's counting on you. It's the only way to lure S.R. out of hiding."

"Isn't that dangerous, eating and drinking stuff when you have allergies?" Logan asked, concerned.

"Oh he knows what's kosher for him to eat or drink and what isn't." Benji held up his right hand. "His gloves have built-in scanners. The instant he touches something it scans it. That's why you'll need to visit a dwarf friend of mine. He'll give you a special cup to trick the scanners, the elf tea, and some emergency equipment—in case things don't go as planned. Jakob," Benji hunched slightly and stared into me. "Listen to me. I'll send you an e-mail soon with details on where and when to meet my friend. It's the safest and most secure way to get you the information. I cannot stress enough the importance of keeping this information confidential."

"You mean don't tell Tiff," Logan said.

Benji straightened. "Yes. She's too vulnerable with her parents and her brother taken. If she knew where I'm sending you, she could be tempted to use the information against us. Don't print the e-mail either. Commit the instructions to memory."

"Here," Benji pulled four red business cards from his pants pocket, handed one to Logan, one to Fleep and two to me. "There's an extra one for your friend—Shig, isn't it?"

I nodded. The card was solid red with his name and e-mail address, benji@thekringlechronicles.com, written in white text.

"Did S.R. direct you to thekringlechronicles.com and tell you to solve a riddle?" he asked.

I nodded.

"And have you solved it?"

"Yes—"

Honk, honk.

"It's my mom," Logan said in a hurry.

"We've got to go," I said, looking up at Benji. He grabbed my arm. I stopped. So did my friends.

"Promise me you'll follow the dwarf's instructions, Jakob."

"I promise."

"Good, now off you go," he said, ushering me toward the exit. "And don't worry. I'll be around Christmas Eve … in case you get into trouble."

I'm smiled at the thought of Benji being around, then confidently walked to the SUV. Everything was coming together. All I needed was the tea and the cup, which would be in my hands soon enough.

Logan rode shotgun and Fleep and I sat in the back while we endured Mrs. Raffo's complaints about how Mr. Raffo had suddenly canceled their ski trip to Colorado.

"We were leaving the day after Christmas," Mrs. Raffo said. And now, without any discussion, I find out that your father canceled the trip this past Friday."

Logan perked up, shuffled in her seat. "Wait, did you say Friday, like this past Friday?" Logan asked.

"Yes! When was he going to tell me? Ugh! He's un-believable," Mrs. Raffo said.

"Did you hear that, *Jakob*? This *past* Friday," Logan said, quickly turning around. She silently raised her eye-brows and pantomimed exaggerated gestures. It took me a minute, but I finally understood what she was trying to tell me: her dad canceled the trip the same day Rick embarrassed me at school. She thought the two were related. For once, I actually believed that Logan might be right about her dad. After all, he did have an elf spy working for him!

CHAPTER 14

I Think Fleep Makes the Wayward List

It was two days before Christmas and it was officially weird—the weather that is. There was an unusually powerful cold front over Florida. In fact, it was so cold that it was actually snowing in parts of the Sunshine State. The town I lived in, Winter Garden, was hovering around a crazy 20 degrees, which meant that if it rained, it would freeze to snow—and that would be awesome. The weather was all my New Jersey-born-and-raised mom talked about on the way back from Sarasota. You're probably wondering how I ended up in Sarasota.

Well, when I got back from The Teashroom, my Dad surprised the whole family with a whirlwind trip to stay overnight in a nearby resort. It was his way of forcing my mom to chill out, even if only for one day. The holidays always seem to wind her up. So, I'd spent the last nineteen hours with my annoying twin sisters and now-relaxed parents ... all the while ready to jump out of my skin and get back to the problems at hand.

As we finally pulled into my subdivision, my thoughts were on Fleep and Tiff. How had they managed to explain Rick's absence? Had the Sanchez's figured out that Rick wasn't staying at a friend's house, that he had actually been taken by magical smoke? And had Clark Cove been taken over by the FBI's paranormal unit? I anxiously inched forward in my seat as my street came into view. Thankfully it looked as normal as ever. That was a relief.

As soon as I got settled into my room I checked my e-mail, hoping to find one from Benji. There was nothing. Bummer, I thought. It was two days before Christmas, and no instructions. Suddenly I felt anxious. I had a plan, but it required the tea. I grabbed my phone and called Logan.

"Hey, you're back," Logan said excitedly. "Are you coming over now?"

"Yeah. What about Shig and Fleep?"

"Shig's gone for the day, and I'll IM Fleep."

"Okay," I said and hung up. I sprinted downstairs, got permission to go to Logan's, and took off.

I saw Mr. Raffo as he was backing out from the garage, probably leaving for The Teashroom. He waved for me to go on in through the open garage, then smiled mysteriously. I couldn't help but stare at him. There was something secretive in the way he smiled. Like he had a secret to tell, but wouldn't. I waved and walked inside.

As I walked into the kitchen, Mrs. Raffo peeked over the refrigerator door at me.

"Mr. Raffo said I could come in," I said nervously then pointed over my shoulder toward the garage. Just then the garage door closed with a loud bang.

"It's okay, honey. Logan and Fleep are in her room."

"Thanks," I said and rushed off.

Logan was sitting in front of her MacBook and Fleep was on the floor leaning against Logan's bed. I got right to it and asked Logan for an update on what had happened the past nineteen hours.

"Nothing, nothing happened," Logan said. "It's been quiet *and* I stayed away from Tiff's house like I promised."

Fleep nodded.

"What about the book, did it roar again?"

"Nope, and no sign of S.R. or attacking smoke. It's been quiet."

"Good."

"Did Benji write?" Logan asked.

I shook my head. "But he will."

"So, what's our plan then?"

"Well, assuming we get the tea, then Fleep and ... hey, where is Tiff?"

Fleep looked at me gravely. "My dad grounded her 'cause she won't tell him where Rick is."

"Great. Well, you and Tiff need to be at the house that's for sale—across the street from mine—around eleven-thirty p.m. on Christmas Eve. I'll have to be asleep at my house for Santa to come. Once inside, find a place where you have a clear view of my living room table through our front window. That's where the special cup with the elf tea will be. If Benji is right—and I'm guessing he is—then Santa will slam the drink. Remember, you can't see him … you'll just see the cup moving by itself. Then text me from your phone. Once I have Santa, you get the gang."

I turned to Logan. "Fleep will tap three times on your bedroom window, then Shig's. That's the signal to meet at my house. Hopefully by then Santa's forces will have sprung their trap and caught S.R."

"Sounds pretty simple," Fleep said.

"All we can do now is hope nothing else happens before then," Logan said.

That evening, my dad and mom went out on a date, so my sisters and I ended up eating dinner with the Sanchez family. After devouring dinner, Fleep and I decided to shoot hoops outside under his driveway lights. As we walked out through the garage, I thought I heard a faint shriek. The vampire owls in Tiff's kitchen. I glanced over at Tiff's dark house but didn't see anything out of the ordinary. Just then a gust of cold air swept under my jacket and up my back, forcing me to retreat into the garage.

"What are you doing?" Fleep asked.

"It's freezing! I'm not playing."

"Oh come on. We'll play twenty-one, and maybe our sweat will freeze," Fleep smiled, dribbling the ball.

"No!"

Fleep jogged toward me then suddenly sprinted past saying, "Fine, then first one to the fridge wins."

"Hey!" I shouted then took off after him with no chance of winning.

"What do you want?" Fleep asked, jerking the fridge door open.

"Whatever," I groaned just as his hand appeared over his shoulder holding a bottle of water. I snatched the water and walked over to the door that led into the kitchen. It was cracked open. I heard voices. His parents were arguing. I peeked.

"He's going to figure it out, plain and simple," Mr. Sanchez said forcefully. It was easy to understand him, but don't ask me what his mom was saying. I could never understand her. Her Scottish accent was thick, and she spoke fast and used strange words when she was angry. I looked over at Fleep. He was closing the fridge door. "Should we go inside?" I asked in a whisper.

"No," Fleep said somberly.

I listened some more. They went back and forth for the next minute. I gathered—understanding only half of the conversation, mind you—that they were arguing about Christmas. Fleep came over beside me and listened in. His dad was talking.

"He's not too young. *Everyone* has one, and he should get what he asks Santa for." Then his mom said something, but like I said, I couldn't understand her.

"Skateboards are too dangerous," Fleep said, translating his mom's response in a whisper. It was weird, but I welcomed the help.

"I had a board at his age," Mr. Sanchez said.

"And you broke your ankle," Fleep said, continuing the translation.

"This will be the *fourth year in a row* that boy has asked for a skateboard. Don't you think he's going to start asking questions—"

"Yes, I am," Fleep said, barely audible. Mr. Sanchez continued.

"—wondering why Santa isn't bringing it? And what are you going to say to him? That there is no Santa?"

I could just see Mrs. Sanchez shrug her shoulders. Mr. Sanchez threw his arms up then slapped his thighs in defeat.

"Great, so he'll think Santa's not real, tell his friends, and *bam,* we have a neighborhood event. Here comes the drama: 'Your son told my son,' and, before you know it, Christmas is ruined for Clark Cove. We may as well start packing now."

Mr. Sanchez stormed out of sight. I could hear pouring. When he came back into view, a few seconds later, he was holding a cup of something hot.

"Let's tell his little brother while we're at it." He sipped. "We can kill two birds with one stone. I mean, how many five-year-olds believe in Santa these days? Right, so how do we do it? You know what? Don't answer that. This is just brilliant, really ... brilliant."

Mr. Sanchez stormed toward the door, the one we were hiding behind. I shoved past Fleep and grabbed him by the arm, but he jerked free. Whatever—if you're going to get caught listening, it's every man for himself. I ran over to the refrigerator, opened it, and messed around, pretending to get a bottle. After a few seconds, I realized Mr. Sanchez wasn't coming and returned to Fleep's side. His mom shouted something, but Fleep didn't offer a translation. It sounded like, "I didn't say that," I think.

Then there was dead silence—awkward silence. Seconds felt like an eternity. I rubbed my face and sighed like I was tired, but I wasn't physically tired; I was emotionally tired, frustrated by all of the Christmas drama. What happened to this being a time of cheer and happiness? I couldn't bring myself to look at Fleep but knew I had to. He was crushed, shoulders sagging, his glassy eyes struggling to hold back the growing pool of tears. His parents had dropped a huge bomb. Of course, their conversation didn't shake my faith in Santa, not in the slightest, because I knew there were unbelieving parents out there. So hearing the argument wasn't a big shock to me. I just didn't expect to hear it from them. And I'm sure that was Fleep's problem.

"Come on, buddy. Santa is real." Nothing. Fleep wouldn't even look at me. "Hey, come on man. You know your dad didn't mean it. He was mad. Parents say dumb things when they're mad. Come on, let's go back outside."

Still Fleep wouldn't move, or even acknowledge me. He just stood there, like he was in a trance, staring into his kitchen from behind the cracked door. I could see half of his face, one eye, and the teary trail down his cheek. Was he angry or sad? Probably both.

"Seriously," I said in a forceful whisper, "your dad's just trying to make a point—that you're not going to believe in Santa if you don't get the skateboard. I think that's pretty cool of him to stick up for you." I had no idea if I was making any sense but I had to say something to my friend. "Come on. We should go."

I grabbed Fleep by the jacket and managed, with a tug, to get him moving. Silently he followed me out of the laundry room. I ended up shooting hoops by myself in the freezing cold for about five minutes while he sulked in a lawn chair. Then he stood and finally broke the silence.

"Rick was right all along. There's no stupid Santa. It's all fake, the whole thing." I didn't say anything. Fleep needed to vent. "And even if Santa is real, he's not bringing me what I want. What am I saying? He's *not* real, and you know what? The more I talk about it, the more I realize it's all just a fairytale. I hate Santa and I hate my lying parents!"

I stopped bouncing the basketball and stared at Fleep. His rant had suddenly turned foul. I couldn't believe my ears. I couldn't believe I was watching and listening to one of my best friends—one of the nicest guys I knew—disrespect his parents. My mouth hung so low you probably could have driven a train through it. I rushed over to him.

"Take it back Fleep! Take it all back. You don't mean it. You don't mean what you just said. I'm telling you. You don't want to mess around with the Wayward List. It's real."

"Made-up Wikipedia garbage—"

"*What?* Not Wikipedia. The Kringle Chronicles Web site. There's a whole page dedicated to the Wayward List …" I hesitated. I was so nervous for my friend. "On the site, there's a silhouette of a large man, Santa, on his knees sobbing over this long list. I clicked on the list and, well, nothing I read was good. Disrespecting your parents is one way to get your name written on that Wayward List." I studied Fleep for a moment and let what I'd said sink in. He didn't say anything, just stared through me with his tearing blue eyes.

"I don't care about some fake Wayward List," Fleep said smugly, then wiped his cheeks.

"It's not fake! Tiff's book even mentions it. I read about the list. It talks about the disposal of kids, Fleep. You know what that means, don't you—disposal?"

Fleep didn't answer.

"Throw away! It means to throw away, Fleep. It talks about punishing and disposing of kids whose names are on the Wayward List." I gripped his shoulders, hoping he'd say something but he didn't.

"Fleep, you have to believe. You have to take back what you just said … all of it! You don't hate your parents or Santa, right? And the other things you said … they just slipped out. You were just mad, that's all. Right?" I asked poking him in the chest.

"Cut it out," he protested and swatted at my hand, missing. I heard a loud engine. It was my parents. They rounded the corner in our SUV. Fleep and I moved toward the garage as they pulled into Fleep's driveway and honked the horn. I waved then turned back to Fleep.

"You've seen S.R., and if he's real, it's only logical that Santa is too. Come on, forget all the stuff your parents said and listen to what I'm telling you. Believe."

"I do believe, in *S.R.* because I can see him; that's what really matters," Fleep said.

"Fleep, don't do this. You need to believe. I need you to—"

Just then Fleep's dad came out with my sisters in tow and loaded them into the SUV.

"Just go home," Fleep said, walking into his garage. I felt betrayed. One of my best friends didn't trust me. He gave me one last look and shook his head gravely as he reached over and pressed the garage door opener. The door slowly closed, reminding me of the falling curtains from a play. I wondered if Fleep's faith would get an encore or if his door of belief had closed forever.

That evening I got e-mail from Benji, Santa's elf spy. It read:

Jakob,

First thing tomorrow morning go to The Kringle Shop in Christmas, Florida. It's not far from you, about thirty minutes drive east. Bring Logan, Shig and Fleep … but by no means are you to bring Tiff.

Once there, look for a little person with a long black ponytail and a handlebar moustache. Tell him Benji sent you. He will almost certainly not believe you, so show him the glasses I gave you. If he still doesn't believe you, then say to him, "Baum is no bum." That's all. He'll have to believe you then. Listen to him, do as he says, take what he gives you, and you will succeed tomorrow night.

Benji

I thought about the Kringle Shop. I knew of it. It was in a town actually named Christmas, Florida. It was where the locals and tourists went to mail their Christmas cards, buy gifts, and whatnot. I glanced over at the time and yawned. It was late, and I was tired, so I shut down the computer—the right way—and climbed into bed.

I don't know why, but I couldn't fall asleep. I mean, just seconds before, I'd felt like passing out at the computer, but now I was wide awake again. I let my mind drift and found myself thinking about the next day, Christmas

Eve. Then Fleep popped into my head. Would he come to his senses? Maybe he'd already talked to his dad. I wondered. I hoped. I couldn't stop worrying about him. Was he the friend Tiff said would be on the Wayward List? I finally fell asleep after about an hour of tossing and turning.

I dreamed.

I stood at the edge of a cliff staring down into a valley and across a lake. I looked up. The sky had an ominous, navy-blue hue. The moon was full, a luminescent medallion in the sky, illuminating the silhouette of a gigantic palace perched on a mountain across the valley. The palace was surrounded by thick, white banks of snow. The wind blew, and the air smelled of burning wood. The palace was beautiful, powerful, but scary. Suddenly I heard a voice.

"You should have told me." It was Fleep's voice. Stunned, I looked around but there was no Fleep.

"Where are you?" I asked nervously.

"You know where I am. It's *your fault* I'm here, Jakob."

"I—I have no idea where you are. I don't even know where I am."

"I'm under the palace, in the dungeon. My side lost, Jakob. You knew your side would win. You knew all along that *you* would win. Why didn't you tell me all this was real? I said no to the greatest present, and it's your fault." His voice fell silent.

I focused on the palace. There was a red glow coming from the windows, and then black smoke billowed out.

"I'm wayward forever!" Fleep's voice shouted. "But you already know that." Then, as it often happens in dreams, the scene shifted. I was now looking into a dark prison cell. Something moved in the shadows. "You should have helped me ... but you didn't," Fleep's voice said, as the blurred image of a wooden creature charged the cell bars, reaching out at me with wooden hands.

I sat bolt upright in bed, my heart slamming against my ribs.

"Fleep!" I said, clawing at my blanket. I reached around and turned on my reading lamp then grabbed my journal and pen. Frantically, I flipped the pages until I found a blank one and then began writing all that I could remember from the terrible dream.

After re-reading what I wrote, I closed the journal. My clock read two-thirty a.m. It was the morning of Christmas Eve. I turned off the light and fell back on my pillow.

"Fleep ..." was the last thing I said before dozing off to sleep.

CHAPTER 15

WE GO TO CHRISTMAS AND PET A POLAR BEAR

I woke up at the crack of dawn Christmas Eve, but not because I was an early riser. Fleep and the stupid dreams had me restless. I thought about calling Logan, but she was probably still asleep. So I sent an e-mail telling her what Fleep had said about his parents and Santa. Logan always started her day by reading the Yahoo.com news headlines and her e-mails.

An hour later we were on a video call on our computers.

"Read what I wrote about Fleep?" I asked.

"Yeah. He really said that about his parents?"

"Yeah! And he *really* doesn't believe in Santa. And then last night I had this strange dream with him in it." I told her about the dream and then Logan really freaked me out.

"Oh my gosh, Tiff was right. Fleep's wayward and I'll bet your dream is a vision or something, like of Fleep's future."

"Don't talk like that, Logan. You're freaking me out. We just need to get Fleep to believe again. And him seeing Santa is the only way. So, are you going to ask your mom to take us to The Kringle Shop in Christmas, or do I ask mine?"

"My mom will drive us," Logan said.

"Did you ask? You know it's the annual brunch today."

"Don't worry, I have a plan. She'll do it."

I heaved a doubtful sigh. "Just make sure. And what about Shig?"

"I already talked to him. He can't come. His mom is making him go to the brunch."

I sighed again. Nothing was going as planned.

"Chill. I'll pick you up in thirty minutes."

"Okay, bye."

"Bye."

I ended the video call. Logan's plan had better be good. Her mom never missed a brunch. I walked downstairs in search of my own mom. It was going to be a tough sell, asking to skip out on the Christmas Eve brunch, but I had to ask, regardless. You see, the Clark Cove moms had their traditions, and the Christmas Eve brunch was the one gathering you did not miss. This year the Sanchez's were hosting it, and there would be the signature items like Mrs. Sugihara's chocolate-covered sushi (although odd, it was always a hit), Mr. Raffo's assortment of teas, Mr. Sanchez's tortilla de papas (potato omelet), and, of course, my mom's apple cake.

Thirty minutes later and much to my surprise, I found myself sitting beside Logan in her mom's Armada SUV on our way to the little town of Christmas, Florida. She was peeling her way out of the parka her mom had made her wear. Moms—they know how to overdo it. Speaking of moms, I'd told mine it would only take us an hour to make the trip to Christmas, so she'd said, "Sure, go ahead, whatever." Now that I think of it, I probably could have asked her for twenty dollars, and she would have said yes; anything to get me out of the kitchen and out of her hair. I shifted in my seat, then looked at Logan and wondered how in the world she had gotten her mom to skip out on the brunch and drive us all the way out to Christmas.

"How did you do this?" I asked.

"I called some of the neighborhood moms and asked if they had any last-minute holiday cards to mail, because my mom and I were going to Christmas. As I expected, almost everyone had at least one thing they'd forgotten to mail. I reminded them that postmarking the cards from Christmas, Florida would make them special, even if they were late. They were all very grateful and gave me their mail. Then I just told my mom and she felt obligated. And here we are, on our way," Logan said with a cutesy smile and shrug.

"That's incredible," I said, and Logan smiled again. Man, she was good.

Forty minutes later I was in the town of Christmas, listening to Mrs. Raffo complain about the freezing cold and how far away we had parked. We walked for another minute or so until we arrived at a split in the sidewalk. To the right was The Kringle Shop, a shoebox-shaped, weathered, red, single-story building with a metal roof and large wraparound porch. It cried out for a new paint job, but was probably left that way on purpose for added character. To the left was the post office—with a long line of people trailing out the door. Most of the people were holding packages or envelopes, and everyone was dressed for the cold. It was unusual seeing people in Florida wearing thick jackets and even hats and gloves. I just couldn't believe how cold it was.

Mrs. Raffo spotted the line of people.

"Ah, will you look at that line," Mrs. Raffo complained. It's funny how adults can loudly hate waiting in lines, yet tell us kids to be patient the moment we complain.

Logan and I veered right on the sidewalk.

"Just where do you two think you're going?" Mrs. Raffo said.

We stopped.

"I told you, I want to get a book or something from the shop," Logan said, pointing to the red building.

Mrs. Raffo sighed then made a beeline for the shop. "Follow me," she yelled over her shoulder.

"As long as there's someone here to keep an eye on you two," Mrs. Raffo said, then trotted up the steps, opened the door, and disappeared into the shop. Logan and I followed. The hardwood floors creaked as I walked inside. There was a red brick fireplace to my left as I walked in. The smell and heat of the burning wood made me smile and brought warmth to my cold hands and face. I took off my jacket and tied it around my waist then looked around, taking it all in. The first thing I noticed was how big and spacious the place was on the inside. The ceiling was so high that I went back outside to take another look at the roof. It didn't add up; the roof was just a single story on the outside … but the inside ceiling soared. It had to be at least double the height of the outside roof. Strange, and not physically possible. I glanced over at Logan. She didn't seem to be aware of the contradiction.

"Jingle Bells" was playing from the speakers overhead, and a giant LCD TV was showing my favorite Christmas movie about an Elf who travels to New York in search of his father. Cool, I loved that movie. I continued looking around.

The theme of the shop, aside from being Christmas, was also rustic and country-like, similar to the shop area of a Cracker Barrel-like country store. Knickknacks and down-home Christmas stuff cluttered the shelves, and tightly placed clothing racks with Christmassy-themed items were everywhere. Mrs. Raffo grabbed one of the workers. Logan's eyes bulged. It was a little person. My eyes searched his shirt and found his nametag. It read *BAUM*. He was the one we were here to meet. Wow, was he interesting looking. His face was youthful, I guess, despite the nasty scars running across his forehead. His hair was pulled back in a black ponytail and he had a handlebar moustache and tattoos that added an element of fierceness. Despite his size, Baum wasn't someone to mess with. He was dressed in red and black camouflage combat pants, black boots, and wore a tactical belt that looked like something from the Special Forces. His tight red t-shirt hugged his muscular frame, and the logo over the left side of his chest read *DT-6*.

"Sir," Mrs. Raffo began then paused, giving Baum the once-over, "well, aren't you cute in that outfit."

Baum crossed his arms then tapped his bicep. He looked at her like he'd heard that line a million times. *Cute,* not a word I'd have used to describe him. *Tough* sounded better. I could tell Mrs. Raffo was bugging him. I noticed an interesting-looking tattoo on his arm. It was two crisscrossed candy canes—forming a kind of X—with a military dog hanging down the middle. I squinted but couldn't make out the name written on the dog tag.

"These two are with me," Mrs. Raffo said, pointing to Logan and me. "I have to get into that awful line at the post office, and they want to buy something from your charming shop, so please keep an eye on them." Baum gave her one of those "Are you kidding me?" looks.

"I mean," she lowered her voice and leaned down, "the freaks. It's Christmas, and all of the freaks are out. Just make sure they don't leave with anyone or—you know—get stolen."

Baum sighed, resigned. "Don't worry, lady. I get it. They'll be safe in here. Just go mail your stuff. When they're done shopping, if you're not back, they'll be sitting on that bench over there."

Baum turned, flipping his long ponytail as he pointed to a black bench beside the checkout counter. Mrs. Raffo turned to Logan.

"Give me the cards." Mrs. Raffo looked at Logan's empty hands. "Oh my blah!" Mrs. Raffo said, frustrated.

That was a new one, I thought. I'd never heard anyone say "oh my blah" before, but it was a good substitute.

Logan frowned. "I thought you had them. Sorry. I guess they're in the front seat," Logan said as her mom stormed away in a huff. We traded shrugs and turned around quickly, expecting Baum, but he was gone. So much for keeping an eye on us. A second later, I saw him clear across the other side of the shop helping a lady, but how did he get so far so quickly? By the dumbfounded look on Logan's face, I could tell she was thinking the same thing. We sprinted over and quietly snuck up behind him while he finished up with the lady.

"Yeeessss?" he said drawn-out-like as he turned around, as if he knew we were there all along. I stared at him for a moment, thinking what to say.

"Benji sent us," I whispered.

Baum regarded me. "I don't know anyone named Benji."

"He said you'd probably say that." I smirked, reached over to Logan and snapped my fingers. "Logan, the glasses." I turned back to Baum. "You see, he gave us a special pair of glasses."

"Oh goody," Baum said sarcastically while clasping his hands. My smile faded.

I snapped my fingers again. "Come on. Give me the glasses."

"Uh, Jakob, I kind of ... forgot them," Logan said sheepishly.

"You what?"

"She forgot them," Baum said walking away.

I trotted up beside him and whispered, "Look, they are special Santa glasses."

Baum stopped and rolled his eyes.. "Santa ... nice, and I guess I'm some sort of an elf."

"Well, actually Benji called you a dwarf!"

Baum stared up at me curiously then said, "You think that up all by your lonesome or did your girlfriend help?"

I glanced over at Logan. She smirked.

"She's not my ... hey!" Baum had walked away—again, faster than humanly possible—and was already helping another customer when Logan brushed up beside me.

"Hey, boyfriend," she mocked as she punched me in the arm.

"Cut it out. We're failing miserably here. And now I can't remember the phrase Benji told us to say."

Logan shot me a cutesy smile. "What would you do without me?"

She remembered!

"Awesome, let's tell him."

As we approached Baum, Logan pointed to the back of his shirt. It was the image of an enormous polar bear, dressed in clothes similar to Baum's but holding a green and white striped device of some type. I'd never seen anything like it. It looked like a cross between a giant candy cane and a power tool. What intrigued me most was the polar bear. It looked so real. I had to touch it. Slowly, I reached out. Instantly my hand felt a cold, windy breeze then the polar bear's white, furry coat. I jerked my hand back. I couldn't believe it, but Logan was my witness. I'd just stuck my hand into the image on Baum's shirt and petted a polar bear. Suddenly Baum turned around, startling us both.

"What do you two want now?"

Logan and I were astonished.

"How did I do that?"

He looked away, glancing around the store, then looked back at me. "Do what, kid?"

"You know, reach into your shirt." He chuckled dismissively, but his anxious glances around the store told me something was up.

"I have no idea what you're talking about," he said.

"Okay, enough with the games. Logan, tell him."

She moved in close to his ear and whispered, "Baum is no bum."

He slowly straightened his back. Then leisurely and deliberately stroked his handlebar moustache. Baum was quiet for another minute as he studied us, then he finally spoke, but not before giving the shop another once-over.

"Took you long enough. And for the record, I'm a Special Forces commando dwarf. Customer service isn't my thing." He looked us over again. "Aren't there supposed to be three of you?"

"Actually four, but Shig and Fleep couldn't come." Briefly, I wondered if his miscount meant Fleep was already on the Wayward List, but then forced myself to concentrate on our mission.

Baum grunted then said, "Well, I'm only cleared to equip three. Follow me."

He led us behind the counter and through a series of green doors, each leading to new rooms that became increasingly smaller. We first entered a small inventory room, then another cluttered storage room, and finally a bare room the size of a closet. The instant he closed the last door, a dim green light shone from above. Baum smiled then rubbed his hand over the far right wall. Upon his touch, a panel of lighted buttons appeared. We were in some kind of an elevator. I looked at the panel again, but it made no sense. The buttons were for floors one to forty-four.

"Do you see the buttons?" Logan asked, tapping me repeatedly on the shoulder like it was a drum.

"Yeah, stop hitting me."

"How is it possible? I mean, forty-four floors?" Logan asked, panicky, as she gestured to the buttons. "It's a one-floor building!" Logan carried on, but her voice was suddenly muffled by a loud swooping sound as the walls around us disappeared and we ascended slowly past the first floor. "What's happening to us?" Logan yelled and smacked me on the back. Enough already with the hitting, I thought. I turned, ready to smack her back, but immediately stopped, startled. She was changing. I pointed at her, and that's when I noticed my arm and hand had also changed. Logan let out a bloodcurdling scream.

We Are Crystal Clear on the Forty-Fourth Floor

I couldn't believe my eyes. Logan was barely visible, just an icy-clear silhouette. My eyes shot over to Baum. He looked like he was completely made of crystal. My hands were too. I'd given up on wondering how any of this was possible. It just was. Even the elevator looked like a box made of ice. Baum reached for the now invisible controls and pressed one, obviously having memorized the buttons. The elevator stopped abruptly, causing me to lose my balance. I grabbed for something to steady myself, then felt the cold wall of the icy elevator. Logan was rocking herself and wouldn't meet my eyes. She was terrified.

"Logan, it's okay. You look really cool," I said, trying to make a bad joke.

"Don't worry. It's not permanent, just necessary," Baum said.

She was still hysterical, repeating, "Not possible," over and over again. I examined my legs, then my arms, and then the rest of what I could see. I lifted my right foot and looked under my shoe. All of me looked like ice. I wondered if, since I had suddenly transformed into ice, I'd be leaking water. No water and I wasn't frozen. Okay, maybe it was a dumb thought, but my self-inspection wasn't over. I made a fist and knocked on my chest. It made a clinking sound. Solid.

"Logan, can we continue?" Baum asked.

"It's one floor ... one floor!" Logan repeated. Baum must have taken that as a yes, because he set the elevator in motion and we continued our ascent.

Logan kept mumbling, her lips quivering. I reached over and placed my hand on her glassy shoulder, hoping to calm her. She didn't respond to my touch. The elevator continued upward, past the roof of the shop. As we ascended higher and higher, I looked beyond the see-through walls and down at the shrinking road, the parking lot, and the treetops. Amazing.

"Logan, this is really cool," I whispered. "Just look around and pretend you're on a carnival ride or something." Logan peeked around hesitantly and, as she did, seemed to relax a bit.

Baum began to explain. "From the outside, yes, the shop looks like a one-floor building. But once you go through that second green door, you are in Santa's Western Hemisphere Command Center. We call this the Crystal Palace. I'm sure Benji told you all about the Palace and my team."

I cut my gaze over to Baum. "No, he didn't," I said slowly, wondering if I'd just gotten Benji in trouble. Baum shook his head.

"Typical. Benji is always downplaying the importance of *the team*. My team, *DT6,* almost caught that thing you kids are calling S.R." Baum stroked his crystal handlebar mustache and thought some more. "Well, maybe now that we have the help of a Pole, this will be the year we finally capture that filthy animal."

"Ooh, he really hates S.R.—" I whispered to Logan.

"You bet I do," Baum said, shaking his head with disgust. "I've spent centuries trying to catch him, laying traps and counter-traps, planting tracers and trackers, but nothing. This plan is the only way. It has its risks, but I think it will work. It has to. That's why you are here. I'm going to prepare you for just about anything." Baum motioned for me to lean down. "You just do your part. S.R. *has* to believe you caught Santa! It will lure the freak out into the open. He won't resist the opportunity."

"I will," I said, straightening. "I'll do my part."

"Good. Let's get your supplies and equipment so you can catch Santa—and I can catch S.R."

The elevator stopped.

"Forty-fourth floor. Now follow me, and don't touch anything," Baum ordered as he exited. "Oh, and don't look down if you have a fear of heights. Messy!"

Follow? Touch? I could barely see the outline of his clear body. The last one off the elevator, I stepped out. Baum and Logan, the little of them that was visible, looked like they were walking on air. The entire floor, everything, was crystal clear: no walls, doors, nothing. Walking took some getting used to, but I managed by keeping my head down. Looking down, and being able to see through the floor past my transparent shoes, made me a little queasy, but it passed once I encouraged my brain to ignore the see-through world and get moving.

As I followed behind Logan, wondering how she was faring, I saw activity below us, under her feet: the slight appearance and quick disappearance of silhouettes. They had to be workers. As we continued on, my eyes adjusted and I began to see the faint outlines of tables, chairs, and even rows of bookcases. Bookcases? I wondered. Were we walking through a library? Just imagine being surrounded by bookcases as tall and long as a school bus. Then imagine a crystal forest of stacked books as tall as a bus. Regretfully, I didn't slowdown long enough to read the titles, but I did count fifteen long rows of books before we finally turned right and walked down a long hallway, then turned left at another stack of books and stopped. Actually, I clanked into Logan then stopped.

"What's up?" I asked, secretly hoping we hadn't chipped each other. Was that even possible?

Logan pointed ahead then continued eavesdropping. Baum was in deep conversation with someone.

I took the opportunity to look around some more. That's when I saw the offices. They ran along the far edge, or at least what would have been the edge of the floor, if it were visible. A large emerald plaque hanging outside an office door caught my eye. It was green, not clear. I had to have a closer look.

I reached the door and completely forgot about the plaque when I saw what was in the office. It was the largest pyramid-shaped display case I'd ever seen. It took up most of the office and reached up to the ceiling. Whatever required a case that big was definitely worth a look-see. I walked straight to the massive glass enclosure. Inside the glass was a giant book. Again, I asked myself what kind of book required a case this grand. I took a closer look. The book was massively oversized. Forget inches. This thing had to be measured in feet. It was easily the size of my kitchen table, and it was closed ... and, oddly enough, familiar. It kind of resembled the book in Tiff's kitchen. There was an image of a man carrying a sack over his left shoulder on the cover. I read the title, *The Kringle Chronicles,* like the Web site. Just then, I heard footsteps running toward me. I looked up and accidentally head-butted the display, causing a clanking noise.

I felt my forehead for cracks. None. Whew!

That's when I heard Baum shout, "No!" then a screeching alarm sounded. I reached up and covered my ears, clanking my elbow against the glass.

A swooshing sound came from my left. Then I saw them. Stone-faced, fierce, icy-looking dwarves dressed like Baum materialized from the floor below, carrying transparent science fiction-looking blasters. Wow, those guys were fast.

"Stand down," Baum ordered, walking between me and the assault team, and smacking down their barrels. "Good work, men. Unit dismissed." The team saluted and dropped back down to the floor below. Baum gripped onto my wrist and forcefully led me out of the office and over to Logan. She quickly ditched a crystal book.

"What were you guys doing over there?" Logan asked as Baum stopped and looked up at me. His face was flush. He was mad.

"Let's make one more thing clear."

I nodded, looking down at Baum.

"Do not leave my side, and do not touch anything. Got it?"

"Got it."

He turned to Logan. "Understand?"

"Yeah, but I don't see ..." Logan said. She stopped short as Baum gave me another disapproving glare. I looked away to the office with the giant *Kringle Chronicles* book, the one I'd just been escorted from.

"What in the world?" I asked, tapping Baum on the shoulder and pointing to the office. Shreds of glass flew from the book, like its pages were being etched. Then a page fanned, and more glass and shavings.

"What are you two staring at?" Logan asked, frustrated.

"Nothing, now follow me. And you ..." he pointed to me, "by my side." Like a submissive dog, I stepped up and parked myself at Baum's side. He was quiet as he led us down a hall. I was dying to know more.

"What was the book doing?" I asked.

"Writing a new chapter."

"About what?" I asked.

"Not about what ... about *whom*."

"About whom?" I asked.

"About you!" Baum said then fell silent, seemingly lost in thought. Again chills ran down my back. Something told me not to ask any more questions. Instead I pondered Baum's words. The book was writing all by itself, and about me. What was it writing about me? I glanced back at Logan. She forced a fake smile. What was that for? We passed more offices on our walk to wherever Baum was leading us, but none of the offices looked like the one that had the giant *Kringle Chronicles* book. Then as we turned left at yet another crystal tower of books, Baum broke his silence.

"Great responsibility comes with being a Pole. You can see and do things others can't," he said softly.

I didn't respond at first. I was too busy looking down past my feet to the floor below. The armed dwarves were still keeping an eye on us.

"I know, like I saw the room," I said.

"What room? What are you two talking about?" Logan asked. "Will someone *answer me?*"

I was about to answer Logan when Baum took me aside.

"It's not a good idea to let the Flickers know what you can see."

"Flickers?"

"Someone like her, a human. They're Flickers because, unlike us, they're only here for a short time ... like the flicker of a light." I looked at Logan. Our eyes met. Flicker or not, I couldn't lie to my best friend. I walked over to her then glanced over my shoulder at Baum. His eyes warned me not to tell, but I had to.

"There's an invisible office over there. I was just in it looking at a book titled *The Kringle Chronicles*," I said pointing. "Looks kind of like Tiff's book."

Baum shook his head disapprovingly. I could see the anger in his eyes. "You're not ready for your own book— too young and immature, too prideful and overconfident." Baum sighed. "But it's not my decision."

"What's not your decision? What book?" I asked, confused.

"Nothing," Baum said angrily then started walking again. We walked for a few more seconds, then turned left again and walked past another room that caught my eye. I stopped short, backing up in astonishment at all of the equipment. I assumed it was a tech and communications room. The big surprise was that it was in full color: there was no icy silhouette or concealment. Two dwarves were working the equipment. The closest one sat in front of a huge LCD with a lot of open computer screens. The second dwarf sat in front of another LCD that displayed a map of Earth. The second dwarf wore a small listening device in his ear and had sophisticated-looking equipment neatly organized around the desk. Just as I stepped into the room, Baum's small but strong hand gripped onto my arm and jerked me back.

"Oh no you don't," Baum said. "It's just an empty room." Logan was right behind him.

"Yeah, Jakob, where are you going? There's nothing to see. Come on, remember my mom will be back soon."

"But I can see them," I insisted, pointing over my shoulder to the room. "And they're not transparent like us," I said.

"What room? Why can't I see the room?" Logan asked, sounding a little perturbed. "You seriously see a room?" she demanded.

I glanced over at Baum. He was shaking his head. He definitely didn't want me to say anything.

"Yeah, it's right there," I pointed. Looking through the room's window, I also saw a large radio tower outside— even taller than the forty-fourth floor. It undoubtedly had something to do with that tech room and most definitely kept low-flying aircraft from crashing into the Crystal Palace.

"Where? I still don't see anything."

"Do you see the radio tower?" I pointed toward it.

"Okay, yeah, I see the tower. It's outside."

"Well, the room's in that direction," I said then turned to Baum.

Shaking his head, Baum walked off.

Logan looked at me crossly then said, "Why are you messing with me?" She walked away before I could defend myself. Great, now they were both mad at me.

I skipped ahead and caught up with them. Just as I reached out to grab Baum's shoulder, the polar bear on the back of his shirt reached out and almost clawed me. Needless to say, I left Baum alone. I followed a little farther until we stopped beside a stack of red and white candy canes lying on a glass table. We were in some sort of a laboratory. The candy canes were interesting—about the length of my arm and the width of a hotdog. They were red and white, and completely visible ... to me anyways.

"Can you ... see them?" I asked Logan hesitantly. She nodded. Our eyes begged to touch the candy canes and Baum saw it.

"Go ahead, these you can touch," he said.

"They're candy canes," Logan said, picking one up. "Long, fat, plain old candy canes."

"Old, yes. But plain, no! And certainly not edible," Baum said, shaking his head. "These sweet sticks are called J-Rays, candy canes that transform into plasma emitters and shoot red plasma bolts."

"Plasma bolts?" Logan said nervously. "But we're just kids."

"Relax. The red forgives," Baum said.

"What does that mean?" I asked.

"One bolt will knock any breathing creature unconscious for thirty minutes. It's not like the green ones."

"What's up with the green ones?" Logan asked. Baum seemed to be lost in thought, staring at the red J-Ray. "Baum, the green J-Rays … what do they do?" Logan asked again.

"Huh? Oh, yeah. The green ones … they're very destructive," Baum said nonchalantly.

"Whoa, we are not destroying anything," Logan said, putting the candy cane back like it had germs.

"Relax, only a pole can operate a green plasma emitter. Besides, they're smart weapons—they know who, or what, wants to hurt you. And you're right; you are not destroying anything anyway. That's our job. So just stick with the red and remember this: as soon as the red stripe drains you'll need to recharge. So make sure you have a lot of extras with you, which reminds me …" Baum began counting on his fingers.

"What do you mean by *recharge?*" I asked. He held his index finger up to me, signaling me to wait, then reached under a table and opened a clear cabinet door.

"One ... two ... and one more makes three," he said, head half inside the cabinet. I'm not a thief, but something was telling me I'd need the green candy cane, so when I saw that no one was watching, well, I swiped it and hid it inside my crystal pant leg.

"You'll need a couple of these ... some of these ... and, oh yeah, a pack of discs just in case," Baum finished.

When he stood back up, he was holding three army-green backpacks and a handful of what looked like miniature Frisbees along with several bags of marbles.

"Backpacks," I murmured.

"No! They're *frontpacks*—so wear them that way. In fact, wear them to bed just to be safe. And if for some reason you find yourself outside, do not take them off—no matter what." He opened the packs and dumped the discs and marbles in, then handed me my pack, then Shig's and then handed Logan hers. The packs were surprisingly feather light, considering they looked filled.

Baum continued. "Ok, here's how to recharge. A transformed J-Ray is a solid white plasma emitter, and the three red spiral stripes are its tubes of energy. Every time you zap out a bolt it requires energy, and the red color drains some. So keep track of your red levels, and be ready with another candy cane if you run out. They provide energy to your J-Ray; just smash one anywhere on the emitter and it will get absorbed. Got it?"

"Okay, I got the recharge part but how do you make it transform in the first place?" I asked.

"Say the word 'Shamira' while holding the hooked part. Likewise, do the same thing to the J-Ray and it will transform back into a candy cane."

Shamira, what does it mean?"

"It's from an ancient language. It means protector."

"Okay," I said. "If everything goes as planned, my team and I will insert, take over, and clear any tangos."

"Tangos?" I asked, baffled.

"Enemy targets," Baum said confidently.

Baum cracked a devious smile then gestured for us to wait one second. He grabbed his ear, listened, then touched his throat. I could barely see a clear strip of tape on his throat, no doubt some high-tech microphone of some sort. "Roger that." He spoke hurriedly then turned to us. "We have to go."

We followed him back around the way we had come, retracing our steps. We continued on, passing the towers of books and walking through the library. The elevator still wasn't visible, but I knew we were close. Baum trotted ahead, then turned around and spoke, trotting backward.

"Jakob, toss me your frontpack."

I threw one. He caught it then unzipped it.

"Listen, I don't have a lot of time to go over all the contents and their proper uses," he slowed down and rummaged around in the pack, forcing us to slow.

"The most important thing is this cup." He held up a shiny, ceramic-looking cup with a snow-covered, hilly landscape painted on it. He dropped the cup into the pack with a loud *clank* then snickered at our alarmed expressions. "It will take a lot more than that to break that cup," he said. He continued rummaging around. "And this is the ancient elvish herbal tea." Baum removed a white parchment from the frontpack, carefully unwrapped it, and showed it to me.

"It looks like dried-up leaves my dad uses to make tea," I said.

"Well, it isn't," he said gruffly, then wrapped it up and dropped it back into the pack. He zipped up the pack and tossed it back to me. "Use seven pinches of tea. No more, no less. See my finger." Baum made a pinching gesture. "Then mix the tea with some water. Once it touches water, it will dissolve. And remember, you have to use the cup. It will conceal the tea."

We entered the elevator. Baum pressed the invisible button pad to return us to the first floor, then cupped his ear again as the door closed. He was receiving another message. He touched his throat to answer whoever it was that called him.

Baum finished his conversation just as we returned to our normal full-color, visible selves and came to a stop on the first floor. The trip down had seemed quicker than the trip up. Baum turned to Logan.

"Your mother just entered the shop." Logan nodded, then the door opened and we exited the elevator with Baum trailing behind us.

Mrs. Raffo spotted us a minute later behind the counter, sitting on the bench and holding the three frontpacks.

"Oh, that's some package you've got there," Mrs. Raffo said while trying to peer inside Logan's pack. "What did you guys buy, army backpacks?"

Logan pulled away. "Mom!" she whined. "It's a surprise." Good cover.

"Okay, okay," Mrs. Raffo said. I glanced over at the door behind the counter. Baum was looking at me, his arms crossed. I half-waved good-bye. He returned a slow nod.

Logan and I were so preoccupied with everything we'd just learned that we barely spoke on the drive home. There was so much to absorb. I stared out the window. Fleep popped in my head. He was so angry with his parents and Santa. I glanced at the clock on the dashboard. Mission time was just over thirteen hours away. I had to make Fleep believe in Santa before it was too late.

Mr. Raffo's Gift
Eats My Comics

"Good timing, mister," my mom's voice startled me as I closed the front door. She was filling plastic baggies with her cinnamon roasted almonds—no doubt for me to deliver to the neighbors. It was another one of my mom's Christmas traditions.

I took off my jacket and threw it on the sofa.

"What do you have there?" She asked, staring at the frontpacks.

"Oh, these, just some gifts," I said, walking to the closet under the stairs.

"They look full. How exciting."

Hey, I wasn't lying. Technically speaking the frontpacks were kind of like gifts—gifts from Baum to me. I walked over to the closet my friends and I called "the fort" and opened the door. Being that it was under the stairs, it was odd-shaped but spacious. An adult could stand comfortably. I left the frontpacks in there and closed the door, coming face to face with my dad.

"Hey, bud. I fished one of the phones out from the bottom of the pool. Any idea how it got there?" I froze for a second then grabbed my jacket, not prepared in the least to answer that question, but I had to—and truthfully.

"Oh, the phone, yeah," I finally stuttered and looked over at my mom then back at my dad. "It started smoking and, well, I kicked it into the pool."

I stared at them, studying their expressions. My mom was easy to read. She was already back to pouring almonds into a baggie. My dad's face, on the other hand, had me shooting glances at the front door, wondering if I'd see the other side of it this year.

"Smoking," he pressed his lips and gave me an appreciative nod. "Nice one. But seriously, big guy—it's coming out of your allowance. Tell me next time, okay? I probably could have fixed it," he said, then ambled off toward his office.

"Sorry," I said. My dad threw his arms up and shot me the peace sign. I looked over at my mom.

She suddenly looked up like she remembered something. "Hey, I almost forgot. Mr. Raffo dropped off a box for you. At first I thought it was one of the weird packages he has you mail. I almost laid it over by the mailbox this morning until I saw it was addressed to you. Must be a gift. It's right there on the table."

It was a large box, big enough to hold a printer, and mom was right, it was addressed to me. After I pulled off the tape, my mom came over.

"Well that's not nice," she said as I opened the top flap. "An empty box. It didn't feel empty."

Was my mom messing with me or could she seriously not see the ancient-looking metal book? I went to pick it up when a ripple moved across the metal cover. It was as if I'd touched water. Unnerved, I jerked my hands back.

"Did you just pretend to touch something?"

"No—I mean, I didn't pretend."

"It sure looked like it," my mom said, reaching inside the box. "*Oh my gosh!* Where did that come from?" She stared at the book for a moment then felt her forehead. "I must be losing my mind. It's the holidays. I haven't been sleeping well." She looked down at the book. "It's beautiful and looks very old."

We stared at it. The front cover was a shiny silvery metal. On the top half of the cover was a giant hand holding an open scroll with ten things written across it. I realized they were the Ten Christmas Rules. A standing polar bear was on each side of the scroll. Below the scroll was a city. I noticed that the tallest building was flying a red and white flag just like the one outside The Teashroom. I turned the book on its side. *The Kringle Chronicles* was written on the spine.

"Let me see that," my mom said, taking the book. "Oh my, this is sterling silver. It looks just like your father's Siddur. Oh my gosh, I hope Mr. Raffo didn't give you his." She turned the book over. "Oh, okay, no, it's not." On the back cover were nine etched reindeer heads with name tags hanging around their necks. Actually, they looked like military-style dog tags. The book obviously had something to do with Christmas.

My mom turned to the first page. "Blank pages. Oh, it must be a journal. Well, take care of it and make sure you thank Mr. Raffo."

I was speechless. The pages weren't blank, they were covered in text and drawings. But I was pretty sure I knew why my mom couldn't see anything—because I hadn't touched the pages. I closed the book and tucked it under my arm.

"I will. Call me when the almonds are ready," I said, running up the stairs to my room. I hopped up on my bed and read the title again, *The Kringle Chronicles*—just like the Web site *and* the book in the invisible room in the Crystal Palace. I eagerly opened the book and began to read. The prologue was titled *In the Beginning*. It began with an introduction to the history of the Poles of Polanshalem, sworn enemies of the giants. Then it talked about borders, treaties, and even had an ancient-looking map of a supercontinent. I read some more and learned that the text I was reading was actually Brewpolan, the official language of the Poles. It looked like a mix of Chinese and Hebrew. I didn't know either language, yet I could read the text. I skipped ahead to the first chapter. It was titled *Survival of the Hanokh*. It mentioned a terrible freeze which occurred after the original garden was violated by Adam and Eve—a freeze that destroyed most of the great beasts, giants, and even man. Lord Hanokh, a Pole of Polanshalem and a great leader to his people, helped them survive. He also earned the trust of those beings not bound by time—the elves and dwarves. Six thousand years passed and the population of beast, giant, and man swelled. New alliances were forged between Earth's creatures, and new borders were drawn. The dwarves and elves remained masters of their domain: the timeless forests, metal-rich mountains, and earthy underground. Man chose the northern highlands near the sea and named their land North Polanshalem. The fierce Mar dragons, largest of the sea creatures, remained loyal to their master, man, and chose the sea along North Polanshalem. The giants greedily claimed the rest of the land. Another five hundred years passed. Then war broke out.

"Jakob!"

Ugh! It was my mom. I quickly flipped ahead to see what happened next. Chapter four was titled *Santa and the Servant*. And there he was—the cloaked, dusty man from my dreams—in a picture below the title.

"They're ready!" my mom yelled louder, but I couldn't stop reading just yet. It was impossible to put down the book. I quickly read the history of Santa and Servant Rupert—or S.R. as we knew him—and it was bad, very bad. Then I came to a part where Santa and his army were preparing to battle his former servant.

"JAKOB!" Man, my mom wouldn't let up. The almonds *had* to be delivered.

Reluctantly, I closed the book and plopped it on my desk beside the stack of comics. That's when something on my desk suddenly made a noise. I whirled around and almost yelped. The book was alive! A silver arm had already grown out from the spine and another arm was sprouting out from the gilded pages. Two skinny, pencil-like legs sprouted from the bottom of the book. And as if things couldn't get any stranger—the thing did a push-up and stood. Two crystal green eyes blinked as if they'd just awakened. Then they widened, and the large mouth grew into a smile. The eyes suddenly looked mischievous. They were staring at my stack of comics. Then the craziest thing happened. The book rushed over to the stack and started shoveling the comics into its cavernous mouth. What do you do when a book comes to life and begins eating your drawings? Nothing! And that's just what I did.

After gorging on the comics, the book changed back to normal. No eyes, no mouth, no arms ... just a book. I cautiously reached out to touch it when the mouth suddenly appeared again and let out the loudest burp I've ever heard. I kid you not, the burp lasted at least twenty seconds. I even heard my mom say, "That's gross, Jakob!" from downstairs. I decided to leave the book for a moment and find Shig and Logan. I had to tell them what had just happened. I rushed downstairs, snatched up my jacket and had it on by the time I reached the door, which opened courtesy of Mom. With the box of almond packs in hand, I walked outside and was met by a gust of wind.

"AWW! *It's freezing!*" I complained.

"Is that jacket going to be enough? You want some gloves and a hat?"

"No, I'm okay."

"Okay, listen, don't worry about Fleep," my mom said.

I shot her a worried look.

"What happened to Fleep?"

"Nothing happened to him, silly. He came by when you were—"

"What did he want?" I asked, still worried.

"His almonds. Don't worry about delivering his package. Mrs. Sanchez couldn't wait for them," she said, laughing.

"Oh," was all I said, but on the inside I was like, whew! My dreams had me pretty freaked out, plus Tiff's dream about one of my friends becoming wayward only added to my anxiety.

After delivering some of the almonds, I made my way over to Shig's. He was out in his front yard wearing one of those oversized blue parkas that come down to the knees and have fluffy fur lining around the hood. He looked like a scientist from Antarctica. I grinned at the sight and gave him his family's bag of almonds.

"You're not going to believe what just happened," I said excitedly.

"What?"

"Logan's dad gave me a book called *The Kringle Chronicles*. It's just like the book in Tiff's kitchen and the one in The Kringle Shop in Christmas. Well, actually, you don't know about the shop—"

"Yeah, I do. Logan told me. She said you messed with her and said there was this book in an office, even though there wasn't."

"Wrong! There was a book and it's just like the book in Tiff's kitchen. Only those books didn't come to life."

"What?" Shig scrunched up his face.

I quickly told him about the book coming to life, eating my comics, and even the burp. When I was done, Shig stared at the ground, thinking hard.

"What if it ate the comics so they'd become part of its story?"

"I don't know. I'll have to look. Did you get my IM about—"

"Fleep not believing? Yeah. I got it. Something is definitely wrong with him. After the brunch, I asked him to come over and help me launch rockets and he said no thanks. Fleep *never* says no to rockets."

That's when I noticed the rockets in the grass. There were three of Shig's smaller ones, about twelve inches in length. Shig saw me looking at them.

"Just trying to keep busy, Jakob. I hope everything goes as planned tonight. S.R. scares me."

"We'll be fine. Just make sure you get some sleep. It's going to be a long night. As soon as I catch Santa, Fleep will come by to get you."

Shig rolled his eyes.

"What? He'll help us, don't worry," I insisted.

"I sure hope so," Shig said, tinkering again with his rockets.

I noticed the palm trees swaying.

"I wouldn't launch those today. It's too windy," I said.

"Leave the rocket trajectory to me. You go hurry up with the almonds," he teased.

I smiled, jogged over to Logan's house and rang the doorbell.

"What's up?" Logan said, opening the door.

I forced a bag of almonds against her stomach.

"Give this to your parents. And we need to talk. Can you meet in front of Shig's?"

"Five minutes," Logan said hurriedly then shut the door.

X DoEsN't Mark tHE SPot

After handing out the almonds in record time (thank you very much), I was standing in Shig's yard beside Logan. She wore a puffy pink ski jacket and kept blowing in her hands to warm them up. As Shig made the final touches on his next rocket, I told him about our meeting with Baum, describing everything in detail: us changing into clear, icy-looking silhouettes, Logan freaking out in the elevator—which drew laughs even from Logan, and about only me being able to see the giant book and the communication tech room. I explained how J-Rays, frontpacks, the special cup, and the elvish tea work. Then I told Logan about the book her dad had given me.

"The cover is solid silver—"

"Is it one of the ones you've been mailing for him?"

"How would I know that? I *don't open* the packages. I just mail them, but check it out … my mom couldn't see the book until I touched it. It's called *The Kringle Chronicles.*"

"I want to see it *now*," Logan demanded.

"Yeah, me too," Shig said.

"Later. We need to talk about Fleep. I think he's made the Wayward List and that means no palace, forever."

Logan looked at me funny.

"What?" I demanded. "What are you looking at?"

"You! You said no *palace.*"

"No I didn't. I said no *presents*," I said defensively.

"Oh, yes you did," Logan snapped back with a chuckle.

I gave Shig a pleading look.

"You did, you said *palace,*" Shig said nodding. "He's made the Wayward List and that means no palace."

I raked my fingers through my hair. "Weird. It's this strange dream I had about Fleep being banned from this Crystal Palace. I've had three really scary dreams since Friday." I told them about the dreams, which they all agreed were creepy.

"Fleep alert!" Shig said suddenly.

Logan and I spun around as Fleep swaggered toward us and handed me a gaming controller.

Logan, of course, went right for the jugular.

"So you don't believe anymore, huh?"

Fleep gave me a contemptuous look then turned to Logan.

"You didn't hear my dad. He flat-out said there's no Santa." Fleep rolled his eyes. "I didn't come over to argue. I'm out of here!" He sauntered off.

We looked at each other concerned. This was strange behavior from a guy who was typically pretty sensitive.

Beep. Beep. A high-pitched horn beeped several times. An old, bright orange convertible MINI Cooper turned right on to our street and pulled up to Fleep. Benji stepped out and said something to him.

"Holy smokes!" I said, shocked beyond all belief.

"What?" Logan asked quickly.

"The last day of school—Friday—that car—Benji was the guy parked in front of the for-sale house, watching Tiff."

"Well, what in the world is he doing here?" Shig asked.

We ran over to them just as Benji walked back to the MINI, reached in, and got something from the back seat.

"It's a frontpack, just like the ones Baum gave us," Logan said curiously.

Benji handed Fleep the frontpack and said, "Wear it to bed tonight." Fleep nodded, and Benji motioned Logan, Shig and I over to the MINI. He got behind the wheel. We huddled around the window and Benji whispered to us, "Be sure he wears that frontpack. I'm making a special exception by giving him one, because he'll need the protection." Just then a voice announced the time over the MINI's speakers.

"It's two p.m."

"I have to go. Lots to prepare for. I'll see each of you later. Peace," Benji said, pulling away in his MINI.

I turned back to Fleep. "Hey," I shouted. "What's in your frontpack?" Fleep stopped on his driveway.

We jogged over and congregated around him.

"A pair of black sunglasses," Fleep said pulling his arm out of the pack. They were the exact same glasses Benji had given me at The Teashroom.

"There's got to be more in there," Shig said. "It looks full."

Fleep searched around inside the pack then tossed it over to me. I searched around too but didn't feel anything—not even a bottom. I struggled to see inside by holding it at different angles—still nothing. As I was about to give up looking, I thought I saw a faint yellow glow. Then suddenly I saw the contents—commando gear: a helmet, elbow and knee pads, gloves, and even boots. I blinked my eyes really hard and looked again, but the stuff was gone. I had to be seeing things. That was the only explanation, or was it? I picked up the pack and gave it to Logan.

"Here, it's empty—I think. I mean I thought I saw stuff," I said. Skeptical, Logan took it.

Shig motioned for the sunglasses and tried them on.

"Cool, they cover my eyes like safety glasses," Shig said then ran off to his front yard. Annoyed, I smacked my thighs. I had hoped Shig would stay and help us talk some sense into Fleep. With Shig there, Fleep wouldn't feel as if Logan and I were ganging up on him—we assertive-personality types always seemed to do that.

Regardless, it was time to continue Operation: Make Fleep Believe. I spoke urgently. "Fleep, you need to believe. I had a nightmare with you in it, and there was this palace with a prison and—"

"I don't care," Fleep said coldly. "S.R. is real! Maybe if I do something for him, I'll get what I want—maybe *he'll* bring me my skateboard."

I couldn't believe my ears.

Logan was stone-faced. "You're joking, right?" she asked. "How can you say that after being attacked by S.R.?"

"I can see *him!*" Fleep said darkly.

"Seriously, you better take back what you said about Santa and your parents," Logan said with a pointed finger.

"No, I'm not taking anything back. They're liars. I hate Santa. I hate him!"

"What are you *doing*? If you don't take it back, you're going to be on the Wayward List for sure," I said.

"No I'm not, because there is no Wayward List," Fleep said angrily.

There was an uncomfortable pause; I honestly didn't know what else we could say to convince him.

Finally I said, "Shig thinks you're not going to help us tonight."

"Well, he's wrong," Fleep said, less irritable. "You guys are my friends, and I'll help you … even if it *is* a complete waste of time."

A sudden explosion followed by a roaring swoosh stole our attention. Logan and I sprinted to Shig's yard. It was littered with bits of singed plastic. One of the rockets must have exploded before liftoff. Thankfully Shig looked fine. He was standing, gazing up through the sunglasses. I followed his gaze and quickly found the other rocket's smoky trail. It climbed for another second or so then arched, deployed its chute, and began its slow descent.

"What happened to the other rocket?" I asked, looking up.

"Exploded about a foot off the ground," Shig said, annoyed. "AWW, NO! It's landing on your roof."

"I told you it was too win—"

"Wow, you have to see this!" Shig shouted as he stared at my roof.

"What is it?" Logan asked. Shig ignored her and turned to me.

"It's your house. Here, put these on. I'm not saying anything until you look," Shig said, handing me the sunglasses.

I slid the glasses on and looked up at my roof. Glimmering under the sunlight was a large red X the size of a car.

"Do you see it?" Shig asked eagerly.

"Yeah," I said, but my expression said something more like, *Duh, how could I miss it?*

"See what? Someone answer me!" Logan was perturbed. She reached for my face, for the glasses, but I jerked back just in time.

"Wait a minute." I glanced around at the neighborhood rooftops, all of which were marked with red Xs. I gasped when I got to Fleep's. His roof was missing the X, and so was Tiff's. I handed Logan the glasses. "Look for yourself," I said. She fumbled with the glasses for a second, then forced them over her eyes and looked around.

"Xs, red ones—on the roofs—all of the roofs. Well, all of the roofs except for—"

"Fleep and Tiff," I said darkly. Fleep shrugged and crossed his arms.

Logan offered the glasses to Fleep, but he refused with a shake of his head. After Logan dropped the sunglasses in the frontpack, I handed it back to Fleep.

"Fleep, those Xs are there to tell S.R. to pass over a house. I read about it in a book Logan's dad gave me. See, S.R. and Santa used to work together, S.R. was actually his servant. Santa would leave presents for the good kids and S.R., well, he would leave a lump of coal for the wayward kids. But as time went on and things got busier, Santa and S.R. split up. It made it easier for Santa to visit the good kids and S.R. to visit the wayward. But then something really bad started to happen. Wayward kids started disappearing on Christmas day. Things didn't look good for S.R. when black dust and pieces of coal were found in homes of the missing kids. So Santa set a trap and caught S.R. turning a boy into coal. There was this huge battle with dwarves and elves, tall men, and even giants and dragons. Oh, and there were five great beings called elements." I stopped.

"Why did you stop?" Shig asked.

"I had to stop reading to deliver the almonds." I turned to Fleep. "My point is, you have to believe in Santa! S.R. might—"

"No more stupid fairy tales," Fleep said.

"Why can't you just believe in Santa?" I asked.

"Easy, because he's not real," Fleep said smugly.

It was pointless to argue with Fleep. I could only hope that he'd take measures to protect himself. "Come on, Fleep. You're in danger. You're wayward. At least do what Benji said and wear the frontpack tonight. Please."

"Fine," Fleep snapped. As I watched my friend saunter off toward his house, I couldn't help but feel an over-whelming sense of gloom. Would my dreams come true too, like Tiff's had? No, I assured myself, everything will turn out just fine. I'll catch Santa and prove once and for all to Fleep that Santa is real.

Then Shig flipped out on me. "Guys, this is bad. We can't do this alone. Fleep needs protection!" He looked over at his house, where Mr. Sugihara was cleaning out his police car. Then Shig took off, mumbling, "We need help."

I didn't like the look of this one bit. I raced after him and caught up just as he was telling his dad about the red Xs.

"You really see a red X on our roof?" Mr. Sugihara asked.

Oh boy, this was bad. I stepped in front of Shig with my back to his dad. I widened my eyes at my friend, hoping he'd get the message to shut up. He brushed me aside.

"It's a shiny red X, but Fleep doesn't have one. S.R.'s coming for the wayward—for Fleep. You're the *police*. You have to stop him!" Shig's eyes were glossy with held-back tears. Oh man, I had to shut up Shig before he put all of our parents in danger.

I started laughing. "Awesome, Shig; you got him. Okay man, I owe you five bucks." Still with my back to Mr. Sugihara, I whispered, "Are you *insane*? Remember S.R. said no parents."

I turned around, smiling. Mr. Sugihara's stare burned through me.

"What are you two up to?" he asked.

"Nothing—I mean—you know—a dare." In my opinion, convincing police officers of anything is one of the hardest things to do … but especially if you are trying to convince them of a lie. They are so suspicious and serious. But I must have been Hollywood-worthy because, in the end, Mr. Sugihara dismissed us with a curt warning to stop fooling around.

I led Shig away and leaned in to support him. He was crying under his breath, trying to conceal it. I snuck a glance over my shoulder at his dad. He was watching us. "You need to cowboy up," I whispered.

Logan was sitting on her driveway with her head buried in her hands. Shig wiped his eyes as we sat down. Logan looked up teary-eyed. My friends looked terrible, and I felt really bad. I wanted to say something that would make them feel better but I wasn't sure what to say. The situation stunk. Now the stakes were raised. Not only were we catching Santa to rescue Tiff's family, we also were saving Fleep. I heard my name being called in the distance. It was my mom, calling me home.

"Guys, I have to go. Don't forget. We all have a part in this. Cowboy up! Just think, we'll catch Santa tonight, and by tomorrow morning Fleep will believe, Rick will be back, the book in Tiff's house will be sealed, and S.R. will probably be on his way to swap places with all of the imprisoned kids. And maybe, just maybe, I'll get a replacement phone for the one I kicked in the pool."

Logan managed a laughing snort through all of the tears. "Did you ask for a phone?"

"No."

"Then I doubt it."

"You never know," I said, walking off. "He's Santa."

I Catch a Commando

Ithrew off the covers and tried to remember if I'd put my jacket and shoes in the fort under the stairs with the frontpacks. It was ten p.m. on Christmas Eve, and I had to do one more thing before going to sleep: sneak downstairs and swap out the cup of eggnog my sisters left for Santa with the elvish cup Baum gave me. I rolled out of bed, stealthily left my room, and crept downstairs to the fort.

I opened my frontpack and took out the elvish cup and tea. Then I silently snuck over to the dining room table for the switch. Grabbing the cup of eggnog, I quickly walked to the kitchen then poured water into Baum's elvish cup. I thought I heard someone walking around upstairs. Because I was in a serious hurry and nervously swapping glances between the stairs and the cup, I accidentally poured all of the tea leaves into the water. They dissolved instantly. I gasped, remembering that Baum had said to use only seven pinches of tea. From what I could tell, there were probably about twenty-eight pinches of tea originally, so I figured pouring out three-quarters of the liquid would fix it. I was certain that would balance things out. I left the elvish cup on the table where I thought Fleep could see it, and was back in my room within minutes, laying on my bed and staring at the ceiling. This was it, we were about to catch Santa. And, with that, I prayed and fell asleep.

A loud thump woke me, not my iPod as I'd expected. Was it Santa? I had to check. My mind raced to my parents—if the noise was loud enough to wake me, they probably heard it too. I threw off my covers, sprinted to the light switch, and flipped it on. Then if my parents were awake, they would think I had made the noise. Sure enough, my dad was walking down the hallway to check out downstairs. He stopped at my door.

"Sorry," I whispered sheepishly.

"You okay? Sounded like you fell out of bed."

I nodded.

"Okay, then go back to sleep, or Santa's not coming."

"Okay, Dad."

He turned off my light and left. Success! I had to get downstairs. I grabbed my iPod Touch and switched it to vibrate to avoid any more noise. I waited about ten minutes or so, just to be sure my dad had settled back into bed, then snuck downstairs ... all the time worrying.

Who had made the noise? If it was Santa, why hadn't Fleep called? Halfway down, my iPod vibrated. It was Fleep calling me via Skype. Finally, I thought.

"Hold on," I answered in a whisper then turned at the second flight of steps that led to the living room. I froze, awestruck by what I saw beside my Christmas tree, beginning with the black boots. I stepped as quietly as I could down the rest of the stairs and stared at the amazingly large figure. Who in the world was lying beside my tree? A large man had fallen flat on his back onto a perfect row of crushed presents. The presents had softened the fall and prevented his head from hitting the floor. I cringed at the thought until I noticed he was wearing a ballistic military helmet.

I stared at the unconscious body for a minute and wondered who the person was—in my house, my living room. He was supposed to be Santa but didn't look anything like what I had expected. Sure, he wore red … but his coat wasn't a coat at all. It was a military-style flak jacket in crimson, gray, and black camouflage, with shoulder and chest armor. I noticed a nameplate on his chest and leaned in closer. It read Santa. Incredible!

Suddenly the secret website, Baum, and the Crystal Palace all made sense. Santa was a soldier of some type. From his helmet down to his boots, this guy was tough.

Around his camouflage pants were two black belts—one worn just above the other—joined by a large, silver buckle. I noticed something peculiar about the belt buckle: it was actually two elaborate buckles, one fitted over the other. The top buckle was shaped like a polar bear's head and had flashing red gemstone eyes. I'd seen the same exact polar bear on the back of Baum's shirt. The initials *S.C.* were engraved in cursive over the bear's head; they had to stand for Santa Claus. I didn't like looking at the other buckle. It was shaped like a creepy-looking goat's skull. The creature's horns bridged a gap between the two buckles and connected to the polar bear. This belt had the initials *S.R.* engraved on it, but there was an X etched over the letters, as if someone had purposely crossed them out. It was weird—I can't explain it, but I didn't want to give the goat buckle anymore thought. I gave the giant man another look. I'd caught Santa! I started a silent victory dance.

A subtle tap on the glass of the front door startled me. It was Fleep, with his nose pressed against the glass, fogging it up with every breath. Something on Fleep's head caught my eye. It was snow. No way, I thought. His hair was covered in snow! I ran to the door.

Fleep mouthed, "Hurry up," then looked over his shoulder again. Once the door was unlocked, he rushed inside and brushed the snow from his blond, wet hair.

"I can't believe it's snowing," I whispered as I poked my head outside.

I gave Fleep a once-over and noticed that he was wearing his frontpack the wrong way. He had it on as a backpack.

"You need to put that on the right way," I whispered.

"Yeah, yeah. Later. Hurry up. Close the door."

"What's wrong?"

"I wasn't alone in the house—"

"Yeah, Tiff was with you, right?"

"No, I mean yeah, but—"

"But what? Where's Tiff?"

Fleep swallowed. "I don't know. One minute she's there and then the next thing I know she's trying to get me to leave. She kept saying 'He's here! He's here!' and I kept saying no he wasn't, that the cup at your house hadn't moved. Then she said 'not Santa' and that it was 'too late.' She took off running and mumbling something about the servant. And like I said, we weren't alone. Benji and some tall guy in a black cloak were there too."

I gasped. "A guy in a black cloak! Has to be S.R." Like from my dream. Tiff must have run off when she saw S.R.

"I don't know, but Benji was upset that Baum hadn't warned you about the consequences of using too much of the elvish stuff." I ran over to the special cup. It was empty. I glanced down at Santa then whirled around.

"Fleeeeep ..." I whispered long and drawn out. "What's supposed to happen if I used a lot of the elvish stuff?"

"I don't know. That's when the guy in the black cloak came up from behind Benji and knocked him out. And I took off!"

I was worried for Benji. I thought for a moment then looked at Fleep. "Listen to me. You need to believe in Santa," I said, nodding gravely.

Fleep looked at me like I was crazy.

"Look, over by the tree. Seeing is believing, Fleep, and you really need to believe."

Fleep looked over my shoulder at the Christmas tree. There was a moment of silence, I assumed from the shock of seeing Santa.

"Uh, yeah, I don't see anything," Fleep said coolly.

"Not possible." I could see Santa as clear as day. Wait a minute. It's probably like what happened to my mom with the book Mr. Raffo gave me. I walked over to Santa, knelt down and touched his boot.

"How about now, can you see him?" I asked, a little frustrated that I hadn't heard a *wow* or *no way* from Fleep.

"Now I can. I had to move over to the right. The columns were blocking my view."

Impossible. Santa was way too large. It was that invisible thing again—I had to touch him for others to see.

"Well come over and look at him."

Fleep was thinking.

"What's wrong now?" I whispered.

"Nothing," he snapped, "it's just that he doesn't look anything like Santa. It's probably your dad in a military costume."

"He's definitely not my dad," I said confidently.

"Have you checked?"

"I don't have to check. He's not this tall," I said in disbelief. "You know that."

Fleep waved me off dismissively. He still didn't believe. "Whatever. I'll go get the rest of the gang."

"Wait," I said in a forced whisper, but I was too late. Fleep was out the door. I didn't like the idea of him being outside on his own, especially with S.R. lurking around.

I gave Santa a curious look and wondered what his face looked like under the helmet. I have to admit, I thought about peeking once or twice while I waited for Fleep to return. In the meantime, I took in the totality of Santa's size. He was a big man and tall—really tall. I needed perspective, so I decided to lie next to him. Wow, he easily was twice the length of me.

"Is he dead?" The small whisper scared me half to death.

I grabbed my chest, gasping, then looked up. Staring down at me was Koji, Shig's little brother! I got up quickly and glanced at the open front door.

"No, he's not dead," I exhaled. "What are you—?"

"I ran ahead."

Ahead? Ahead of whom? It didn't matter. I shook my head.

"Well, go home and go back to bed." I waved my hand over his head like a Jedi. "You are dreaming ... I am not here ... you are not here ... you have to go home ..." I whispered with authority.

Koji smacked my hand. "If I'm not here, then why do I have to go home?"

I pressed my lips. Smart kid.

"Besides, Jedi mind tricks don't work on me."

I quickly grabbed Koji by the arm as he brushed past me on his way to Santa. Oh, no you don't, I thought as I pulled him back.

He leaned forward, captivated at the sight. "His jacket says Santa. Is that really him?"

"Yeah, it's him."

"But he looks like a soldier."

"He looks like a *soldier?*" Logan whispered from the door as she quietly walked in with Shig and Fleep. I was secretly relieved to see Fleep back safely.

I launched into Shig as soon as he came inside. "What is *he* doing here?" I asked, slightly raising my voice and pointing to Koji.

"He woke up when we were leaving and said if I didn't bring him, he'd tell," Shig said.

I sighed. Nothing like blackmail from a ruthless six-year-old. "Fine, whatever. Just keep him quiet."

"You did it! You really caught him," Logan said, barely suppressing her excitement.

"Unbelievable! He doesn't look anything like I expected. He doesn't even look like a regular soldier. He looks like—" Shig couldn't place Santa's look.

"A commando? Special Forces?" I whispered.

"Yeah," he answered, still lost in thought.

"Did you look under his helmet?" Logan asked.

"No, I was waiting for you guys," I said.

"Well, we're here, so let's see." Logan's whisper was filled with anticipation.

I nodded and bent down to reach for Santa's helmet just as we heard a loud thump from above. Someone was up—walking—coming down the stairs!

We Almost Get Busted

We panicked. I looked at the front door, but we wouldn't all get out in time. There was nowhere to hide except behind the Christmas tree. I squeezed in, sandwiched between Logan and Shig, and hoped whoever it was wouldn't see us.

"I see you guys." Dang! It was my little sister, Jordan. In chorus, we sighed and grumbled as, one by one, we came out from behind the tree. I rolled my eyes when I saw Jordan watching us from the stairs. What was with all the little kids playing detective—tonight of all nights?

She settled her suspicious gaze on Santa's huge, sleeping body then jerked as she read the nameplate on the jacket. "Santa!"

She looked at me, teary-eyed. Uh-oh, I knew that look. I charged at Jordan, hoping I'd be able to get a hand over her mouth, but didn't make it in time. She let out the loudest, bloodcurdling girl-scream I've ever heard her make. There was absolutely *no* way my parents were sleeping through that scream.

"You killed him! You killed Santa!" Jordan shrieked, then turned and ran up the stairs.

"No, Jordan! Stop!" I whispered as loud as I could, but it was no use. She was already up the second flight of stairs. I heard footsteps coming from my parents' room. "Get him in the fort," I ordered my friends in a forced whisper then snuck up the stairs. Before I got to the top, I heard my dad telling my mom that he'd handle it as he went into Jordan's room.

"What's wrong, honey?"

No answer. Jordan was crying.

He asked again. "Jordan, what's wrong? Why are you crying?"

"They killed Santa." Her voice faltered.

Oh, this was bad—really bad. I snuck back downstairs. Logan was struggling with one of Santa's legs.

"You guys need to hurry up," I chided.

"He's just a *little* heavy," Shig said gruntingly. Fleep and Koji were struggling with the other leg.

"This is not good," I said under my breath then ran upstairs. As I approached the top step, I heard my dad. He was still in Jordan's room.

"Baby, you had a bad dream. Santa is not dead. He's probably delivering presents as we speak, so go back to sleep, okay?"

"But Daddy, Jakob's downstairs with Fleep and Logan and Shig and Koji and dead Santa." She'd stopped crying. "Go downstairs and check."

"I think I'll check on Jakob first, but not until I get you back to sleep," my dad said.

Well that was good news—my dad wouldn't leave Jordan's side until he was certain she was asleep, so her antics actually bought me some time. I went back downstairs to help my friends.

Things were looking better. Santa was almost to the closet. Logan barked an ultra-quiet order to stop so I could join in. I quickly grabbed Santa's other arm. I nodded and silently mouthed a countdown from three, and everyone heaved. We'd gotten maybe two feet when Santa's helmet slid off, quietly landing on the carpet.

We all froze for a second, captured by the sight of Santa's strikingly bald head. I set down his arm and quickly knelt beside him.

"I can't believe it," I said.

"Wow. Forget everything you know about Santa," Logan said in an awestruck whisper. "He's young, not old … tall, not short … muscular, not plump. *And* he dresses like a Special Forces dude, not in a red and white coat."

His face was also unlike anything I'd expected. There were no rosy cheeks and white beard; instead his skin was dark, his features exotic and finely chiseled. But it was his expression that intrigued me the most. It was a combination of commanding, yet gentle. He was handsome and strong, but peaceful too. He was even smiling in his sleep. Slowly I reached out and touched his face. It had this glow to it. I was in complete wonderment. I stood, still looking down.

"We don't have time for this. Admire later. We have to hide, remember?" Shig—once again cool and collected—reminded us to get a move on.

It was a struggle, but we had managed to get Santa almost completely into the closet when Logan dropped his leg, lost her balance and crashed against the wall. At the sound of the crash, I dropped Santa like a lead weight and beelined it out of the closet—hoping to create a diversion for my dad's inevitable awakening. On my way, I spotted a shiny metal object next to where Santa had fallen. It was a silver tag on a chain. I snatched it up, shoved it in my pocket, and ran up the stairs, pounding my feet heavily. Sure enough, my dad was waiting for me at the top of the stairs as I started up the second flight. Perfect, I thought. Pretending to be caught in the act, I stopped short and looked guilty.

"What are you doing? And why are you dressed?"

Doh! I hadn't thought of a cover story.

"I um ..." I stalled and thought.

"And what was that thump?"

Jordan peered from behind him. "I told you, they killed Santa."

My dad glanced over his shoulder and shushed Jordan, then looked down the hall toward his bedroom.

"Whisper, Jordan." I could tell he was frustrated. "You're going to wake Mommy. Well, Jakob?" he asked, eyeing me suspiciously.

"Yeah, it was me. I was—"

"Killing Santa," Jordan whispered.

"Dad, tell her to stop it! She's crazy," I whined in whisper mode. He gave Jordan the look, and she quieted down. Finally, I thought. And, just in time, I finally came up with a cover.

"I was putting your present under the tree," I said, kind of embarrassed-like.

"What present?" Jordan asked, crossing her little arms. "He doesn't have any presents. Daddy, go downstairs," she begged.

"If it will prove that you had a bad dream, then let's do it," my dad said.

My dad winked at me. I winked back. Wait, what was I doing? This was a bad idea. The gang was probably still trying to get the rest of Santa into the fort. My dad brushed past me with my devious-looking sister clinging to his back.

"Dad wait, you can't go down there. My present—it isn't wrapped and—"

By the time I caught up with them, they were already downstairs, staring at the tree. I casually looked to my left at the closet door, the door to the fort. My eyes bugged out. Santa's black boot was sticking out! I ambled over to the door, leaned against the boot and pushed it in with my foot. My dad turned and faced me just as the closet door closed pretty loudly.

"You have some explaining to do, Mister."

Oh no, did he see the boot? My heart slammed against my ribcage, and my head was beginning to throb from the tension. "Dad, I can explain." I just didn't know what it was I was explaining.

"You'd better." He held up the empty elvish cup. "Did you drink this?"

Whew.

"I was thirsty," I confessed. I hated being so sneaky with my dad. Jordan was ogling the cup.

"What were you thinking? Santa hasn't even come and you drank his eggnog? At least refill the cup." He handed me the cup. I took it as I glanced around the tree. The gang had hidden the presents. Good thinking.

"Hey ... that's not the cup Mommy put out for Santa. She used her snowman cup. I know. I helped her," Jordan said accusingly. I froze and watched my dad. He bent down and leaned toward her.

"Didn't you hear me, Missy? Santa hasn't come. See, look under the tree. Those are our presents, not the ones from Santa. Jakob hasn't even had the opportunity to kill Santa." Dad winked at me.

"They must have buried him!" Jordan said sadly.

"Dad!" I protested, still whispering.

"Alright, that's it. I'll deal with this in the morn-ing—off to bed, let's go." My dad scooped up Jordan and trekked up the stairs. He stopped halfway up, turned around and whispered, "Don't forget the eggnog."

I nodded. After they left, I tapped the door once, then twice to signal all was clear and walked to the kitchen. I could hear my sister telling my dad that I had just used a secret knock on the door to the fort, and he had to go back down and check.

"Everyone must be in the fort," she said.

I heard him pause at the top of the stairs. I leaned over by the open refrigerator and looked up at my dad. He took the last step, then turned around and looked down at me, smiling. I knew right then and there that I was in the clear. I stood up, raised my index finger to my temple, and made circles like the *crazy* hand motion. He nodded and that was it for Jordan, at least for the time being.

I shifted gears and began to think of ways to wake Santa. Water, I thought. A splash of water should wake him. I walked back to the living room, carrying water in the elvish cup and eggnog in the snowman cup. My dad wouldn't remember that the cup was different. After I placed the eggnog on the glass table beside the sofa, I walked to the closet.

"… not Santa," Fleep whispered to Logan as I entered the closet.

"What in the world—"

Logan held up her hand to my face, gesturing me to shush, then turned to Fleep.

"We know what your parents said, and you need to get over it." Logan paused.

"Jakob, try the water."

I shot Fleep a mistrusting look, then carefully stepped over Santa's legs and settled down beside his head. I still couldn't believe how big he was. I looked back. Everyone was watching from the closet door. I took a deep breath.

"Come on, Santa. We need you."

I began with sprinkles of water.

Nothing.

I escalated to drops, then to a slow pour, and, finally, just dumped the remaining water on his face. Still nothing.

"Why isn't he waking up?" Logan asked, worried.

"Because I did something stupid. Something really stupid," I said, shaking my head regretfully. "I accidentally gave him too much tea."

I stood, shoulders sunken.

"How?" Logan begged. "You were only supposed to give him seven pinches."

Shig patted me on the back. "It doesn't matter now. He just needs some time, you know, to sleep it off. He'll wake up, he has to."

"I hope you're right," I said.

"Look, Shig and I will do some recon, see if we can find the reindeer and the sleigh. Maybe there's a Santa first-aid kit or something," Logan said.

I was already shaking my head. It was a great idea, but there was no way was I letting Logan go on a recon mission.

"Nope, not happening," I began, careful to keep a low voice. "S.R. is out there. I should go."

"Yes, it is happening." Logan replied with determination as she tossed me the flashlight. "You need to be here in case he wakes," she said in a forced whisper, then turned to Shig and motioned for him to follow her. Shig turned to me for approval.

I shrugged my shoulders as if to say, "Whatever." There was no sense arguing; she was right. I felt terrible that Santa wasn't waking up and had to think of something. I nodded. "OK, but take Koji home too and, hey ..."

"Yeah?" Logan said, stopping.

"Be careful."

After they were gone I returned to the closet and remembered my *Kringle Chronicles* book. Maybe there was something in there that would tell me how to wake Santa. I told Fleep to wait while I went to get my book. When I came back to the closet, Fleep was staring at Santa.

"I need light," I said, showing Fleep the book. While Fleep stood beside me, shining the flashlight, I skimmed through looking for a mention of anything that could possibly help us. About a quarter of a way through the book, I found something that stopped me short—my comics. They had been absorbed onto the pages, and looked like they had always been part of the book. I passed at least ten pages of comics then stopped. The next pages were blank. It wasn't the invisibility thing, because I was holding the book. Maybe I had to rub the pages. Nothing. Odd, I thought. Then the really weird happened. The book vibrated so strongly that I dropped it. Only it didn't fall. It floated.

"No way!" Fleep said. "Now that's cool."

Then the pages fanned backwards to the first blank page and, amazingly, text appeared. It was as if an invisible hand was writing.

CHAPTER
21

We Read as
My Book Writes

After Fleep steadied the flashlight on the book, I noticed the oddest thing. The text was in my own handwriting, and read from a first-person perspective, as if I'd written it. It read:

I didn't know it at the time, but the moment Santa had felt his knees tremble, he'd pressed down on his belt buckle. That sent an alert to the nearest listening post, which was Baum's location in Christmas, Florida—Santa's Western Hemisphere Command Center.

Remember that communications tech room, high above on the forty-fourth floor, with the two dwarves? Well, they were tracking Santa and monitoring holographic interfaces when the alert came across the screens.

The black-bearded dwarf, Ira, tapped his finger on one of the holographs, which created an image of the state of Florida. He double-tapped the image, and the holograph zoomed in on the Central Florida area, then beyond the roads and lakes, and finally settled on a single house in Winter Garden—my house. The dwarf stared at the holograph for another second, hoping the alert would reset. Sometimes Santa accidentally hit the polar bear belt buckle, what with all the lifting presents and such.

But with every passing second, the dwarf's hope for a false alarm faded. He looked at the timer on his holograph. Thirty seconds had passed with no response from Santa. That was confirmation enough: the alert was real. The dwarf reached down and pressed a silver holographic button. A mini-microphone slithered out from his tiny earpiece. Ira's voice was deep and monotone.

"Crystal Palace to Dasher," he said.

"Dasher, go." The reply was a raspy whisper over the speakers.

"Resetting Polar Bear alert. Attempt to contact Sierra Charlie."

"Vixen and I are uncloaked. We have a lock on Sierra Charlie's beacon and are en route," Dasher said.

"Wait," Fleep said. "What does Sierra Charlie mean?"

"It's military talk. It's on the Military Channel all the time. Sierra stands for the letter S, and Charlie is for the letter C. Sierra Charlie is Santa Claus," I said, looking down at Santa. The red polar bear eyes weren't flashing. They'd been reset. No way. Things were happening as we read.

I looked at the book. Another block of text had been written. I read fast.

A faint alarm began sounding as Ira spoke: "Crystal Palace to all units: Sierra Charlie is off the grid. Repeat, Sierra Charlie is off the grid. This is not a drill."

He pressed the silver button again, then drove his hover-chair over to the other dwarf's station to study a particularly large holograph. It displayed nine sets of vital signs like heart rate and body temperature. There was a silhouette of each creature being monitored, six looked like Clydesdale-sized reindeer, and three were undeniably human. The reindeers' vital signs suddenly spiked, and the reindeer images morphed into human silhouettes. The animals were actually humans, using cloaking devices to hide their identities.

Ira pointed to another holograph that looked like an aerial view of my house. There were six blue dots between mine and Shig's house, and two more in my back yard. The elves zeroed in on two red dots which had just appeared and were slowly moving toward the blue.

"Natsar, look," Ira said to the other dwarf.

"I see them. They're approaching Dasher's team." Natsar double-tapped on the holograph. It zoomed in on the two red dots.

"A human boy and girl," Ira said.

I slammed the floating book closed.

"What are you doing?" Fleep whined.

"Logan and Shig! They're talking about Logan and Shig in the book," I said in a strong whisper. "Remember, they're doing recon outside." Just then the book fanned open to the page where we'd left off.

"Come on, it's telling us to keep reading. Logan and Shig will be fine. Let's read," Fleep said. Reluctantly, I went back to reading.

Baum walked in the room. Natsar and Ira stopped what they were doing and saluted.

"As you were," Baum said, returning their salutes. "Do we have visual?"

Natsar shook his head.

"We're working on it sir. Two human children may have seen Dasher uncloak."

"Not important. Those children are going to see a lot more before the night is over. Dwarves, you are now part of Covert Operation: Catch S.R." Ira and Natsar looked surprised. "Unfortunately I'm shutting down the mission and issuing new orders: extract the primaries—Santa and Jakob."

"What!" I gasped then stepped back from the book.

"They're coming for you," Fleep grinned.

I couldn't believe Fleep. "This isn't a joke. We're reading text that is magically appearing in a floating book, and you're joking around. They said they're coming after me."

"Come on, what could possibly happen?"

"I'll tell you what's going to happen. Commandos are going to come through that door." I tried to sound calm, but I was freaking out.

"Come on, this is the best stuff I've read all year. Let's read some more!" Fleep said.

"Fine," I said, then stood beside Fleep and read.

"Tell them NEGATIVE on assault until I get there. I want perimeter containment on the trap house since Santa is still inside, and warn Dasher that Benji is battling enemies inside the vacant house west of their location. Advise them to use discretion. And get me a visual!" Baum barked.

"Crystal Palace to Dasher," Ira said.

"Dasher, go."

"That's negative on assault. Establish perimeter containment on trap house, Santa is inside. Top requesting video, and Benji's engaging enemies inside the vacant house to the west."

"Bad guys to the west, roger that."

Baum studied the holograph for another minute then stared at the nearest speaker as it crackled.

"Team six, Crystal Palace."

"Crystal Palace," Ira answered.

"Six is good to go. Standing by for Top," a rapid, surfer-dude-like voice said through the speakers.

Baum gave the thumbs up and ran out of the room. TOP was military slang for MASTER SERGEANT, and that's what Baum was—master sergeant of the Special Forces Kringle Elite Team Six, otherwise known as KET6.

"Roger that. Top en route," Ira said, then maneuvered his finger and opened another holographic image.

A large three-dimensional rocket of sorts—with six small, human silhouettes—appeared. Ira watched as the silhouettes lined up in the container. He clicked on each one, which brought up six new holographic windows. Each window profiled a team member, their handle (or nickname), and their vital statistics. This was Baum's Special Forces team.

"Vitals good. KET6 prepare for launch in five, four, three, two, one." Ira grabbed and pulled down on a holographic lever, and with that, KET6 was launched in their ballistic transport from atop the Crystal Palace en route to my neighborhood.

I wanted to slam the book shut, but what good would that do? Nothing. I wasn't in control and it scared me.

REINDEER
ASSAULT OUR FORT

The thought of being whisked away by Santa's Special Forces didn't bother me as much as the thought that they wanted to abandon the mission because Santa was unconscious. S.R. was outside my house, scheming and planning who knows what, and we had to stop him. Giving up wasn't the answer and definitely seemed out of character for Baum and the rest of the commandos.

I held the flashlight beam on Santa while I stared and silently begged him to wake. He didn't. Then I remembered what Benji said about the frontpack protecting Fleep, and I felt a sudden urge to put mine on.

Where was my frontpack? I followed the dim circle from the flashlight beam, unexpectedly found my shoes and quickly put them on, then spotted the frontpacks on the other side of Fleep.

Fleep was completely absorbed in reading from my floating book. I, however, had decided to stop reading and start doing. And, frankly, reading what happened to people in real-time was creepy. What if something terrible happened to my friends? It was just as bad as watching it take place. No thanks!

I shifted around Fleep, careful not to step on Santa, then grabbed the frontpack with the crisscrossed straps— the one I'd hidden the green J-Ray in. I shouldered the frontpack then handed Fleep the flashlight. I was unnerved by what I'd read in the book and put my frontpack on so fast you'd think I was being timed in a competition. After snapping everything in place and making sure it fit firmly against my body, I gave Fleep a onceover. He was still wearing his frontpack as a backpack.

I rolled my eyes. "You need to put that on the right way," I said.

"Okay, here." He passed me his flashlight, and I steadied the beam on him.

After Fleep finished, I aimed the flashlight into my own frontpack and searched for the green J-Ray. The quicker I had it in my hand, the better I'd feel.

I finally found the stout, green and white striped J-Ray buried deep in the frontpack. With a firm grip on the hook, I barely whispered, "Shamira." I was expecting it to vibrate kind of like those vibrating stuffed animals everyone has as a little kid. The ones with the *press here* sticker. Well, forget that. This thing felt like a blender puréeing ice. I gripped it with both hands and held on as the candy cane silently vibrated for a few more seconds then morphed into something I never expected. It was a pointed crystal rod that partially coiled around my wrist and up my arm. At the end of the coil was a hanging piece that looked like a plug of some sort. But what did it plug into? Three illuminated green energy tubes, the life source of the J-Ray's power, looked like veins. It looked more like an alien device. I'd expected a blaster like from Star Wars. After all, Baum had said the thing would produce plasma bolts. Oh man, it was amazing, surprisingly light and flexible. I was able to bend my wrist and aim the J-Ray. "Awesome," I said, unable to contain my excitement.

Fleep had been absorbed in the book, not listening at all, when suddenly he looked up and put his nose in the air.

"Holy smoke. It smells minty in here."

I hadn't noticed it in my excitement, but the smell of spearmint was emanating from the transformed J-Ray and now overpowered the closet. Weird, but cool.

Just then, we heard a faint noise outside the fort. I peered out and saw Shig and Logan. I smiled and let out a sigh of relief, then quickly motioned them into the fort. At first I thought about telling them what we'd read in my floating book, but then it dawned on me: how did I know for sure that everything we read really happened?

Sure, the blinking red eyes on the polar bear belt had stopped flashing at the same time as in the book ... but that was all I knew for sure. No, I decided that first I'd let Logan tell us what happened outside. Then I'd tell her about the book.

Logan sprinted past Shig, wearing a smile from ear to ear, and we learned why the moment she entered the fort. She whispered in what sounded like a million words a minute. Koji was back home and I understood the weather report—it was snowing and there was at least an inch of snow on the ground and, yeah, it smelled minty in the closet. She finally started to tell us about the reindeer but was talking way too fast.

"Slow down." I had the dim circle from the flashlight on her. "What did the reindeer do?" I asked.

"They morphed into commandos," Shig said, animated, then lowered his voice. "It was, well, like the coolest special effects I've ever seen. One minute there are these six huge Clydesdale-sized reindeer. Then the next thing you hear is a voice call out, 'Now, Dancer!' Then it was Prancer, then Comet, and then Cupid and Donner, and Blitzen. You should have seen it. Each of them morphed into a tough-looking soldier wearing commando gear like Santa, and carrying a green and white striped blaster like the clone troopers from Star Wars."

"Like the DC-15S blaster?" Fleep asked, wide-eyed.

"No, the big ones—like the DC-15A!" Shig and Fleep were Star Wars freaks like me.

I regarded Logan. It was time to tell her about the book.

"Well, actually the reindeer uncloaked," I said.

Logan eyed me curiously. "How do you know?"

"Put your frontpacks on first." Logan and Shig wasted no time and had their frontpacks on in a matter of seconds.

"Check this out," I said shining the flashlight on my floating *Kringle Chronicles* book. I told them about the book and how it wrote things down as they were happening.

"Incredible!" Shig said admiringly.

Logan brushed past me, almost knocking me into Santa. "Hey, be careful," I complained.

"My dad gave you this book—a floating book?" I could tell by her tone she wasn't happy.

"Yeah, it's incredible, isn't it?"

"Yeah, incredible," Logan said sarcastically.

"Now what?" I said, trying not to sound like I wanted to strangle her.

"My dad! He has weirdoes in yellow suits building things, an elf spy working at The Teashroom, and now he gives you a magical floating book."

"Logan, he's a spy!" It all made sense now.

Logan regarded me, processing what I'd said.

"Just not the kind of spy you thought he was," I said, talking with my hands. Logan nodded, relieved that her dad was one of the good guys in this battle.

She locked eyes on my arm. "What in the world is that?"

"A green J-Ray."

"Baum didn't give us green ones. You swiped it?"

I shrugged.

"Remember what he said about the green ones. They're dangerous. Make it transform back."

"No. S.R. is out there," I said defensively, then told them what I read in the book: that Baum was aborting the mission and coming to get Santa and me. I had to stop S.R.

"Jakob, going after S.R. by yourself is suicide. If what you say about the book is true, then we can figure things out when the commandos get here. Just put the J-Ray away. Please," Logan said.

I sighed. "Fine, but I'm not giving up on the mission." I stared at the J-Ray and said, "Shamira!"

After it finished its vibration thing and had transformed back to a cane, I stuffed the J-Ray in my waist. Fleep and Shig were staring at me.

"What's the deal with the green J-Ray?" Shig asked curiously.

I had just finished explaining the difference between the red and green J-Rays when two commandos stormed into the fort with frightening stealth and speed, brandishing green and white striped blasters. Logan and Shig instinctively reached for the sky then moved closer to me. Fleep took cover behind my floating book.

The commandos were tall and, like Santa, wore the same tactical gear and protective equipment over their uniforms—the same half-head ballistic helmets and cool-looking black goggles. If you looked really close at the goggles, you could see the heads-up display. I wondered what the rubber-like turtlenecks they wore were for. It looked like part of a wetsuit or something. And what did they have in their bulging pockets?

"Clear," the commando closest to me said. I could tell by the way they'd scanned the closet that their blasters weren't out for us.

"It's okay, we're the good guys. You can put your arms down. I'm Dasher," the biggest one said, pointing to himself, "and this is Vixen." Holy smoke, I thought. He was *the* Dasher from my comics. And Vixen was a female commando. A very *pretty* female commando.

"Awesome," Logan grinned at me. Vixen removed a small silver disc from her belt, the size of a silver dollar, and flipped it in the air. It transformed into a silver Frisbee-looking disc. Hovering above our heads, it casted a dull red light that illuminated the closet surprisingly well.

I glanced at Vixen. She had just finished listening through an earpiece when she dropped her blaster and said, "Perimeter is clear!"

Dasher immediately dropped his too, and the coolest thing happened. In midair, the blaster automatically holstered. Impressive.

Dasher and Vixen knelt down by Santa's side.

"He won't wake up. We've tried water but—" Shig began.

"No worries. He'll wake once he's in the armored personnel carrier," Vixen paused. "I mean the sleigh."

Just then, two more commandos entered the fort.

"Prancer ... and Dancer," I said slowly.

"How do you know their names?" Fleep said.

"Uh, it's on their jackets." I pointed. "See, he's *Prancer* and she's *Dancer.*"

Logan and Shig looked at me skeptically.

"I don't see it," Fleep said.

"Yeah, me either," Logan added.

"Shig?" I asked. He shook his head.

I thought about touching their nameplates to see if it was the invisible thing. But, on second thought, they were fierce looking and probably wouldn't take kindly to me touching them. I regarded Dasher. "How come I see—?"

"Pardon me, Jakob," Prancer spoke with a British accent. She turned to Dasher. "Baum is on the ground."

I glanced over at Logan. She mouthed the name *Baum.* I shrugged then watched Dasher. He lightly pinched his throat with his thumb and index finger. It was the same thing Baum had done at the Crystal Palace.

"Dasher to Comet and Cupid."

"Comet here, Cupid's with me ... go." The loud reply sent painful shock waves through my head. I fell to my knees holding my ears. It was like I'd turned my iPod volume to full blast with my ear buds still in. No one else was feeling this effect.

"What's happening to him?" Logan pleaded.

"His abilities are maturing. It's our presence," Dasher said.

I glanced at my friends. They didn't seem to hear Comet's voice. I'm not saying that I suddenly developed some super-hero listening ability where I could read people's thoughts because it wasn't like that. But I clearly heard Comet's voice. It was like I had a listening device in my ear even though I didn't.

"Dome the neighborhood, house by house. We'll dome the trap house from the inside," Dasher said with urgency.

"Roger that, doming in progress." I heard background noise behind Comet's voice. A swish, like a bottle-rocket taking off.

"Vixen, take care of doming this house," Dasher commanded.

She nodded.

"Dancer, Prancer, ready the package," Dasher continued his rapid-fire orders.

"Roger that," Dancer and Prancer said, moving over to Santa.

Prancer was holding a silver disc, the size of a serving dish, and looked like he was typing on it, but I couldn't see any keys from my angle. Then Dasher turned, blocking my view of Prancer.

"Dome the neighborhood?" I asked, confused.

"Dome—the moment we get outside, you'll see that

your house and every other house on this street, minus the vacant one, will be domed."

"I still don't understand."

"A red shield will surround the homes and prevent our nemesis from taking further hostages. Once the domes are up, it's sleep time for eight hours for anyone inside. Now, let's go. Operation Catch S.R. has been aborted. We're here to extract you and Santa."

"Okay," I said, distracted and trying to see around him. Then I suddenly realized what I had just agreed to and quickly corrected myself. "I mean no; I am *not* going anywhere with you guys," I said in protest.

"Yes, you are," Dasher said then looked up. It looked like he was reading something from his heads-up display. Logan, Fleep, and Shig moved protectively in front of me. Dasher looked down at us and blinked. "There's no time for this. Radar indicates Baum and the rest of his team are across the street. They're engaged in a pretty heavy firefight."

Actually that was good news. It meant S.R. was close. "Guys, let's do what he says." Logan looked over her shoulder at me, her eyes full with worry. I winked. I had a plan.

"The package is ready," Prancer said. The package … Santa. I hadn't been paying attention to Dancer or Prancer, but I could see Santa had been moved to a long silver tube-like chamber. That must have been the disc Prancer had.

"Let's move out," Dasher said. I quickly grabbed my floating book and stuffed it inside my frontpack just as Dasher grabbed and ushered Logan and me out of the fort. Shig and Fleep followed.

"Wait! I need to talk to him—Santa—as soon as he wakes," I pleaded.

Dasher nodded. He brandished his green striped blaster and led the four of us toward the living room, taking cover behind one of the columns in the foyer.

"Take cover behind the table," Dasher said, pointing his blaster toward the front door. The four of us knelt. Vixen tossed a red, rubbery, brick-sized thing into my living room, then did a commando run with her blaster aimed forward and took a position beside the living room window.

"What are they doing?" Logan asked.

"They're trying to see if the exit's safe," Shig said.

"And wake Jakob's parents in the process," Logan said.

I tapped her on the shoulder then pointed to the red thing Vixen had tossed. It had changed and looked like a brick of red Jell-O. There was a red force field bubbling up at the ceiling and creeping its way through the house.

"The doming barrier is up. I guess that's why they've stopped whispering," I said. After a minute, Vixen moved over to the front double doors and exited, taking cover outside behind a concrete support pillar. A gust of cold air

carrying snow flurries blew in just as Dancer and Prancer ran by with blaster rifles trained forward. Between them was the hovering silver tube-like chamber that carried the still-unconscious Santa. It looked like one of those photon torpedoes from Star Trek. They exited and turned left into an area of large bushes. Dasher, still behind the column, turned and motioned for us to move out.

"Let's move," I ordered the gang. As soon as we got outside, Vixen ushered us into the bushes. That's when I noticed Dancer typing on the invisible keyboard on the silver chamber.

Prancer was gone.

I'd forgotten my jacket and worried the cold would be a problem when the frontpack suddenly got warm. It was like I had a personal heater strapped to my chest. The frontpack was mysteriously warming my body.

Dasher exited my house with the strong red glow of the dome behind him. The light was so bright it made his uniform and protective gear look red. "You three, take off the frontpacks and go home. Jakob is coming with us," Dasher commanded. The gang protested. I stepped forward, quieting the lot. It was time to reveal my plan.

"I already told you, I'm not going with you guys. We have a friend, Rick Lang, and his family to rescue."

I noticed Shig was wiggling and reaching behind him for the clasp to take off his frontpack, and Fleep had shouldered his.

"Shig, stop it! And put yours back on the right way," I said to Fleep then turned to Dasher. "Look, S.R. is over there, and we all know what he can do. So no one is going home, retreating, or evacuating. And no one's taking off their frontpacks until we catch him."

Dasher's dark brown eyes studied me. "Is that what the Pole commands?"

I looked at Dasher incredulously. Was he seriously asking me for confirmation on what I'd just said? I ran with it. "Yes," I barked.

Dasher began issuing new orders to his team, including the change to catch S.R. It was like all of the sudden he was taking orders from me. Why? Because I was *the* Pole?

Dasher came nose to nose with me. "This doesn't change the fact that I am still ultimately responsible for you. If we don't fare well in our attempt to capture the Servant, *we will* tactically disengage and evacuate. Understood?"

"Yes," I nodded. "But I still don't understand what this is all about."

Dasher continued. "Servant Rupert wants his belt of power back."

An image of the two belts Santa wore flashed before my eyes, including the one with the nasty goat head and the crossed-out initials. Suddenly it all made sense, and I knew what Dasher was going to say next.

"They each had a belt of power until S.R. abused his for evil. Santa took it back and S.R. has been trying to get it ever since," I finished for him. "That's what this is all about."

Dasher nodded then pinched his throat. "Sit rep?"

Sit rep, more military slang. It meant situation report, he was asking for an update. "Prancer here. I just got to the APC. It's been sabotaged. I need Comet." Prancer was speaking so loudly we could hear his voice over the device inserted in Dasher's ear.

"Comet here. I copy. En route."

"No way!" Shig said. "Santa really has an APC, an Armored Personal Carrier."

After a few minutes Dasher commanded, "Damage report!"

"We have power, but it looks like it might be the stabilizers," Comet updated him. "I'm on it." I figured Comet must be the engines expert.

Another voice interrupted over the speaker. "Blitzen to Dasher."

"Go!"

"Reading multiple bad guys inside the vacant house. Baum and team look like they're about to be overrun. Permission to attack?"

"Negative, Blitzen!" Dasher interrupted. "I see them. Deploy the heat-rays and keep your heavy plasma cannon trained on the front door of the vacant house."

"Roger that," Blitzen said.

Who was Baum fighting? I had to know. That meant getting a better look at the house across the street, so

I left the cover of the bushes and ran over to the pillar opposite Vixen. Perfect, I could use the pillar as cover and still see everything—even the rest of the commandos.

I can't explain how, but I knew exactly who was who—even from that distance. Cupid had just finished firing what looked like a large Roman candle at the house across from Shig's and began riding some giant disc-like thing back toward my yard. A second later, a red force field encapsulated the same house, forming a dome. Amazing. Donner and Blitzen were behind a giant live oak tree, manning plasma canons trained on the house across the street.

I looked across the street at the vacant house. The front door was open, but it was pitch black beyond that. Then Benji and Baum stepped into view. They were in the foyer with their backs to the open door. The commando dwarf was blasting away at something. Yellow blasts of energy flew back at them from the darkness inside. It was a miracle they weren't hit. Benji struggled to move, and the small dwarf supported him. That's when I realized that Benji was hurt. What were the commandos waiting for?

Then I saw *him*, the cloaked man—if he even was a man. I shouted, "It's S.R.!" I broke from cover and ran through a row of four-foot-tall hedges. A second later, with the transformed J-Ray in hand, I yelled, "Attack! Attack!"

And then I tripped and fell face first into the snow. Clearly, I still had some work to get used to this hero thing. Still prone, I got up on my elbows and brushed the snow from my face. I saw the door slam shut behind Baum and Benji. They were trapped in the house. Then I felt myself sliding backward on the snow. It was Vixen, dragging me to ... Dasher.

S.R. Gets His Goat

"Are you out of your mind?" Dasher said as I was dropped at his feet.

"It's, it's S.R.—attacking Benji and Baum." I was out of breath from the excitement and thrill of the charge, even if it was short-lived.

Dasher tapped his helmet. "I have communications with Baum. He'd call me if there was a problem. Trust me, Baum can handle himself. Besides, Servant Rupert is not over there," Dasher said firmly.

"Yes, he is. I just saw him," I insisted then turned to Vixen. "I'm not seeing things."

Dasher eyed me, sighed, then fiddled with his goggles for a second. "Nothing. I don't see him and—"

"But—" I began, but Dasher held up his hand, stifling my interruption. I grunted in protest.

"If he were there, I would still see through his invisibility," Dasher said.

"But you can't see S.R. now," I snapped. "He's in the house! Gear up before anything else happens and get ready, we're attacking," I said to my friends as I pulled a combat helmet out of my frontpack. They shot me a look as if to say, where in the world did you get that? "Yeah, I know. I can't explain how this thing can hold so much, but it does. I've touched the frontpacks, so you should be able to see everything now. Dig in," I said, pulling out a flak jacket too.

A few minutes later we were all geared up, much to the chagrin of Dasher—probably because we looked like a miniature version of his team, from the boots to the goggles and the communication links. Not to mention we looked cool too, thanks to the gear auto-sizing. The uniforms automatically adapted to the size of the wearer, making us look like official soldiers ... just half the size.

"Comet to Dasher." Comet's voice came across the speakers inside my helmet. "Stabilizers are toast, we are no good here. Returning to battle."

"Roger that! Crystal Palace," Dasher called back to the dwarves at the Western Hemisphere Command Center.

"Crystal Palace ... go!" I heard the dwarf respond.

"APC dead. No ETA on fix. Request immediate evacuation."

"Negative, negative. You are too hot! We're reading a mobilized, battalion-sized force underground, precisely two hundred feet west of your location," the voice from the Crystal Palace replied.

Dasher sighed. His face was deadpan, but I could tell things weren't going as planned. "Roger that! We'll need close air support," Dasher said.

"Air support confirmed, Crystal Palace out."

Just then I saw a revitalized Benji, along with Baum and a bunch of other Special Forces commando dwarves, running out of the house and firing blasters over their shoulders. I saw what they were firing at ... and froze. There were about ten at first: icy, spiked skeleton heads with long, ice-skeleton bodies and frozen-liquid wings. They were the frightening creatures I'd auto-drawn in my comics. If snow angels could be evil, this is what they'd look like. They were shooting deadly-sharp icicles from their wrists in our direction. It reminded me of the way Spider-Man shot his web.

"Ice-skulls! Set blasters to heat clusters and open fire!" Dasher shouted just as Prancer rejoined us under the tree.

Dasher's team peppered the sky with laser bolts. The bolts exploded into yellow energy clouds that consumed the ice-skulls, liquefying all but their heads.

My friends and I grabbed our J-Rays. We quickly uttered *Shamira*. Then we stared at the transformed machines helplessly; we had a problem.

"Uh, how do you use them?" Fleep asked, perplexed.

Thankfully Prancer was listening to us. "Flick your wrist, like it's a wand!" he shouted.

I aimed and flicked. A green light emitted from the crystal rod and swooshed out, blasting an ice-skull into ice cubes. Cool!

"Aim for their heads!" Shig shouted.

Prancer heard Shig. "No, definitely not the heads! They explode and rain down nasty shrapnel ice. Aim for their necks—their body will freeze if you hit the right spot and they'll come crashing down. It's a small target, but with all the video games you kids play these days— you can hit it."

We aimed, flicked our wrists, and zapped; it sounded like a hundred helicopters flying above us. It was cool at first, and felt like I was in some virtual reality video game ... that was until our position was hit with a volley of icicles from above. The tree we were under was decimated. How none of us were hit was beyond me. Vixen and Prancer shouted, "Ice-skulls! Hit the snow."

We dove. Just as I dared myself to raise my head and look, chucks of ice and ice bones fell on us. Two spiked ice-skull skeleton heads fell inches from Logan's face. She screamed. Utterly freaked out, the four of us stood and wiped off the ice. I glanced over at the vacant house. That's when I realized we were in serious trouble. Ice-skulls were pouring out, now thirty at a time, from the front door of the house. Benji, Baum, and the Special Forces team were being suppressed by attacking ice-skulls.

Dasher looked over to check on us. "Is everyone okay?"

"Yeah, but Benji and—we can help them," I begged.

"Not happening," Dasher said. He ran, took cover in the bushes where Vixen and Dancer were guarding Santa's tube, and motioned for us to do the same.

I yelled over the plasma blasts. "But we can help Benji and Baum—"

"No, Jakob, there are too many ice-skulls. We'll handle the rescue!" Vixen shouted, never losing sight of her targets. Dasher looked at Vixen. Their quick communication ended with a nod from Dasher, then Vixen shouted to me between shots, "Take your team and get Santa to the sleigh. It's an APC—armored personnel carrier—parked by the side of your house. After you secure Santa, engage your armor. There are too many ice-skulls to battle them wearing just this." Vixen knocked on her metal-plated flak jacket.

I threw up my arms in surrender to her insistence. "Okay—but which side of my house?"

Vixen, almost as if reading my thoughts, was already pointing toward Shig's house.

"Your friends will not see the APC, but you will. Just push the silver tube into it. Once it's inside, Santa should wake and all this will end."

This will end. That was more than enough incentive to get Santa to the APC as soon as possible. Logan and Fleep took one side of the silver tube while Shig and I took the other, and we all pushed. Thankfully the tube hovered effortlessly. As I guided the tube I realized for the first time, despite the ongoing battle, how beautiful the neighborhood was under a blanket of white snow. The neatest thing was seeing the palm trees draped in snow. It was so unnatural and ultra-weird. We rounded the corner of my house when Logan shouted in a panic.

"Where is the APC?"

I looked for a reaction from Fleep and Logan, but they looked mystified too. Vixen was right, I was the only one who could see it. It was big and white, like the snow beneath it. It almost looked like a tank, but without a cannon. I could see two portholes on the side of it.

"I see it," I shouted. "About thirty feet away. Keep pushing. It's right in front of us. As soon as I touch it, you'll be able to see it. Trust me."

We were inches from the APC when a tall figure in a dusty hooded cloak—the man from my dreams—stepped out from the shadows and showered us with a thick cloud of black powder. We couldn't move. We were all frozen stiff. Wide-eyed, I gazed upon my attacker. His black hood concealed most of his face ... but I could see the familiar evil frown, the whiskers on his cheeks, and the long braided goatee. It was S.R.—my dream was coming true! He reached down and typed something onto the tube's keyboard. Golden symbols appeared on the tube briefly, then the bottom opened and Santa fell to the snow. I tried to speak but couldn't.

"For me?" S.R. said jubilantly in his distinctive Scottish accent, motioning to Santa's sleeping body. Black dust fell from his cloak. If I could move, my shoulders would have sunk.

"You shouldn't have," he continued gleefully. "I owe you a great debt of gratitude for this, Jakob." I looked past him, trying to see beyond the dusty cloud. Our eyes met for a moment.

S.R. craned his head backwards. "What are you looking for? Oh, dear me," he said mockingly. "That's right. We were supposed to trade, but I seem to have forgotten Tiff and her useless family."

He had Tiff?! It seemed like a lifetime ago that she and Fleep had run away from their watch post at the house across the street. I felt bad; I'd assumed she bailed on us because she was afraid of S.R., but he'd actually caught and held her captive.

"Let's forgo the whole ransom thing, shall we? I have something better in mind." He chuckled and then, with lightning speed, grabbed the ugly goat-head belt Santa was wearing. Instantly something went WHIIISH! An electric charge struck and sent S.R. flying back. He wasted no time getting to his feet then shuddered like you do after you've eaten something disgusting.

"Well, well. Fat-face has new security. But there's more than one way to skin a cat." He reached under his cloak and produced a cube of coal. Within a few seconds the coal transformed into a black-and-white Alien Workshop skateboard. I had a sickening realization of what was about to happen.

"Who wants this?" S.R. said flatly.

Fleep's eyes widened. "I do!" he said, brushing past me. How was *he* able to move?

"Me, too!" Koji said, bursting out of the bushes. What? Koji was supposed to have been returned safely home. Clearly the miniature Houdini had figured out an escape route.

S.R. was reaching out to offer Fleep the skateboard, then pulled it back once he saw Koji.

"Oh, my," S.R. said, sounding more like a growling animal than a man. "*You* may certainly not have this. Mind you, I would love to give it to you, but ..." S.R. paused and sighed, "you are, sadly, too young to accept it. You wouldn't understand your choice, but Fleep does. He *chooses* to not believe in this has-been anymore." S.R. kicked Santa's boot. "He *chooses* to believe in me," he said slowly, wickedly.

"But I—" Koji began.

S.R.'s eyes grew bright yellow. I was afraid for Koji.

"Go home!" he growled. And, with that, Koji did what any kid with enough sense would do. He ran, fast. I only hoped he was running home.

"Give me the board," Fleep demanded, grabbing for it. S.R. held it out of reach.

"Of course. But one small task first," he said, looking down at Santa. "Remove the goat-head belt and give it to me."

No, Fleep. Don't do it. He's using you. Don't touch it, I begged with my eyes since I couldn't speak.

He did it. Fleep removed the belt from Santa unharmed and gave it to S.R., then reached out and grabbed
the skateboard like a starving child reaching for a chocolate cookie. Just as eagerly, S.R. wasted no time clasping
on his coveted goat-head belt. He paused for a moment
to lovingly rub a finger over his now-scratched-out initials, then his eyes angrily flashed yellow again. I noticed
the goat eyes on the belt were lit yellow as well, and it
seemed to be giving him more power. S.R. held out an
open hand, outstretched to Fleep.

What was he doing? Then I saw the horror that
chased chills of fear up my spine.

My dream was coming true!

Fleep studied the skateboard, flipping it over several
times and rolling the wheels, entranced by his new toy
and never realizing that he was disintegrating. I watched
as Fleep's legs began their transformation into tiny, fine,
black particles. He was being sucked into a forming lump
of coal in S.R.'s hand. Fleep's disintegrated lower half was
now serpentine; he looked like a genie being sucked into
a bottle. Seconds later, Fleep's frontpack fell to the snow,
and he was gone … just like the wooden creature from
my dream.

I struggled to move. I wasn't scared anymore. I was
breathing heavily, angry and full of rage. Set me free. I'd
burn the very flesh off of my skin to get Fleep back. My
eyes were drowning in a pool of tears.

"He takes the board willingly and disappears. My
first wayward in more than five hundred years. Any more

takers? I can use the help. Things are about to get ... complicated. I hate complications," S.R. said as he placed the coal in his black, soot-covered sack. "No one? What a pity. The Wayward List is not what it used to be."

Enraged, I tried to speak. S.R. walked toward me then stopped suddenly, almost stepping on Fleep's frontpack.

"Aye, now that would probably hurt," he said, stepping around it carefully as if it were a land mine. He came within inches of my face and snapped his fingers, sending more soot into the air.

Suddenly able to speak, I cried out. "Let me go! *Fleep!*" A flood of tears ran down my face.

"On second thought ..." S.R. snapped his fingers again, and I was silenced. "There's no time for a chatty debate or moral reflection on what is happening here. It's simple, really. You either believe in that buffoon lying over there, or you do not. And if you don't believe in him, well, let's just say it's only a matter of time before your name is added to the Wayward List. And once you're on the list, you're fair game," he said, walking around us, throwing up his arms. "He comes to those who believe, and I come to those who are on the list." He laughed victoriously. "Before I depart, I feel obliged to impart a great deal of gratitude for your efforts. Without you and your band of misfits, I would not have this!" He patted the goat-head buckle. "My belt of power!"

He quickly looked down at Santa and studied the remaining belt, the one with the polar bear eyes.

"What a pity to leave such power with such an in-competent. I'll relieve him of the burden. My belt will protect me." He didn't sound too sure of himself, but reached down anyway and touched the one that remained on Santa.

WHOOSH! A flash of blue light rippled from Santa's belt and struck me. I fell to the snow, unconscious.

A Dragon Forces Us Out of Time

I heard the muffled sound of rapid plasma blasts as Dancer's blurry nameplate came into focus. She didn't tell me how long I'd been unconscious, but it couldn't have been too long since the fighting was still going on.

"Are you okay, Jakob?" Dancer asked, almost yelling. She was scanning me with a handheld device. "Are you okay, Jakob?" she asked again, then touched the device several times.

I felt groggy and sore all over. Kind of like the time when I had wrecked my bike going over Fleep's skate ramp. My entire body had ached for a week.

"I think so," I answered, a little unsure.

"Here, sit up, but don't stand until I'm done." She glanced over at Logan and Shig. "That goes for the rest of you too. Stay put." She held my face like the doctor does just before he asks you to open wide. "Jakob, you took the brunt of the discharge."

"Um ... I ..." I stammered. "I don't understand."

"The shock," Dancer said tenderly. It was hard to believe she was a fierce commando. She was so gentle and caring. She continued scanning me and touched the device a couple more times, then looked around like she was looking for someone. Her face was suddenly awash with concern.

"We delivered the little one to his bed, but where is the other boy?"

Shig visibly jerked. "The little one—that's my brother, Koji! Is he okay?"

"Yes. He's in that domed house, in his bed and very safe," Dancer said, pointing to Shig's house.

I could see the weight of the world fall off of Shig's shoulders. He had obviously seen what had happened with Koji and S.R.

"But the other one—Fleep, isn't it?" Dancer asked.

"He was taken, turned into ... like, coal," Logan's voice faltered, then the tears ran.

Dancer frowned. "Once again the Master of the Wayward List wears his belt," she said darkly, then stood and quickly scanned Logan and Shig with the handheld device. She walked back to me. She didn't have to read too far into my expression to realize how I felt. The situation was bad, very bad. I felt disappointed, hopeless, and sad. I wanted to cry and did.

"Don't lose hope, Jakob. All is not lost." There was a loud explosion followed by more blaster fire. "The battle still rages," Dancer said, pulling me to my feet.

Logan was already up and helping Shig. I hadn't noticed Comet and Cupid before, but I was glad to see them. They were watching for threats. I looked down at the footprints in the snow. Specks of black dust were everywhere. Then I saw Fleep's frontpack and lost it. I cried hard. Logan and Shig walked up beside me, and we all cried together for our friend.

"I feel ashamed. I should have done more," I said, wiping away my tears.

"You couldn't help Fleep," Dancer said. Her words were soft and kind, but they didn't help ease the sadness I felt. I collected Fleep's frontpack and gave it to Dancer. Then I noticed someone else was missing.

"Where's Santa! Did S.R.—" I said, worried.

"No, Santa's in there." Dancer pointed to the APC. I could tell that Shig and Logan still couldn't see it. "He should have woken up by now, but he's still unconscious," she said with a worried frown.

Dancer reached inside the APC. She must have looked strange to Shig and Logan, holding her hand up in midair and reaching for nothing. "I've tried everything I know." Slowly, Dancer removed the silver chamber from the APC then typed something on it. That changed the silvery top of the tube to glass, revealing the resting Santa.

None of this would have happened if I hadn't been so reckless with the elf tea. I raked my fingers through my hair in frustration, then slammed my hands in my pant pockets. That's when I felt the tag in my pocket. I'd completely forgotten about it. I pulled it out and examined it.

"Santa's dog tags," I said and passed them over to Dancer. She took them silently.

"It's my fault—I think I know it all, and look at us now. Look at him," I said as I approached the chamber. Santa's chest rose and fell with each breath. I leaned in over his head.

"I don't know if you can hear me, but I've made a mess of things. I thought Rick was S.R., I gave you too much tea and did this to you, Tiff's gone, and now I've lost one of my best friends." I sniffled. "Please," my voice faltered, "please, wake up. We need you. I need you. You're supposed to make everything right," I pleaded.

I noticed that some of my tears had actually permeated the glass tube and pooled on Santa's forehead. Without thinking and more embarrassed than anything else, I reached through the solid glass and wiped the tears. Logan gasped.

Dancer grabbed my arm, not forcefully. It was more like, *take it easy.* "Jakob, best you leave him for Benji. You should—"

"You're not surprised?" I asked. "My arm passing through solid glass?" Dancer let go of my arm then gave me a meaningful look.

"No," she said, shaking her head, "I'm not." Shig knocked on the glass then gave Logan a shocked look.

"Why can I do all of these things but can't even wake Santa?" I asked.

Dancer ignored me then did the same thing I'd just done—reached through the glass into the chamber. She untangled the dog tags then put them around Santa's neck. "Let's go. We have to stop the Servant before he escapes." Dancer pushed Santa's tube back into the APC then motioned for me to lead on.

"Ice-skulls are everywhere, and we have no idea where the Servant is," Dancer said. "You *need* to engage your armor! On your frontpack, there are two straps that extend around your waist. Pull them out and snap the clasps together! Hurry Jakob," she said running ahead.

Logan and Shig trotted up beside me as I was feeling for the straps.

"You okay?" Logan asked. I looked at her mournfully and shook my head.

"It's Fleep … it's Santa … it's everything," I said, stopping.

"I know. Don't take this the wrong way, but sulking about our loss isn't going to solve anything," Logan said.

"But I've made some really bad choices."

Shig grabbed me. "You know, a friend once gave me wise advice."

"Yeah, what's that?"

He regarded me. "Cowboy up!"

Any other time I would have grinned. They were true friends and meant well, but the best place for me right now was under a rock. I hated myself and carried the blame for all that had gone wrong.

"Trust me, I wish I could," I said.

"You can! I mean, seriously, look at you. You can fight S.R.'s smoke and see things we can't. And do I have to remind you that you just put your hand through solid glass? This is your destiny man, your purpose. You are a Pole! So cowboy up. Let's get Fleep back ... *Pole style!*"

Shig was right. There was something in his encouraging words that lifted my weary spirit. I was meant to help my friends, meant to fight S.R. and rescue Fleep. He may have been a lump of coal, and was probably safer that way for the time being, but it wasn't permanent.

"We're getting Fleep, Rick, Tiff, and that belt of power back. We're fixing this," I said, then reached down to engage my armor. Two straps, I thought. I felt around my waist some more as I jogged ahead, but I couldn't find the straps Dancer was talking about.

"I found them," Logan announced excitedly, like we were in competition. "Where the frontpack hits your hip—they're retractable and clip around the back like a belt."

I found the straps and snapped them in place, then sprinted after Dancer. But I didn't get far.

Seconds after I engaged the frontpack, it started to vibrate and my legs felt like they were made of lead. The heaviness spread until my entire body felt as stiff as a rail, and all I could move was my eyes. Then I felt something that, if I *had* been able to move, would have made me jump out of my skin. It felt like a snake was coiling around my legs. I looked down and saw white gooey, marshmallow-like stuff oozing out from the frontpack. I thought I'd accidently hit a wrong button and caused a glitch, till I looked over and saw the same thing happening to Shig and Logan. The white stuff slimed up over my whole body, and was now all the way up to my chin. It was weird because it felt like heavy whip cream and, I kid you not, smelled sweet. I didn't know what it was, but I knew it wasn't anything bad. I squeezed my eyes shut and held my breath as it continued up my forehead. Seconds later, after I was completely enveloped, the wetness evaporated and the goo transformed into a hard armor.

Slowly, I peeked, then widened my eyes and blinked. I was in some kind of helmet, looking through a holographic heads-up display, or HUD. The HUD projected a grid about a foot from my face in 3-D. I turned my head. I was free. I could move.

I did a quick self-inspection. I was in a snow-camouflage suit. The whip cream-like stuff had turned out to be some kind of liquid armor that hardened into a protective white shell. Even the frontpack, which was still on my chest, had transformed. I tapped on it—solid metal.

I glanced over at Shig and Logan. Whoa! They looked incredibly high-tech. The helmet followed the contour of the head and slightly bulged over the eyes like bug eyes. That's when it hit me. My comics. I'd drawn the suits before.

I noticed the J-Ray was missing from my arm. Hesitantly, I opened the frontpack, and my HUD went nuts with data. A bright yellow targeting cursor locked onto an array of gadgets inside the pack, while the HUD scrolled with data identifying each one's name and usage. Somehow the green candy cane had returned to the frontpack. I grabbed it, shut the case and thought the word *Shamira*. It instantly transformed into a J-Ray. But something new happened. The hanging part at the end of the J-Ray was plugged into my armored suit. I faced Logan and Shig.

"Let's roll!" I commanded. Clad in our white armor, we ran toward the front of my house, not prepared in the least for the sight that waited ahead. Ice-skulls covered the vacant house like bees on a beehive. It was an intimidating site considering how outnumbered we really were. For one thing, it made me appreciate my armored suit and J-Ray. A bright red glow from the protective domes colored the snow and everything else in the neighborhood an eerie shade of red. Piles of misshapen ice, once part of the ice-skulls' anatomy, lay everywhere, also reflecting red. It looked like a sea of red crystal shards. The commandos and dwarves were spread out in teams of two, each blasting trails of plasma bolts at the attacking ice-skulls.

I crouched at the sound of multiple explosions—like fireworks—then felt chunks of ice-skulls clank against my suit. I glanced over at the nearest commandos. They were taking cover behind a pile of ice-skull remains. One saw us and hurried over.

"Jakob, Logan, Shig." It was Dancer. She fired her blaster up at an ice-skull. "Repeat after me: *Armor commo, on.*"

We repeated her words. A mechanical voice inside my helmet replied, "Armor communications ready."

Now that the communications function was engaged, Dasher issued several more commands that turned on several of the suit's features like auto shield, auto scanning, auto targeting, and 3D touch. The technology was overwhelming, and I wondered why the settings didn't all just come on automatically by default. Dancer quickly explained that most of the commandos were self-confessed control freaks and preferred to set the HUD settings manually, tweaking each one to their individual preference. In between blasting ice-skulls, she went on to explain how the 3D feature allowed me to select images displayed on the holographic heads-up, sort of like using my finger as a computer mouse to select objects on the grid and zoom in closer.

Just as I was about to test out the 3D feature, Shig shouted, "There he is!"

I looked in the direction Shig was pointing. My tracking system locked onto the object. I tapped on the 3D image like Dancer showed me and zoomed in on the running figure. Sure enough, it was S.R. and he was running straight to Tiff's house. We gave chase and sprinted across the street, reaching the driveway just as S.R. stopped and turned around. My suit's computer system alerted, "WARNING, WARNING … redirecting all shield-energy forward." S.R. fired a yellow blast from his belt. I didn't have time to move. The shock of the blast scrambled my HUD and knocked me on my back. But thanks to my shielded armor, I didn't pass out this time. Shig and Logan's voices grunted through my speakers. They'd been hit too, but looked fine. I locked my eyes on S.R.; he was on the move again, darting inside Tiff's house. Enraged with thoughts of what he'd done to Fleep, I gave chase and recklessly stormed through Tiff's front door, where I was met by a cloud of dust in the shape of a large hand. My targeting system maintained a lock on S.R., tracking him as he disappeared down the steps of Tiff's book. I fanned at the smoke, dispersing it like a cheap magic trick, and raced on to the kitchen. S.R. had made a huge mistake; I was mad and *nothing* was going to stop me from following him down into the book.

Boy was I wrong.

I had made it just past the dining room table when the book's protectors, the skeleton owls, attacked with claws outstretched. I jumped back in fear, remembering how rabid they were, just as Baum and two dwarf commandos brushed past me and effortlessly blasted them to smithereens. Bones clattered to the floor.

"Forget you're wearing armor, kid?" a bald, gray-bearded commando said. His name plate read *Zola*.

"Yeah," I said, noticing that they weren't in armored suits, just flak jackets and goggles. Show-offs.

Baum stared at me. There was an awkward and uncomfortable moment before I finally got the courage to say what I needed to.

"Baum, I'm sorry. I used too much tea—I should have been more careful," I said.

Baum regarded me. "We all make mistakes, kid. Just don't make anymore tonight."

I nodded then remembered S.R. had escaped.

"S.R.," I said insistently. "He's inside the book." I ran over to the book and pointed down. "Down the stairs."

Then the same loud roar that Logan and I'd heard a few days ago growled from the book. Baum ran into the kitchen and pulled me out. Something was wrong; the fierce commandos suddenly looked nervous.

Baum locked his eyes on the book, then turned and frowned. "Let's go, Jakob. We're not going down there."

"Why not? It's just some animal. You guys can take it."

"That's not just some animal," a dwarf named Seif said. He had the most trusting face and looked more like a professor than a commando, with his perfectly round glasses and soft eyes.

I stopped.

"Then what is it?" I asked.

"A traitorous Mar spike dragon," Baum replied, ushering me through the living room. That's right, the same

Mar dragon I'd read about in my copy of *The Kringle Chronicles*. They were sworn protectors of man, but S.R. had one working for him. As we got to the door, Logan walked in with Shig on her heels.

Baum released me and used his arms to block the way. "Oh no! You three—out of here now," Baum said, motioning for Logan and Shig to turn around. "We have to leave, now!" Baum nudged me.

"Wait." I stopped. "Do you guys hear that?"

It was music. It was coming from inside the book and getting louder. No one moved. "I've heard this. I know this song, *The Bells* something—"

"It's *Carol of the Bells*," Baum corrected me. We listened.

Ding dong ding dong ding,
Ding dong.

Oh how they pound,
raising the sound,
o'er hill and dale,
telling their tale.

Gaily they ring,
while people sing,
songs of good cheer,
Christmas is here.

Merry, merry, merry, merry Christmas,
Merry, merry, merry, merry Christmas.

At the end of the second chorus of "Merry, merry, merry, merry Christmas," the voices suddenly faded and were replaced by the sound of a man with a Scottish accent chanting, "The Servant becomes the Master," over and over again. It was creepy, but also infuriated me because I knew it was S.R. chanting.

"I have to seal the book. Get out! NOW!" Baum shouted. Before I could utter a protest, something leaped out of the book. My stomach turned. Two feet from me was an emerald green, scaly dragon with giant webbed feet, silvery claws, and a spiked tail. It was smaller than I expected, no bigger than a large dog. But it was still ferocious. It lunged at Baum. The two commandos instinctively fired at the creature. It stunned the dragon for a second but the creature wasted no time getting up. It seemed to be guarding entrance into the kitchen.

Baum turned to Zola. "Supercharge the plasma cannons. I want one trained on this front door."

"Roger that," Zola looked at me, then ran off outside with Seif.

"This house is off limits," Baum barked, never taking his eyes off of the dragon while herding us outside. Just as he closed Tiff's front door, something crashed against it on the other side. The dragon was trying to get out. "Now get across the street to Logan's yard and hide."

"Wait, what are you doing?" I asked, concerned.

"I going to deal with that dragon, then seal that book before anything else comes through it. Now do as I say and find some place safe."

"But we don't want to hide. We—"

Baum grabbed me by the arm, which didn't seem like him, but I'd obviously made him mad. "Listen, I'm not Dasher and I'm certainly not part of your security detail. All of you will do as I say and you will do it now!" Baum released me with a shove. I don't know what made us move faster, Baum yelling at us or the fact that Zola was aiming a glimmering, white plasma cannon in our direction. It seemed like a lot of drama for a dragon the size of a dog, but whatever. We sprinted and made it to the edge of Tiff's yard when something told me to glance over my shoulder. Just as I did, the Mar dragon crashed through Tiff's front door.

"Get down!" I shouted. We dove into the snow as splintered wood and shards of metal clanked against armor. I rolled over and sat up. Whoa! The dragon was bigger, a lot bigger, now about the size of a horse and growing before my eyes. The beast scanned the group of commandos. He was searching for someone. He locked eyes on Baum.

"Now!" Baum's voice yelled through my speakers. The cannon erupted on cue, firing a long, multicolored stream of energy. It reminded me of the nuclear gadgets the Ghostbusters used to capture ghosts. The dragon flapped its bat-like wings then sprung, barely avoiding the first stream. But the second stream of plasma found its target, landing a terrible blast to the dragon's chest. The beast bellowed in pain then fell like a rock, landing on its side. It lay motionless.

271

I scrutinized the creature and felt uneasy. Was it playing possum in a ploy to lure the commandos closer? Seeing Zola and Seif with their cannon trained on the stiff dragon validated my suspicion. It just didn't feel right. The fight was too easy. I looked around. The commandos still had their blasters trained on the dragon. I'd feel a lot better once someone confirmed the beast was dead. I started thinking ahead. What if it got back up? They'd need help.

I looked down past Shig's house at the battle raging between Dasher's team and the ice-skulls. The commandos were occupied but doing a good job of containing the icy creatures to the area around the vacant house. "Come on guys," I said, then led Logan and Shig in a sprint to Logan's yard, happy to put distance between us and the dragon.

Just as I turned around to look back, the dragon leaped up and began spewing softball-sized fireballs out of its mouth. I knew it! A fireball struck the closest plasma cannon—Zola and Seif's. The cannon exploded into a ball of white and green light, sending the dwarves flying backward. My helmet tracking system locked onto the little commandos; a green assessment bar appeared beside their images, indicating ninety percent health. They'd been hurt, but not badly. Two more dwarf commandos came up from behind me and blasted the dragon.

I couldn't believe my eyes. The dragon was now the size of a school bus ... and still growing.

"Baum to Dasher!" Baum said.

"Vixen here—Dasher is down."

What? No! My heart sunk.

Baum's voice interrupted my thoughts. "Get me more plasma cannons trained on that dragon. Fire until they drain."

"You cannot stop me, Baum!" The dragon's garbled voice growled. "Your weapons will drain, and when they do—"

A swooshing sound followed by colorful flashes of light pelted the dragon. Three of Dasher's commandos had already repositioned their cannons. They were amazingly quick, but the dragon was amazingly tough. It did a funky shake, kind of like a dog does when it's wet, then howled a flaming breath that consumed the commandos' second plasma attack. The beast was agitated. Its eyes glowed red with hatred. Then it tensed its enormous leg muscles, roared, and spat several bowling-ball-sized fireballs. Two laser cannons from Baum's team exploded on impact. The commandos went flying through the air, but their armored suits saved them. It sure made me appreciate my suit.

Something about the dragon's behavior bothered me. It wouldn't leave Tiff's yard—almost like it was protecting something.

Shig brushed up to my side. "There's something weird about that dragon."

"I was just thinking the same thing."

We straightened up as an armored Baum approached. "Something's wrong," he said.

Now what? What could be more wrong than a dragon attacking us?

"The domes are fading and we can't stop it. We have to move this battle before they fade out. We can't put innocent civilians at risk."

"Move it where?" I asked, dumbfounded.

"Out of time."

CHAPTER 25

WE GROW UP

Baum reached up into the air, seemed to grab something invisible, then stared at the dragon. Oddly, I saw fear in its eyes. Seconds before, it had been a ravenous, menacing beast ... but now the gigantic creature was scared stiff by whatever Baum was about to do. Baum jerked his arm down. At first it sounded like paper being torn, then there was a loud pop—like the world's largest soda had just been opened. A small tear had appeared in the air above Baum's head, and a blue ripple of light shot out from the opening and struck the dragon. It flew back fast and with force, like it had been kicked in the chest by an invisible giant, and ended up wedged between several palm trees in Tiff's yard. Then there was a sucking sound, as if someone had turned on a giant vacuum. Without hesitation, Baum grabbed something invisible in the air and sprinted down the street like he was running with a kite. Baum went all the way down to my house, crossed the street, then ran back to us. When he finished, my jaw dropped—he had made an odd-shaped, giant black hole in the air above our street.

There seemed to be some sort of tornado spinning inside, no doubt the source of the powerful suction. Several of the commandos, along with a horde of ice-skulls, had already been pulled into the black hole. We ran to Logan's front porch and held onto whatever we could find as the wind swirled around us.

"Are you guys seeing this?" I shouted while bear-hugging a pillar.

"What?" Shig said, sounding out of breath and sharing the door handle with Logan. "That Baum just tore a hole into thin air? Yeah, I see it!" he shouted. Logan shook her head slowly, like she'd seen a ghost. Yep, she saw it too.

Everything that wasn't either a building or rooted in the ground was being sucked into the hole. When even the dragon was pulled free from the palm trees and swallowed up by the hole, I realized that resisting the vacuum was pointless.

Baum came out of nowhere, startling us.

"Let's go," he said, then waved at me to jump in the hole.

"Go where?" I asked.

"Out of time," he replied curtly.

That made no sense. How could you go outside of time?

"Well, what about the dragon? It's probably on the other side waiting with its mouth open," I said.

Baum shook his head. "No. It will be back in Tiff's yard."

"Are you sure?" I asked disbelievingly.

"It's protecting the book. Look, trust me. Now go!" I gave Baum a leery look then ran toward the hole. I dove in like I was diving into a pool, only this pool was a whirly sea of blackness. I expected to descend into a whirlwind, but surprisingly that didn't happen. I ended up doing a somersault and landing right back where I started ... in Logan's front yard. It was like I'd jumped through an open window that led to nowhere. Thankfully Baum had been right. The dragon was back in Tiff's yard, pacing and spitting up fireballs.

But something wasn't right with me. I felt different. I sat up and was startled by the sight of my legs. They were huge—I mean compared to their size seconds ago. I was bigger, like grown-up bigger. My armored suit was gone but I was still wearing commando gear. Just as I stood, two unfamiliar commandos tumbled into me. The three of us grunted and complained as we crashed to the snow. We quickly stood and exchanged looks. They were in their late teens, maybe seventeen, and dressed just like me—in tactical gear from head to toe with frontpacks and green J-Ray's. The male was Asian. The female was tall, tan-skinned, exotic ... and slightly familiar.

"Jakob?" the male said cautiously.

"Shig? Logan?" I asked, eyeing them—searching for my friends in their grown-up faces.

"Yeah!" Logan said excitedly.

Holy smoke, it *was* them. A hug was the first thing that came to mind, but a nearby explosion canceled that idea.

Baum hopped through the hole next, and was transformed into a large muscular version of his dwarf self. I couldn't take my eyes off of him.

"What, never seen a tall dwarf before?" He grinned, then fiddled with something that looked like a high-tech remote control.

Slowly, I shook my head. But the strangest thing was not his height; it was his total lack of surprise about us. He didn't find it odd that minutes ago we were kids and now we were grown?

Baum pointed the remote at Logan's roof just as a huge roar interrupted our reunion. The dragon was on Tiff's roof, roaring and spitting fireballs at attacking commandos. Without warning, a chorus of blaster fire erupted from behind us, blasting the dragon off his perch.

"Whoa! Logan, your house," Shig said. Logan and I turned around. My jaw dropped. The front of her house looked like some futuristic castle. Steel battlements were built into the roof, and extending between elaborately arched parapets were unmanned sentry cannons. So that's what Mr. Raffo's hazmat workers had been up to— building an assault system. I noticed most of the cannons pointed toward the street—like he knew where the attack would come from. He *so* had to be a spy for Santa.

"Your dad did good, Logan," I heard Baum say through my speakers. "These cannons are no ordinary cannons. They're heat-ray and plasma cannons. The ice-skulls hate them!"

I was about to say something to Logan when I spotted several armored commandos across the street trying to flank the dragon. But I wasn't the only one that spotted them. In one swipe, the beast's massive spiked tail struck the commandos and sent them flying through the air.

"No!" Logan yelled.

"They'll be fine," Baum said reassuringly. "Their armor knows what to do. Now re-engage your armor—all of you. You lose it when you leave time."

"Look!" Shig pointed across the street at the commandos.

"They look like armadillos," Logan said. "Giant, rolled-up armadillos."

Baum had been right about the commando's armor knowing what to do. It had turned into an armored ball. The commandos were holding their knees to their chest when the armor transformed back. They continued their attack, concentrating on the dragon's left rear leg. Maybe they'd found a chink in its scaly body. Maybe with our help and a little diversion the commandos could finish the dragon. I looked at my friends then gave myself a once-over. We were grown-up and capable. Surely we'd be able to help out.

I cleared my throat. "Come on guys, they need help."

"Oh no you don't," Baum said forcefully.

"But we're grown-up—"

"Maybe on the outside, but not on the inside. My job is to keep you and Santa safe, no matter the cost. Understand?" Hey, at least he didn't yell at me again. I guess he was just temperamental. Unhappily, I nodded ... then had an idea.

"What about the book?" I asked.

"Yeah," Logan said excitedly, "while your team distracts the dragon, we'll sneak inside and seal it."

I could tell Baum was considering it.

"Come on, it's no more dangerous than dodging fireballs out here. Please," I begged.

We heard loud screeches coming from Tiff's house. More bad news: a steady stream of ice-skulls were flying out from where the front door used to be. My bet was they were coming from the book in Tiff's kitchen. Robotic parts moved quickly as the heat-ray and plasma cannons on Logan's roof blasted to life again. Baum shook his head. I knew what that meant: stay clear of Tiff's house.

Before I could plead our case, Baum shouted, "Logan, Shig, find cover." He glanced at me. "You're with me," he grunted then pointed to Tiff's house. We watched the horde of ice-skulls heading our way. "Baum to Crystal Palace!"

"Crystal Palace," a deep, raspy voice answered.

"What's the status on my evacuation request?"

"Negative, your LZ is too hot. There are ice-skulls everywhere," the raspy voice replied. *LZ*, more military slang. It meant Landing Zone.

Baum raked his fingers through his long black hair. He was contemplating something.

"Broken Arrow! I say again, Broken Arrow!" he said firmly.

There was a long pause before the Crystal Palace finally answered.

"Broken—" the voice stammered then regained its authority. "Broken Arrow confirmed!" I didn't like the way the raspy voice had answered Baum. Something was wrong. What was *Broken Arrow?*

Logan and Shig did as Baum instructed and hid in Logan's yard, behind a row of bushes. I stayed with Baum, crouched behind a splintered palm tree, blasting ice-skulls.

"What's *Broken Arrow?*" I asked after zapping the head of an ice-skull into smithereens and watching the secondary explosion. I'm sorry, I knew I was supposed to hit them in the neck, but it was so cool zapping the nasty things and creating my personal fireworks display. I just had to make sure they weren't too close.

Baum stopped blasting, hesitated, then finally answered. "If it were just the dragon, we'd be able to handle it. But the ice-skulls ... there are too many. We need Santa, but he's not coming. I've called in multiple air and artillery plasma strikes on our position."

"I'm … I'm not sure I understand," I said.

"*Broken Arrow* means I want this place leveled. All we can do now is hope the Crystal Palace will use discretion."

"What about our parents?" I asked.

"They'll be fine. Time doesn't exist here." I gave him a blank stare. Baum continued. "This is a timeless dimension. How do you think Santa delivers all of the presents in one night? Your parents remain in their original state."

Baum returned to the turkey shoot, blasting the ice-skull creatures from the sky. Their remains were everywhere, some falling several feet from me as I ran behind Logan's giant oak. I had crouched there a hundred times before with Fleep and Shig, playing our NERF wars. How I wished all of this was just a simple kids' war game, but it wasn't. I left Baum and went back to Shig and Logan. I told them about Broken Arrow.

"We can close the book. We're not kids anymore. We're bigger and stronger," Shig said.

"Baum will go ballistic for sure if we even leave my yard," Logan said.

Shig frowned. "Yeah, you're right."

"Santa's the only one who can save us," Logan said.

"Aye, he is!" I knew that voice. I spun around.

"Benji!" I shouted excitedly, then rushed over and gave him a huge bear hug.

"Easy now, you've got some strength there," Benji said, reminding me of my new physique. I couldn't take my eyes off him. Then he pursed his lips, and the news

I so hoped for was actually more bad news. "Santa will not wake."

"What?" Logan said in disbelief.

"I'm sorry, Jakob, but I've done all I can. You gave him too much tea."

You gave him too much tea. The words were like an ice pick to my heart.

"What have I done?" I mumbled. "It's over. S.R. won and I helped him."

Benji held up Santa's polar bear belt. "Not if you put this on."

"What?" Baum and I said in chorus. I hadn't notice Baum walk up, but I was suddenly glad he did. Benji ignored Baum.

"You're the Pole." Benji made a fist. "The belt will give you the power you need to destroy the dragon and pursue S.R.."

Baum regarded Benji with disdain. "What have you done? Are you mad? What if Santa wakes? You've left him powerless!" Baum reached for the belt, but Benji was quicker.

"It's not your decision, Baum," Benji said deliberately. "Jakob, please, put it on." He held the belt out to me.

"I can't wear that. It's … it's …" I stuttered. "It's not mine." I backed away from Benji like he was trying to hand me a cobra snake.

"You're wrong, Jakob. It *is* your belt. You're the Pole. You're next in line … you're Santa."

"What?" This time the chorus came from everyone but Benji.

Baum threw his hands up in the air. "Benji, what have you done? You should not have said that now. Give me Santa's belt before you make things even worse."

I didn't stick around long enough to find out if Baum got the belt. I was too freaked by what I'd just heard. I took off for Tiff's house to do the one thing I knew would help us—close the book once and for all. Zapping the ice-skull creatures from the sky on my way, I pushed aside Benji's words.

Just as I reached Tiff's yard, the first Broken Arrow strike arrived, in the form of a giant plasma strike. It struck the street in front of Shig's house, destroying a cluster of ice-skulls that were trying to flank Baum's commandos. A second, third, and fourth strike arrived in quick succession, shelling down the street. The earth shook. I'd never been through an earthquake but imagined that this equaled about a seven on the Richter scale.

"Jakob! Fireball!" Baum's voice rang out over the chaos.

The evil dragon had hocked a fireball at me. I'd always wanted to do one of those slow motion back-bend moves like I'd seen in the karate movies, but never imagined I'd be forced to do one to avoid a dragon's flaming spitball. The maneuver half-worked. I arched my back and avoided losing my head, but fell flat on my back. At least I got to watch as the beach ball-sized fireball flew over me. It struck a house and disintegrated on impact.

I got up, gave Baum the thumbs up, then—needing no further motivation—armored up.

The dragon clawed at the air then spread its large, bat-like wings and flapped in protest, probably because it had missed me. The beast started heading toward me slowly, dragging its right hind leg. It was hurt. That was the first piece of good news all day, but who was I kidding ... it was still alive, big, and determined.

Some of the cannons on Logan's roof had been destroyed, but the remaining heat-ray cannons still zapped the ice-skulls, evaporating them from the sky while explosions from the Broken Arrow plasma strike kicked up snow and dirt.

"What are you doing, Jakob? Get back here," Baum's voice ordered over my headset. I glanced across the street at Baum and my friends. I was glad to see that they had activated their armor.

"Jakob, the belt!" Benji's voice called. He was beyond freaking me out with the talk about me being next in line for Santa. I ran toward the gaping hole in Tiff's house, blasting ice-skulls all the way.

I was about ten feet away from Tiff's front door when Baum's loud voice echoed in my helmet. "Broken Arrow! Fox in!" I stopped. What was Baum talking about? I knew a lot of military slang but *fox in* was new to me. Curious, I looked over at the other commandos and my jaw dropped open. Their armor had transformed into something that looked like spinning tops, and they were drilling themselves deep into the ground, driving deeper with every passing second.

I heard Baum shout, "Baum command override Jakob. Fox in." He said the same thing for Logan and Shig. My HUD instantly scrolled, reading off several pages of instructions, then suddenly I felt like I was inside a simulation ride. Baum had instructed my armor to dig into the ground. My arms automatically wrapped around my knees and pulled them to my chest as I spun into the ground like a whirling cyclone. A few seconds passed. Then just as my HUD read "95 percent foxed," I was struck by a jolt of electricity that scrambled my heads-up display.

Whatever was happening aboveground was not good. After several more minutes of earth-shaking bombardments, there was finally quiet. Baum's order to "Dig out!" came through my helmet speakers and, after another spin ride in reverse to dig out from the dirt, my armor transformed back to normal.

Aside from the homes, which were unharmed, my once-picturesque neighborhood was now transformed into an apocalyptic landscape. The dragon had not survived. It was lying on its side. Craters were everywhere, as were icy skeletal remains—evidence of the ice-skulls' demise. Several destroyed cannons were sparking.

I was still determined to get to the book and close it before something else came through. Once inside Tiff's house, I beelined it to the kitchen, grabbed one side of the massive book and heaved it shut. I thought I'd managed to close it before anything else came though ... but unfortunately I was too late. A small, orange dragon the size of a lizard was staring up at me beside the book. I slammed my fist down hoping to splat the dragon but missed. Tiff's book was shrinking—not as fast as I'd hoped, but soon I'd be able to take it and run.

"You may be big, but I see you for what you are, you foolish child," the dragon scoffed in a menacing, growling voice. The animal was standing outside the pantry closet and had already grown to the size of a Chihuahua. It stared at me. "Stupid boy. I'm the protector of my master's book. I *will* stop you." It nipped at my heel. I kicked the dragon into the pantry and slammed the door shut. Finally, after enduring another minute of empty dragon taunts, I collected Tiff's now normal-sized book and bee-lined it outside to where my friends stood. Holding up the book triumphantly, I cheered "I did it, I closed the book!"

Then the scariest thing of my short life happened ... and I soon realized my mistake of not squashing the lizard-sized dragon when I'd had the chance. The roof to Tiff's house exploded and the head of the fiery orange dragon emerged. The *giant* head. It crashed through the walls that confined it, then swept its massive spiked tail and decimated what was left of the house. The huge beast regarded his fallen counterpart dragon with a flaming roar to the heavens.

We all stared, feeling helpless against a creature of such incredible size. Then Benji turned to me and said forcefully, with no room for questioning, "I think *now* would be a good time to put this on." It was Santa's belt.

I stared at it for a second. He was right. It was now or never. The first thing I wanted to do was send one of those electrical blasts from the belt like S.R. had done to me.

Just as I clasped the belt buckle on, the dragon turned to me. Eyes full of rage, it exhaled a huge plume of fire.

"Do something, Jakob," Logan pleaded.

"I'm trying but nothing is happening! How does it work? Am I supposed to feel different, because I don't feel any different. Should I think what I want it to do?"

Baum shook his head at Benji. He disapproved of me wearing the belt. Don't get me wrong. It was creepy wearing Santa's belt, but it's not like I planned on keeping it. I'd return it once the second dragon was dealt with. I just needed to figure out how to turn it on, but it was fast becoming too late.

The dragon crouched down to attack. Then, just as it sprang, it was hit by a huge blue light that sent it sliding on its side down the icy, crater-ridden street. That's when I saw him, Santa, in his red and black camouflage armor suit. He was huge in stature—as big as the dragon he was battling and carried a luminous crystal sword. The dragon rose quickly, spun toward Santa, then roared and charged. Santa quickly sprinted toward the beast as it spat three fireballs at him. Just as Santa and the dragon were about to collide, Santa's sword grew to a blinding, brilliant, white light—so bright that I was forced to look away for a moment. But I quickly managed to focus back on the battle and found Santa in the air above the dragon, coming out of a somersault. He landed to the right of its back end, then jerked back on his white crystal blade, severing its spiky tail. The dragon spewed a painful roar of fire high into the air. Santa quickly stepped toward the dragon's head, preparing to strike it at the neck, when he was struck in the back by a newly-grown spiked tail. Evidently, the dragon was able to regenerate its tail—like a chameleon, but in only a split second. Thankfully the spikes didn't penetrate Santa's armor, but the force of the blow sent him flying.

As he landed, Santa transformed into an armored ball, just like the commandos had done before, to protect himself from further blows. The dragon lunged forward and clawed at the ball, but then stopped and looked at it cock-eyed. You could almost see the beast thinking ... where was the crystal sword? Surely, it wasn't with Santa inside the armored ball.

Eager to destroy its enemy's weapon, the dragon took its eyes off Santa and greedily looked around for the sword. In that split second, Santa emerged from the ball, holding the giant, glowing sword. As the dragon jerked back and spewed a deluge of flames, Santa was ready and stood his ground. He held up the sword and repelled the flames back into the dragon's face. Thankfully, that was the last sensation the dragon would ever experience, as his head was consumed by his own flames and turned to ash. The massive lifeless body crashed to the ground.

We erupted in cheers and sprinted to Santa. When I got there, I heard him mutter instructions as he held the sword handle inches from his mouth. The white light from the sword grew brighter, so bright that it forced me for the second time to look away. But I willed myself to look back; I did not want to miss this. Through the light, I could see Santa's twenty-foot silhouette shrink back to size. Within a few seconds, the light faded to reveal Santa just how I'd seen him in my house. His armor disappeared, and he turned to Baum and smiled.

"How is Dasher?"

"Dancer reports he'll be fine," Baum said. That was good news.

"Baum, I've made a terrible mess." Santa pointed to the dragon several feet from me. "Will you coordinate the clean-up please?" I couldn't believe what I was hearing. He was so nice and gentle. Baum smiled, nodded, and began barking orders.

That left the rest of us—Shig, Logan, Benji and me—alone with Santa. I was really nervous. For all I knew, I was in big trouble, like criminal trouble ... jail trouble ... Santa jail. In addition to my own worries, the traffic of voices inside my helmet speakers was almost deafening as the Special Forces team jumped into action. I guess Santa knew this because he reached out and fiddled with my head armor then removed it. He did the same for Logan and Shig, then turned to Benji.

"Benji, I was not supposed to drink so much elvish tea, nor was Servant Rupert supposed to get his belt back," Santa's voice was not angry, just stating a fact.

"We had an unexpected turn of events," Benji said softly.

"Yes, we did. In the future, let's be sure to communicate more clearly to our young friends. You're lucky the effects of the tea wore off as quickly as they did."

"Aye, sir. But if I may point out, sir, that even though Servant Rupert may have his belt of power, we have his book. And with his book, we know the way to his fortress," Benji said confidently.

"I'm not convinced that that was a fair trade, the book for the belt," Santa said lightheartedly.

Santa leaned into me. "And as for you … I believe you have something that belongs to me." I quickly unclasped the belt buckle and handed it to Santa.

I leaned in and whispered to him. "But why do you wear it? You defeated the dragon without the belt."

Santa gestured for me to come closer. "This belt is nothing more than fancy metal and high-tech gadgetry. But sometimes even magical folks need something to believe in."

"But how did you defeat the dragon?"

"Jakob, you will learn that our magic, the most powerful of all magic, is in here." He tapped on his chest.

"And S.R.'s belt uses a different kind of magic?"

Santa nodded. "Yes, made by the elements. It is not as strong as what is within you, but it still grants great power to the one who wears it. We must get it back and will," he said optimistically. "Then we shall liberate the captured souls the Servant holds."

Captured souls. My thoughts went to Fleep. I should have done more. I didn't even need some dumb belt to beat S.R.; the power had been in me all along. I could have saved Fleep.

Logan stepped in front of me, full of determination. "Let's go then."

"Logan, it is not that simple. I need the help of the five great ones, the ones who forged the belt. But unfortunately four are nothing more than statues without their faces."

"Oh my gosh, faceless statues? Wait ... are they the statues hanging in The Teashroom?" Logan asked, dumbfounded.

"Sadly, yes. Servant Rupert stole their faces and kidnapped their brother during our last battle. Preparation and—"

Suddenly distracted, Santa stopped speaking. Great, he was looking at me. I hid behind Logan. I didn't want him to see me crying.

"Jakob," Santa said, stepping toward Logan and me. Logan moved out of his way. I couldn't blame her. He was so gentle, but also so commanding. "You've been so brave. Why such sadness?"

I sniffled. "It's Fleep. He said you weren't real. He didn't believe. He—"

"He chose not to believe. Jakob, Fleep's lack of belief is not your burden to carry." He shook his head. "Belief is born with the soul and shielded by innocence, until it is finally challenged by maturity and you are left with a simple choice: belief or disbelief. Believing in me was Fleep's choice to make."

He squinted his eyes, as if he were reading my mind. "Now dry those tears," he said, wiping my cheek. "Is there anything else you want to know?"

I hesitated at first. I had a million questions, but one had perplexed me since the moment I laid eyes on Santa. Carefully, I chose my words and said, "If you and I are Poles, then we're related, right?"

"Yes."

"But how's that possible. Your face, I mean your skin is—"

"A different color than yours?" Santa said with raised eyebrows.

I nodded as Santa knelt before me.

"Come now, Jakob. You are thinking like a Flicker. You are part of an ancient race and, in time, you will learn to think like *a Pole* and realize the difference between appearance and truth—between what seems to be true and what really is true. Soon you will see eternal reality and truth for what it is, a magnificent color beyond belief that is deep inside here," Santa said knocking on his chest.

"*That* is the color, *our* color, *a Pole's* color." Santa regarded me. "Understand?"

"I think so," I said a little unsure.

"Right then, well I better be off. Your training begins when I return," Santa announced.

I looked at Santa, surprised. "What am I training for?"

"To be my replacement, of course!"

"But I can't go anywhere. My parents—"

"Will never know you left. One of the few times being out of time actually works to your benefit. Besides, it's *my* turn to grow up with my parents." Perplexed, I shook my head. Was Santa still a boy like me? "It's your turn, Jakob. I'll explain more soon, but *first* I must deliver the presents. Merry Christmas!"

As I watched him leave, I had a feeling Christmas would never be the same again. Boy was I right, but that's another story.